Truth & Conciliation

Truth
&
Conciliation

A Historical Novel

Berend Mets

naledi

Truth & Conciliation

NALEDI

Naledi,
Gansbaai
7220

First Edition © Naledi 2025   www.naledi.co.za

Text © **Berend Mets**

Set in 12 on 15 pt Adobe Garamond Pro

Cover design: Creative Partner

First Edition, First Print: January 2025

Printed and bound by Print on Demand, Pty. Cape Town.

ISBN 9781067234461

AUTHORS NOTE

Truth & Conciliation is a novel and to construe the book as anything other would be a mistake. The characters are of course fictional but many of the events such as the demolition of District Six, the Soweto Riots, and the Trojan Horse Massacre are factual. A few real people like Archbishop Desmond Tutu appear and the things said of them are historically accurate, but they never intersected with the characters portrayed here — that is the art of historical fiction.

Truth & Conciliation takes place in Cape Town during the Truth and Conciliation Commission hearings held there in 1996. Readers may find some of the language used politically incorrect, but it holds true to the time.

The Truth and Reconciliation Commission was constituted by an act of South Africa's Parliament and ratified under the new presidency of Nelson Rolihlahla Mandela. One of the first of its kind; the TRC would become an example that many other countries would follow in the hope-filled search for a peaceful resolution of past conflict.

†

†

To err is human.
To forgive,
Divine

†

1

District Six, Cape Town, April 1966

The breakup began as a whispered rumour, was spelled out by warnings daubed on to dilapidated walls, and then materialized in a feared letter; sometimes discarded in dismay, but more often than not read again and again to be tucked away anxiously against the day of reckoning, when squat bulldozers grunted up the cobbled streets of District Six — the mixed race area had been declared "Whites Only" by the *apartheid* government and needed to be levelled.

Down with the stately Horstley Building, the Public Baths, the rows of derelict tenements that had condemned the slum for destruction. And, out with its varicoloured residents: the Africans, Coloureds, Asians, Dutch, French, English, Koreans, Indonesians and Malays who had made *Canala Dorp* their home over centuries. Gone to make room for new development — for this was prime property situated on the slopes of Table Mountain at Cape Town City's heart, adjacent to the docks.

The Synagogues, Churches and Mosques would stay, but the faithful must go; off to Langa and Nyanga townships on the dust whipped Cape Flats or away to the homelands: Transkei, Venda or Zululand.

And if the citizens of District Six didn't have their furniture and belongings packed and ready and out of their houses on the date described in their letter, the bulldozers would bury it all for good: furniture, crockery, cutlery; books, wills, and identity papers — all added to the dust heap of history.

"Promise, Promise," Marja had opened the window of their cottage bedroom after she heard the heavy thud of the diesel engine labouring up the slope and leant out to look down the road. "They're finally coming," she adjusted the window and walked round into the kitchen where Promise was helping feed their three year old son at the melamine table.

"Aikona, Aikona, Promise shook her head. I thought it wouldn't be so soon. Vorster has only just declared this a 'black spot'." She collected the grey shawl around her slim brown shoulders, "I thought we had more time to get our things together."

"Well now we haven't," Marja leant over Willem who was eating his putu pap, pulled her yellow sarong higher to better cover the scar that marred her sallow skin; her long black hair platted in a ponytail arranged, just so, to cover the ugliness from view, and brushed away a gob of porridge at the corner of Willem's mouth.

"Mama, I have had enough pap. I want to go and play now," the slender boy sputtered.

"Aikona, aikona," Promise said.

"Nee, nee Willem," Marja agreed.

"I want to see what that noise is outside," Willem ran porridge flecked fingers through his mop of tousled brown hair; no trace of either of his parents apparent as he slid from the kitchen table seat and pattered out on to the stoep in his denim dungarees despite their admonishments.

They heard a police whistle, the barking of dogs, the clash of a steel forklift against unforgiving stone and saw a house across the cobbled road from theirs, stricken, the roof collapsing, razed to rubble in a scatter of sand. Their opposite neighbours had pushed their meagre belongings out on to a piece of open veldt and stacked them higgeledly piggeledly in the rush to save what could be from decimation at the hands of the South African Police who were loudly ordering the drivers to destroy, destroy.

"Kry hulle uit. Get them out. Get them out. They have received the eviction letters. They must move out. Continue bull dozing! Now. I order you. Now."

The police officer sounded familiar to the couple; they had joined their son on the veranda. Clad in the blue tunic and trousers of South African's finest, his police pistol still holstered in brown leather at the hip, he rested his one hand on its handle, raising the other to point at the bulldozer's driver who had faltered at the mayhem he had caused.

"Gaan aan. Go on. Go on," the officer yelled over his shoulder in Afrikaans and then turned to continue walking to the threesome gathered on the stoep, a police entourage in tow. He removed his cap, showing his receding hairline, wide glasses, and accentuated nose, quivering over a bushy handlebar moustache; his thin lips downturned to a sneer in order to shout once more, "die hotnots moet uit."

"It's Pieter Marais," said Marja covering her lip sticked mouth with matching red tipped fingers. "He arrested us for the Immorality Act four years ago, right here," she pointed a tapered foot in the direction of the front door, the copper bangle at her ankle glinting sharply in the rain-washed sun.

"Five years, Marja, not four. I remember he had the hollering hots for you. I could see that when he gave evidence in the Magistrates Court, against you."

"Ja, nee. But now I think we have other problems, he's coming over here with two officers, and two bloody Alsatians. I can smell them already. It brings back bad memories."

"Good morning, Promise Madiba and Marja de Koning, we meet again it seems," Marais had tucked his cap under his arm, "may we come on to the stoep, I have something to communicate to you."

"What is your business with us?" Promise stood erect, elbows out, her knuckles pressed in tight at the waist of her black skirt.

"I see you have a boy here. And what is your name son?" Officer Marais crouched down to Willem, who had risen up from the rattan chair he was sitting on to answer in a pinched voice.

"My name is Willem, sir."

"A fine name. How old are you?"

"Mom?" the bright boy uncrumpled his dungarees by stroking down with one hand while reaching for Promise's with the other, "it's three. I am three years old," Willem held up the correct number of fingers.

"A well-mannered boy," Officer Marais resumed his erect posture, "best he stay outside while we talk inside. Can we proceed?"

"No," Promise said, "only if you keep those stinking dogs outside and one of you looks after Willem."

Once the two policemen had been seated on the couch in the tiny lounge, Marais continued, his voice raised and lowered as the situation dictated while the crescendo of bulldozing ebbed and waned outside in a cacophony of grit and dust.

"Promise Madiba, as the owner of this house, did you get the letter telling you that you will be evicted and must make other arrangements?" Marais said.

"I am neither denying nor affirming this fact."

"Well you are a citizen of Pondoland, in the Transkei. The letter will have said that you must plan to move back to your homeland. Have you?"

"I am neither denying nor affirming it." Promise fixed a steady stare on Marais, her mane of tawny ringlets floating at the shawl tightened at her shoulders.

"Not that it matters, we can make the necessary arrangements. Now," Marais swivelled his glare to take in the African masks on the walls, the soft animal hides underfoot, the prickly zebra skin on the sofa he was sitting on and the green tiled kitchen he could see through its open door, "I cannot see any evidence that you are planning to move out. No boxes packed, the house fully furnished, what plans have you made?"

"We are not leaving. Never. This is my house. I

paid for it." Promise stirred in her wicker chair.

"The government will arrange fair compensation. It will be paid out to you; but did you fill out the paperwork for it?" Marais reached to get up but remained on the couch. He stroked his moustache with his holster hand, pale fingers parting the brown hairs lovingly. Marais looked at Marja who had moved to stand in the kitchen doorway appreciating her soft silhouette, "and what is to become of you *my mooiste*, my pretty, and of the fine young boy. What indeed?"

There was a great crunching sound that engulfed the cottage coming from next door. The house shuddered. It felt as if a battle tank was making its way through the detritus; waging a war against its own people. Dirt blew in the open kitchen windows mixed with weeping and cries of anguish from the neighbours. A wailing and a ululating of such tenor that the officer sitting next to Marais couldn't set his face against it and bowed his head with shame.

Nonplussed, Pieter Marais shouted to gain the upper hand, "Okay, to business," and rose to his full six feet. "This house will be bull-dozed today. I will give you till midday to clear out your things. Put them on that excuse for a plot across the street." He pointed in the direction of the front window through which they could see people hustling to pile their cupboards and chairs and tables, propane burners and kitchen appliances; one was pumping at a bicycle tire, another sat in an armchair, her face hidden under a towel, shoulders trembling.

Distracted by the forlorn scene, Marais seemed to lose it for a moment, but then continued gruffly. "A lorry will come to pick youse up and take you and your belongings to Langa Township... some flats have been set aside there for youse. Youse being one of the first batches." He puffed out his chest, put on his cap but continued looking out the window. "But that is only a temporary arrangement, until plans are made for Pondoland; there will be many more evacuees to come. That I know for a fact."

"I will NOT move. You and your National Party Government can go to bloody HELL!" Promise snarled. She had arisen from her chair; her hazel eyes burning. "Amandla," she raised her clenched fist.

"Calm now Promise, calm now," Marja said as she moved closer in and took Promise's clenched fist in her own. She turned and looked Marais in the eyes finding a willing connection. "Can we have some time together to discuss this please?"

"I wish I could Miss de Koning, but there is no time. We have to have a decision now. If Promise refuses, she will be arrested with the full force of the law." Marais indicated his fellow officer with a jut of his squared jaw, who came immediately to standing attention, ready to obey.

"Aikona, aikona, aikona, what about the law? The law of the whites not the blacks. I spit on your laws. I will tramp them into the dust," Promise seethed.

"Yes, we know all about you Promise Madiba, on file at Caledon Square Police Station. A big file. Do you wonder why we are here today, in this street?"

13

"Mama, Mama," Willem had barged open the front door leading from the stoep he had been left sitting on, "why are they bashing down the houses. I am scared."

"Come here Willem, nothing to be scared of. They are going to build nice new ones, but first you must move for a while," Officer Marais bent down and caught the child by the armpits under his outstretched hands, enveloping the little rib cage carefully between his palms, and raised the boy's featherweight to shoulder height to look into his eyes. "Brown, just like my own, and your skin; just a tan, too much sun for a boy in sunny South Africa. Hah! Now be a good boy and I will take you back to the stoep." Marais put the boy down, took his hand and walked him back to the rattan chair he had been sitting on, clearly visible by the others, through the window, and returned, closing the front door behind him.

"And what will you do Miss de Koning? Will you be arrested too? The boy will have to be put in a foster home then. Detention without trial can go on and on and on. I think you know that, after all... I think I recall... a police record, for prostitution. I see you have turned away from that for other things," Marais for once exchanged his scowl for an almost, charming, smile, his moustache following suit.

There was a pause in conversation, necessitated by another building's collapse. The four participants regarded the demolition through the lounge window; the scraggly plot across the street kept filling with more scattered households. The noise and filth and fumes of mechanical destruction; the anguish of losing the place you have called home — hopelessness and uncertainty hung heavy on the air, undispelled by the gathering south-easter.

None in the room could be unmoved by such wanton cruelty, but Marais had his orders, and needed to carry them out. He straightened to the task.

"Sergeant Botha, please arrest Promise Madiba for failure to vacate the premises earmarked for repossession. Promise Madiba, I warn you to keep quiet and to go quietly for the boy's sake. If you do, you can say goodbye to Willem on the stoep and Botha can accompany you to the police van waiting round the corner. If not, we will take you away in handcuffs in front of the boy. Further, to this conversation, and upon my honour, I will do my level best to ensure the safety of Miss de Koning and your handsome son."

Promise slumped, her proud bearing punctured as she stepped towards Marja still framed in the kitchen door and pushed her gently out of sight of the police officers and into the kitchen. Promise closed the door with a slam.

"These shits. What are we supposed to do?" Promise said as she backed up against the enamel kitchen sink and bent forward clasping her hands together behind her neck in distress. Marja moved to stand in front of Promise, breathing rapidly, cupped her hand underneath Promise's chin and raised her face to touch her lips with her own.

15

"I don't know," Marja kissed Promise again, but this time lingered longer. "I don't know my love. But I don't think it is going to help if we both go to prison."

"Aikona," Promise said, "but I cannot let them bulldoze down my house without protest. I cannot." She shook her head from side to side, pulled out a white handkerchief that had been tucked in at the wrist of her black pullover, and blew her nose snottily.

"So you will abandon your son and me to our fate?" It was Marja's turn to hang her head, till Promise lifted her chin to raise their eyes to the same level again; hazel meeting brown in a customary glance that dilated their pupils.

"Yes. I can't help but, and keep my self-respect. I must do this. I must," Promise stood back. Thought better of it. Stepped forward, put both her arms around Marja's shoulders in a warm embrace, held tight for a while as their breathing rhythm slowed, gave a final clench expelling both of their breaths, and then marched out of the kitchen and into the lounge where the two police officers stood waiting.

"Alright Officer Marais," Promise said, "let me get my things in a bag, spend time with Willem, and then you can take me away. Under extreme prejudice! I protest this gratuitous violation of our human rights."

†

After Promise had left, led away between the two officers and the two Alsatians, Pieter Marais stayed behind to talk to Marja. (The boy had been given a lollipop and remained on the small porch watching the bulldozers at work around him.)

Marais had asked for a cup of coffee and sat himself down again on the zebra-skin couch. Sipping gingerly, he looked over the cup's rim at Marja's pretty face.

"*Jislaaik, wat kyk jy my zo?* Why are you looking at me like that?" Marja asked as she settled into a kitchen chair brought into the lounge, her silky sarong shaping her breasts.

"Well you and I have come a long way," Marais continued in Afrikaans.

"What do you mean by that?"

"Well, aren't you half Indonesian? I know that you were a prostitute, in fact married to Henry Plaatjies the Mongrel's gangster boss until he was killed at the Langa Riots."

"*Ja, nee* so what of it? That's no crime."

"Ja, and then you were prosecuted under the Immorality Act with that Doctor Willem Jansen and hence the boy's name."

"We were *vrygestel,* freed, despite you serving as a witness for the prosecution. No thanks to you, *geen dank daar!*" Marja spat out.

"And then Doctor Jansen fell, climbing on Devil's Peak. I followed all that in the newspapers," Marais took another sip of coffee, now that it was cooler, and swilled it about and continued. "And now Promise will be out of the way for a very long time, if I am any judge of the matter. The Special Branch have files on her and will surely put her in prison."

Marja puffed her cheeks and cinched her right hand over her wrist so tight that her veins set out against her dun skin. She fixed Pieter with a stare.

"Well," Pieter stammered, "I see an opportunity here for the both of us; or for all *three* to be more correct. A change of colour so to speak. I have always liked you from the very first day I met you. I can't help it. That very first time, during the police raid, when you were working at the Riad and we nabbed the white ANC sympathizer you were... ah... *servicing* in contravention of the Immorality Act. That day I fell in love with you. Full stop. I have never forgotten it. I have always had feelings for you Coloured girls. But especially you."

Marja barely arrested her recoil back into the wicker chair and wrung her wrist repetitively. Pieter reached over to stop the motion; his hand moist on Marja's.

"You know it will be much better for the boy, if he is classified White, not Coloured. More opportunity. He can certainly pass for it and so could you," Pieter released his hand and lounged back on the couch, his hands behind his head.

Pieter and Marja were oblivious to the bedlam reverberating through the window; their eyes searching each other out.

"I have a proposal. It is within my power to get you re-classified as White. We'll figure it out at Caledon Square Police station once you have... aah... 'lost' your passbook in the move." Marais hyphenated the word 'lost' with two index fingers in the air. "Then you can become my wife, the boy is taken care of, and we won't break any laws: the Mix Marriage Act for one," Pieter raised an index finger, "nor the Immorality Act," two fingers, "which you are an expert at, it seems. But there is one absolute condition," index finger again, "Willem will be called Pieter and you will promise to never tell him the truth, never," Pieter Marais bent forward and stilled Marja's wrist-wringing again with a now clammy hand.

"Now, thank you for the coffee. Think on it, here is my telephone number. I suggest you pack all your belongings, move them outside. I will get Sergeant Botha to help you. The bulldozers will be here around midday. I am so sorry, but these are my orders and I must obey."

✝

2

Truth and Reconciliation Commission University of Western Cape Bellville, August 1996

The Truth and Reconciliation Commission had had almost weekly sessions since its inception at East London in April of 1996. Helmed by Archbishop Desmond Tutu or his deputy, Doctor Alex Boraine, the TRC was constituted by an act of parliament ratified under the new presidency of Nelson Mandela and operationalized from the Commission's Cape Town Headquarters on Adderley Street.

The Commission straddled three subject areas. The Human Rights Violations Committee, The Amnesty Committee and The Rehabilitation and Reparations Committee, all of which could be accessed by submitting an extensive application form before a decision was made whether an applicant was asked to attend a hearing.

To ensure country-wide accessibility to the Commission, suitable venues had been organised throughout South Africa. And, because the hearings were to be a transparent process bringing live radio and television broadcasts to the newly constituted, post-apartheid nation, the Truth and Reconciliation

Commission entourage grew to become a veritable roadshow of vans, trucks, police vehicles, taxis and private cars engaged to transport the commissioners, reporters, translators, broadcast equipment specialists, and administrative personnel across the vast country from venue to venue.

The objective of the demanding exercise was reconciliation through truth-telling by the victims and the perpetrators.

On the one hand, the victims (or their family members) through the Human Rights Violations Committee, could relate their stories to confront the perpetrators with the crimes they had committed in order to establish the truth behind the atrocities enacted; bringing a measure of resolution to the victims from the fact that their voices had been heard.

While on the other hand, the perpetrators, through the Amnesty Committee, could ask for amnesty from future criminal or civil prosecution by telling their stories; at the same time often purging the turmoil in their hearts in the process of revealing their truth.

The atrocities that the Truth Commission was adjudicating had been committed on all sides of the apartheid fight.

The African National Congress's armed wing, Umkhonto we Sizwe had shot, tortured, placed landmines and bombed; the South African Police and a nebulous 'third force' had executed 'dirty tricks' killing, brutalizing and maiming to undermine resistance movements, while the Inkatha Freedom Party and the Pan African Congress and the Afrikaner Weerstands

Beweeging had acted in the same vein — often innocent bystanders becoming the victims of the violence that had infected the nation.

Like a sweeping sepsis, the infestation had threatened to overwhelm the country, running the risk of a descent into civil war were it not contained. The contagion needed to be purged. The truth needed release, so that the people's wounds could start to heal.

†

The Main Hall at the University of Western Cape had been set up in the usual fashion by the TRC administrators.

On the raised stage, backdropped by rich wood panelling, a semi-circle of green-baized tables were arranged for the five commissioners conducting the hearings. Opposite them, and to the left of the stage, the same arrangement was in place for those who would be presenting their testimony, while to the side of both, television crews had placed the necessary cameras to film the proceedings. Masses of bundled wiring flowed all over the stage from the microphones placed at each seat to be fed into electronic relays, and then on to be conducted over the lip of the stage down to the set of three grey telephone-booth like boxes, on each side of the hall, that held the translators — English, Afrikaans, Zulu, Xhosa, Venda, Basuto or whatever tribal language was needed — to be transmitted via earphones to all Commission participants and to those audience members who wanted them; everyone accommodated in the vast hall and gallery that angled up at the back to the rafters.

For the benefit of the audience, both present and those watching via television, an enormous green, yellow and black TRC placard had been attached to the crimson curtain that backed the stage announcing the Commission's intent: TRUTH. THE ROAD TO RECONCILIATION which was flanked by two newly constituted South African flags: an amalgam of a black and yellow V upheld by a green Y (the ANC colours) complimented by a white border above, and below of which ran respectively red and blue bands (the Dutch and British flag's colours).

To create an atmosphere of healing, green potted palms were stationed around the stage and a 'consoler' was provided by the TRC to sit next to the testimony-giver during the proceedings to provide psychological and physical support throughout the traumatic experience.

A South African Police detail was assigned to each hearing to protect the participants; before audience members were allowed into the building at the start of the day, sniffer-dogs and their handlers walked the rows and rows of readied seats, searching for hidden bombs, for there were many who decried the proceedings and would have liked to see the Truth and Reconciliation Commission fail.

Often, especially if the Archbishop was present, clad in his purple cassock and papal cap, the proceedings would commence with a prayer and a few motivational words of comfort and thank you, after which a praise song would be sung by those congregated, accompanied, in the University of Western Cape's main hall, by the magnificent church organ that reached up along its eastern wall.

†

Doctor Pieter Marais, the young Assistant District Surgeon for Cape Town Central, chose his seat in the audience carefully. He wanted to experience the Commission first hand, but unobtrusively, and certainly *not* become immortalized on T.V. The problem was — as witnessed on Sunday's weekly SABC television broadcast about the TRC — that most in the audience were Black or Coloured and so Whites stuck out like sore thumbs. Tall with a dense crop of brown unruly hair cut like a helmet to cover his ears, he had hidden it all beneath a black felt fisherman's cap offsetting his fastidiously trimmed full beard nicely. (He had thought of shaving his beard off completely, but the unweathered skin that this would surely expose, was likely to attract unwanted questions back at work.) And rather than wearing the maroon University of Stellenbosch blazer which he thought would stand out to much but loved, he wore his dark blue medical school version and complemented this with a grey shirt and dull tie.

The reason Pieter wanted to visit personally but not be recognized was because he had a guilty conscience. A dark secret that he still shuddered at whenever it came to mind. Last week Sunday's TRC broadcast on television had brought that back again in sharp focus. Over and over it churned. It literally made him sweat. The Truth Commission had South Africa's medical profession in its crosshairs. The South African Broadcasting Company had interviewed a clutch of medical scholars at the University of Cape Town. They had discussed the case of Steve Biko, killed in detention. At the Port Elizabeth prison in Walmer where Biko had been imprisoned, the District Surgeons had not only given false witness but also falsified certificates denying the fact that Biko had been tortured. The UCT academics claimed that the medical profession had a range of complicity in these crimes against humanity, stretching from not providing appropriate medical care to the imprisoned, to aiding and abetting torture, or providing false witness to the causes of death in detention. The august doctors had suggested a separate TRC for the medical profession, or, at the very least, that doctors who had transgressed should come forward and submit an application for amnesty, rather than be subpoenaed in a court of law, and (the academics had suggested) before it was too late. The deadline for Amnesty Applications was likely to be May 1997, just nine months away. *A gestational period* Pieter remembered thinking to himself as he sat down in a back row in the shadow of the organ and donned his headphones, after removing his cap and placing it on his crossed legs in front of him.

†

Archbishop Desmond Tutu, the embodiment of truth, rose from behind the green-baize table. He had a purple skull cap nestled firmly in his brush of white curly hair. His bright eyes sparkled through distinctive gold rimmed glasses as he tamped down his matching soutane, steadied the gold cross swung free on its neck-chain and with his upstanding, paused. He addressed the audience, his brown face fetching a conciliatory smile.

"Welcome... welcome," Tutu raised his hands into a prayerful position, "Please stand for a short prayer... I give thanks to God. I give thanks to our rainbow nation. I give thanks to you all for being here. We put our trust in the Almighty to guide us. Please sit." The Archbishop smiled beatifically, as the audience regained their seats, but remained standing, "I want to make a few points before we proceed today," his voice could be heard clearly where Pieter sat, in fact throughout the amplified auditorium.

"The raison d' etre for this commission is the opening of wounds, cleansing them so that they do not fester, and doing so, so that we have dealt with our past as effectively as we could... we have not denied the past... we have looked the beast in the eye."

The Archbishop paused, glanced at the majestic church organ on the left wall of the hall and raised his eyes heavenwards, seeming to draw from the fidgety anticipation that emanated from the audience in front of him for the strength to continue.

"We are a wounded people because of the conflict

of the past. No matter on which side we stood we all stand in need of healing." Tutu spread his arms out to include his fellow commissioners "we on the commission are no superhuman exceptions, we too need forgiving and we too need to forgive. Today, because of the graveness of the subject matter at hand, I wish to leave a full prayer for later." The Archbishop brought his left hand to his mouth, its gold ring reflecting off of his glasses in the bright T.V. lights, before continuing.

"I am aware that we have heard much about torture in men, but when it occurs in women that takes a different perspective altogether," he looked down at his notes, "Miss Promise Madiba," and then up, "will you please rise and raise your right hand to take the oath."

A slender women, with doe-like eyes, her fawn shaped face stressed by the grey ringlets ponytailed back by a red doek, rose slowly and then raised her brown lined palm for all to see. She was wearing black but for a set of pearls at her throat and ears.

"Do you swear that the evidence you will give before the TRC is the truth and nothing but the truth so help you God?"

"I do."

"Thank you very much. Please be seated."

"Thank you, Your Worship," Promise replied and took a sip of water from the glass that had been readied on the table, next to the box of tissues.

"Miss Madiba, you have provided an extensive written statement for the TRC and we can hear as much or as little as you wish to provide here. We know deeply how difficult it is to talk of such things. We ask you to take your time and please to speak clearly into the microphone for the translators. Your English is perfect but if you wish to speak in Xhosa, I speak that language too."

"I will speak in English."

"Then, please know, you are not alone. We are all with you in this hall, and Martha is beside you," Bishop Tutu nodded at the raven haired Zulu woman sitting next to Promise, "she can help you through this. Mother Martha is very good at her job."

"I am well enough to proceed."

"Please proceed Miss Madiba."

"The whole sorry story started when the South African Police pigs came to bulldoze down my house in District Six. I protested of course. I refused to leave the house so they arrested me. That was always the plan, I believe.

"I was head of the banned ANC Women's League for Cape Town and they wanted me put away and interrogated. The apartheid government wanted to break my will, my human dignity, by using psychological torture against me. They took me to Caledon Square Police Station at first, directly into solitary confinement. After a few days, my head covered with a sack, they took me in a police van for a thirty minute drive. I think now it was Victor Verster prison they took me to, and back into solitary confinement." Promise stopped, and trembling, sipped some water. Martha put her arm around her shaking shoulder and shushed softly in Promise's ear.

"I went crazy; I was so lonely. Day in... day out, a ray of light through a shaft in the prison cell was the only clock I had." Promise traced a half arc in the air with her index finger over the red-lit microphone in front of her. "No one to speak to but myself; my mind started playing tricks, I cried and cried. I started hurting myself. I pinched my inner thigh till it bled, to distract myself. After any number of days, *that* got the guard's attention. I asked to be let out to see people. I wanted to become human again. I screamed and screamed till I could no more. I was hoarse; I lost my voice. I was threatened with rape if I didn't stop and then... I was. I was blindfolded. He felt, and smelled, like a White man."

The audience could no longer contain itself; cries of "shame, shame, shame," and a few high pitched ululations erupted from all round the hall. Promise sat back in her chair and looked straight in front of her; Archbishop Tutu had bowed his grey head on to the green-baized table to sob. Martha drew Promise to her, massaging her shoulder, and wiped her eyes with a tissue till she could recompose herself and continued.

"And when I was obviously pregnant from the rape, I was sent to Pretoria Central where Steve Biko died. Here the depravity was even worse. When I went into my prison cell the guard showed me the blood on the wall. "Do you know why that is?" He asked "No," I said. "Because women will not tell the truth." They wanted me to give up the names of

29

other members of the ANC Women's League. But I never did. I never did." Promise looked defiantly out at the audience; many women nodding their heads in affirmation of her bravery, others clucked their tongues. She continued in a lower voice, "at least I was not in solitary anymore but I was accorded no privacy. I could not go to the toilet but had to pee in a pot in front of the police guard and I was getting bigger and bigger. In the summer months they took away my clothes, except when I walked in the prison yard so I fashioned an apron from a plastic bag that I found there, instead, to keep my modesty in my cell."

Promise undid the red doek and let her grey-flecked hair fall to her shoulders and continued, "They threatened to poison my baby if I didn't give up the names. I said aikona, aikona, life is precious. One white guard at least, seemed to agree. He started arguing with the others: 'Let's leave her alone, she has suffered enough.' I think it was him; his name was Willem funnily enough, who saved my baby girl. Because it was Willem who called the doctor to come and assist while I delivered. I asked for privacy, just me and the doctor. But they said no and stood around laughing as I delivered in pain. Laughing..." Promise petered out in a whimper. "Then after I breast fed my beautiful baby for three months, they took her away."

"Shoo, shoo, shoo, no way to treat a mother," a Xhosa woman stood up at the front of the crowd waving a hanky in dismay. Others joined by waving

30

their handkerchiefs in sympathy. "Aikona, aikona, aikona, aikona" a chant started in the hall echoing back through the public address system via the open microphones until the Archbishop stood up, raised his two arms in the sign of benediction and pronounced, "we feel your pain, we all feel your pain..." Order eventually restored, Miss Madiba was asked to continue her testimony if she was still willing to do so.

"Having my baby daughter taken away from me was unbearable torture. They told me she could be returned to me for a while but only if I would become a State witness, otherwise, she would be turned over to my family. My family? 'What family?' I said. 'Your family in Soweto' they said. This surprised me Your Worship. That they knew so much about me was scary. 'Yes' they said. But I could not turn State witness against my ANC family...."

Doctor Pieter Marais could not listen anymore, he tried to switch off, as this testimony and the dilemma it posed ran too close to the bone. Too close to why he had come to visit these proceedings in person in the first place. He focussed on the crowd instead and his eye fell on Officer Thembisa Dlamini. The Xhosa policewoman who served at Caledon Square Police Station whom he had only recently encountered when he visited prisoners who needed a doctor as part of his District Surgeon's duties. She must be part of the police detail assigned to the Truth Commission whenever it held meetings in Cape Town. *That was good, he would look her up and sound out her thoughts on the proceedings. She seemed level-headed and bright. In a strange way she was almost attractive, now that he saw her profile at a distance.*

Pieter turned his attention back to the testimony which seemed to be closing. Miss Madiba was relating that after she was released from jail, she was immediately banned so she escaped to an ANC camp in Zambia, and, after a few years, to exile in London where she had made a new life, returning only to South Africa to present at the Truth Commission. Promise ended with a rousing address.

"I have been to the heart of darkness and back, but we have triumphed. Amandla," Promise raised her fist. And many in the audience rose and raised their fist and responded in unison, "NGWETHU, NGWETHU."

Pieter exited quickly during the hubbub, ducking so as not to be caught by a panning television camera.

†

3

General Practice, 1996

Pieter liked the early morning drive from his flat
in Table View that took him along Table Bay to
his General Practice in Tamboerskloof, the munic-
ipal district that led up from the botanical gardens
established by the Dutch East India Compagnie,
centuries ago. It was a well-established neighbour-
hood of Cape Town, lying in the lee of Table Mountain, that had undergone a bit of a renaissance lately,
what with the scrapping of the *Immorality Act* and
the many other *petty apartheid* laws by P.W. Botha's
government in 1986. Over the last ten years the staid
area had become quite fashionable again and ever
more thoroughly mixed; there was no longer talk of
having a Black side and a White side to the medical
practice in the converted house that Pieter was pay-
ing a hefty mortgage on. *Just one entrance for all in
the new South Africa*, he thought. *Not an east side nor
a west side entrance* that he had experienced during
his medical school training at Tygerberg Hospital,
the massive fort-like edifice erected in Parow, built
to serve the surrounding Cape Flats. *We should all
be on the same side. If only that were true,* he mused.

Today he first had to turn off at Paarden Eiland
though, away from the frigid Atlantic ocean that

33

curled on to the long stretch of sandy beach that was arrested at Cape Town's Harbor wall. He drove his royal blue Citi-golf up over the railway tracks on to Church Street leading down into Woodstock to turn up Albert Street lined with an assortment of 19-to-20th century buildings serving as shops, eateries, petrol stations, clothing stores and the like, and then gunned at speed, around the circle passing the Voortrekker Road turn off that led to Tygerberg Hospital some twenty kilometres away, and turned, instead, up the steady slope of Durham Road to his destination: The Salt River Mortuary.

Here, Doctor Marais was well known. He was a regular. Part of his role as an Assistant District Surgeon, he provided services as a Medical Examiner. Arriving at the vertically barred, twin gate manned by an attendant in the concrete guard house, always gave him pause though. It reminded Pieter of a similar set up in Angola — the source of his present preoccupation and the cause of his impairment; a psychiatrist had diagnosed that he had gone *bossies* when he had served in South Africa's bush war on the border — a mental condition that was not yet well characterized but considered not unlike that experienced by many veterans of the Viet Nam war. All Pieter knew, though, was that he frequently experienced recurring flashbacks, and panic attacks, and today anxiety was again kindling.

He shook his thatch of curly hair, took a horn-rimmed comb out of the seat pocket of his pale safari suit, and combed a few strands of errant hair behind his sweating ears, before completing the roll down of the car-window to speak to the guard.

"Goeie môre Doctor Marais," the coloured man had approached the car with a clipboard in his hand, "Please sign here." He straightened up and pointed, "please park over there."

"Where?"

"Right next to that blue police van; they'll match nicely," he lisped through his missing front teeth.

Having grabbed his brown attaché case off the front seat, and locked his car, Pieter strode to the front door, up the angled gangway used to trolley the white-plastic covered corpses into the building. He was warmly greeted, but checked and logged in again nevertheless, before walking into the business end of the building. The cavernous autopsy room which was fed by the recently dead.

Before arriving in the autopsy room the corpses had been catalogued and numbered with a cardboard tag attached to the big toe and stacked in stainless steel racks in the adjacent airconditioned unit to await a final diagnosis or identification for disposition. Be that incineration, to a family grave, or to be buried unmarked and unknown if no one had come forward to claim the deceased and they lacked positive identification — one of the primary problems that the busiest mortuary in South Africa had to deal with.

Doctor Marais was here to determine the cause of death for criminal cases. For the forensic cases that had come in overnight, and not for the pathological cases sent from Tygerberg Hospital or Groote Schuur Hospital, just up the street. There were far too few fully trained forensic pathologists to do all the work required and so the State had hired non-specialists with some forensic training, to help relieve the fearsome workload; a result of the gang-related killings that had infested the crime ridden city for decades. No wonder then that the mortuary staff referred to Cape Town — better known as the Mother City — as Murder City.

"Only one today for you Doctor Marais," said Hannes the mortician. "I have put him out for you ready and *klaar*." A scrawny tan coloured man with an outsize smile creasing his pock-marked, almost hairless, cranium, Hannes had tucked his green scrubs into white blood-spattered boots and was leaning on a side table, layered with forms, a stack of Polaroid photos already set to one side.

"Good, I see you have the police photos," Pieter donned a fresh green surgical gown, its left white cuff obscuring his wristwatch, and got into white rubber boots, his name imprinted on the back of their gleaming surface with Koki pen. "Let me see," Pieter hated looking at the gruesome killing scene, it often brought back — in a flash — the Caledon Square Police Station, or the border scene he wanted to erase from his mind, but he needed to correlate the method of killing with the post-mortem he was embarking on, so that he could properly defend his forensic diagnosis in the court case that would undoubtedly follow this investigation. Hence the need for meticulous, painstaking observation and documentation that was the nature of this work.

"It looks like he is lying in the veld," Pieter was studying the top photograph.

"Yes, they found him on Signal Hill, no clothes, and it looks like he might have been tortured. It looks like a gang killing. Probably not a vigilante killing; the Moslems set some-one on fire with petrol last week after shooting him in the head."

"And why do you think he was tortured? I see he has been beaten around the head from this photo, and there are knife wounds on his chest and hands," Pieter put back the last Polaroid on the desk and turned to his assistant.

"Put on your gloves doctor, and I will show you."

A post-mortem required complete concentration so Pieter demanded absolute silence while he worked, just a to and fro calling out between Hannes and himself of findings to be documented and indicated with pencil marks on the front and back view of the human figure that imprinted the documentation, in triplicate, that accompanied every case. Pieter became aware of the transistor radio parked up on the windowsill tuned to Springbok Radio: "This is the nine o'clock news. The Truth and Reconciliation Commission meets for the second day in Bellville at the University of Western Cape."

"Agh, please, Hannes, please turn it off, I have heard enough of this. I need to concentrate." Pieter put on his gloves and approached the corpse. "But what do you think of the Truth Commission, do you think it's serving any purpose?" Pieter examined the prostrate cadaver starting at the head and lifting each eyelid in turn.

"Doctor, I think there is a lot of trauma. A lot of soul-baring. Ek sê. I've been listening during breaks in the work. Some call it the 'Kleenex Commission.'"

"Why?" Pieter was probing each of the stab wounds in the victim's chest with his gloved finger, calling out his findings for Hannes to jot down, searching for the cause of death.

"Because of all the Kleenex tissues the families are using up — boxes and boxes. But I must say the way some have been tortured is just too terrible. By the S.A.P. and the ANC," Hannes jotted down the findings, but his upturned grin had turned to a rictus.

"Yes, just note down that there is a three centimetre penetrating laceration, left lateral to the manubrium sterni, my finger goes deep into it, I think we will find that caused the cardiac tamponade which finally killed him. But we will see when we open the chest."

"Got it, but I think these *bras* have practiced some of the torture techniques they learnt from the TRC on this fellow," Hannes pointed his pencil at the murdered victim's scrotum, "look there are clip marks there and the skin looks burnt from the electricity."

"Anything else? But why would they torture him?" Pieter palpated the man's abdomen and ran his hands down his legs feeling for broken bones.

"For information. Where the gang has hidden

their guns, or money? They capture their victims, tie them up, put a bag over their heads and take them to one of the gang member's safe houses and extract information. You can see they used the helicopter torture on this man."

At the word, Pieter's narrow features blanched pale, his swarthy skin turned tallow, sweat ran freely down the furrow between his shoulder blades.

"Doctor, you look ill."

"It's alright Hannes, go on."

You can still see the red chafe marks at the crux of his elbows and at the back of his knees where the broomstick was stuck to dangle him in a ball between two tables. They must have spun him round and round many a time to cause such damage to the skin, ek, sê. Just like a helicopter propeller. Only he flew nowhere! Just to the mortuary in a police van. Aitsa!"

"Okay, Hannes, I see it. Please note those facts on the diagram and pass me the scalpel."

Doctor Marais pared the anaemic brown skin away from the breastbone to reveal the rancid fat and cartilage beneath, extending the cut to create a y-shaped incision coursing up both sides of the crime victim's neck. Then, having broken each rib with a steel snub-nosed plier, he removed the sternum from the chest revealing a pericardial sack filled with congealed blood, ladling this out to provide a measure of the exact amount. Then Pieter examined the collapsed lungs noting a bloodied rent on the right side and again measured the quantity of blood collected in the pleural cavity to make the final diagnosis of the likely cause of death, already starting to rehearse how he would describe this in court.

"Your Honour, I think the cause of death was a knife inflicted cardiac tamponade complicated by a haemo-pneumo thorax; in layman's terms, a 'stabbed heart' a very common cause of death here on the Cape Flats..."

Pieter's reverie was broken by Hannes.

"Okay boss, now for the skull. Let me help you saw it open; he has injuries to the face we must investigate..."

The one hour procedure over, Pieter sat down at the little desk in the corner, with a cup of coffee, to finalize his notes. He was known for his particular nature and always took his time to make sure that the report was accurate before signing it, knowing full-well that it would become a legal document once completed. He hesitated before placing his elongated signature. He thought back to events at the Caledon Square Police Station six years ago. He had had to sign a medical certificate then too. A witnessing that had provoked his anguished attendance at the Truth Commission yesterday. The sweating between his shoulder blades could not be erased by another sip of coffee. He'd have to make time for a windsurf today if the wind was strong enough this afternoon, that helped relieve the stress. A bit. Pieter sighed, signed, stood, said goodbye and thank you to Hannes and exited the mortuary, stopping to take a few tranquillizing breaths outside.

He looked up at the great mountain range that

dominated the southern suburbs: Devils Peak, on the left with its craggy top, a grey nipple on a brown breast; in front, the massif of Table Mountain, no cloud, not yet, covering it today. The mountain stretched wide and flat-edged across his view, like a curtain backdropping a stage where people played out their lives. And on the right stood Lion's Head, its bare top curving out, its green flank falling to the dark blue Atlantic ocean he had driven along this morning. Time to resume his commute to his practice — up along Anzio Street past Groote Schuur Hospital on to De Waal's Drive, carved along the lower slopes of Table Mountain, and then down to the Gardens in the City Bowl, and up into Tamboerskloof and into a side road off-of steep Kloof Street, where he had found a suitable house to start as a General Practitioner some six years ago.

Situated in the heart of Cape Town, on Easton Road, the house was built in the Old Cape Dutch style. It was probably a converted farmhouse from the Victorian era, and sported an ornate, white-plastered gable alongside a stucco tiled veranda covered by a dark tiled roof. Fronted by a solid plastered wall, no gate barred access along the black and white tiled walkway up to the varnished, oak front door. Doctor Marais had converted the rooms inside to efficiently manage his private practice. There was a place for his secretary, Suzanne, to welcome the patients and seat them in the waiting room to one-side. Another room was the pharmacy. Yet another the treatment room for small procedures, and yet another for emergencies, where patients needing initial treatment could be managed before transfer by ambulance to Groote Schuur Hospital. And then there was Doctor Marais's office and Sister Jordaan's next door. Together they managed the busy practice five days a week. And it was busy. Doctor Marais was considered an outstanding GP with a long patient waiting list; ever more people wanted to join his practice, so much so that he was considering taking on a partner; his forensic and prison practice was taking up a lot of his time.

"Do you want a cup of tea before you start, Doctor Marais? We have a lot of patients waiting. Did the autopsy take longer than you thought?" Suzanne handed him a note as he walked into the house.

Pieter turned to regard the girl. He found her pretty and always smartly dressed. She had her brown hair fashioned in the page boy style. Slim, she reminded him of a springbok; a pointy nose and fine, almond face. She had thin lips with an almost perfect smile revealing pearly teeth.

"No thanks Suzanne, I had a cup of coffee before I left," Pieter looked down at the note, "I see they want me at Caledon Square."

"Yes, they have a prisoner who is sick."

"I'll go over lunch time, but I better get on with it, I'll try to catch up. Point out the first patient and I'll bring him/her in myself."

"It's paediatrics this morning doctor, you always seem to forget that."

Pieter bent closer to Suzanne so no-one sitting in the waiting room could over-hear them, not that that was too likely given the constant howling that emanated from the room, "I want to forget, I don't really like children, especially when they start screaming when I am trying to examine them, but that's my job, so I just grin and bear it."

"Well today is not going to be a good day for you then, I am afraid. You should have hurried up at the mortuary. Sister Jordaan has already given the children the injections they're due, we didn't want them to have to wait even longer till after their visit with you."

"Oorait, please bring in the first child and parent. I will move it along." Pieter straightened up, went into his office, and sat behind his desk ready for the flow of patients that would dictate the rest of the day. He picked up the patient chart in front of him. *He loved being a doctor, despite what he had said to Suzanne about children. He had often wondered where his wish to become one stemmed from. It had not come from his father, Colonel Pieter Marais, the station commander of Caledon Square Police Station. His father had wanted him to go into the police force. Nor his mother, Marja, she wasn't involved in medicine either, but ever since he told her of his wish had been supportive and encouraging. In fact, now that he thought back on it again,* Pieter laid down the patient's chart on the desk in front of him, *she had said something really puzzling once: "you'll take after your father, he was very good at it," and then covered her mouth and then touched the scar on her chest* — a Dutch doctor and Xhosa nurse had saved her life after she was stabbed in the heart at the Langa Riots. *And then when he had asked her about it. She had corrected herself, "no, no, I meant that like your father you will be good at whatever you do. Look how he is rising to the top of the police force. You will do the same in medicine. I know it." Pieter had watched her carefully at the time. He was in matric at Tygerberg High School and couldn't decide which University he would apply for should he want to study medicine. University of Cape Town or Stellenbosch University. "Which one do you think mom?"*

"Pieter if you do as well in the matric exams as you did in mock-matric, you have a very good chance of getting into both. But if you ask me?"

"I am asking you mom?"

"I would say Stellenbosch. I think it will suit you best. It's more Afrikaans and Dutch." He had thought at the time: 'Dutch?' what did that have to do with the situation? Pieter sat back in his chair bothered by the fact that no patients seemed to be arriving and was puzzled all over again. *He had watched his mother after she said that — oh how long ago? yes, 1980, 16 years or so — she had put her hand over the scar on her chest and then shown signs of distress. Marja started kneading her left wrist in the crux of her thumb and index fingers, so he had left it at that. But he had wondered then whether she was telling 'the whole truth and nothing but the truth' — echoes of yesterday's Truth Commission could not be expelled, and had churned over and over, during his restless sleep last night, despite*

the soothing crash of waves, that the opened windows of his flat afforded. And now, given his predicament, he needed to find out so much more about his father....

There was a knock on the door, and Suzanne shepherded in a mother and child. Covered by a Muslim chador, Pieter barely recognized her till she broke into a radiant smile, "you don't recognize me, and you performed the delivery. Don't you have a chart to read about us?" she swept in to sit in the curved chair stationed in front of his desk cradling a little boy in a colourful outfit, who, on cue, set up a spirited wail.

"Yis, ja, I'm sorry Mrs Shabla, how could I forget. Just a bit distracted, but how are you?"

"I am well, Allah be praised, but the boy, not too good," She tightened her clench around his squirming midriff, "he's been vomiting and his pooh smells off."

"Any sweating or fever or coughing?"

"A bit, he's been coughing and sometimes his chest looks tight and the nurse measured his temperature outside and says it's up."

"Okay let me take a look. Let's put him on the examination table behind you and we'll figure it out. What's his name?" Pieter guided the two to the back corner of the office after he had slung his stethoscope across his shoulders.

"Khalid, after his father."

"Okay Mrs Shabla, let's take off his clothes, you can keep the nappy on and we'll lie him down like this and take a look." Pieter leant over the boy while his mother held the wriggling infant around the shoulders and then listened to the child's heaving chest with his stethoscope. He remembered how he had been taught at Tygerberg Hospital to listen most carefully on the *inhale*, because then the child could not bawl, making it possible to discern lung pathology from the breath sounds. Similarly, he palpated the fat little tummy, again on the inhale, when the abdominal muscles couldn't strain against his steady fingers allowing him to feel for a liver or spleen or even the coiled askaris worm in the intestines which he thought he palpated. It was the thrill of such findings, the art of the practice of medicine, and the detective work needed to make a diagnosis, *or to find the truth*, Pieter thought, that still fascinated and enthralled him. He was so glad to be practising medicine.

"Well, Mrs Shabla, I think I know what Khalid's problem is," Pieter unbent from over the examination table, his stethoscope still dangling from his neck, its chrome head finding position over the middle button of his safari jacket, bouncing as he talked, "he has worms. Not a big problem. We'll take a stool sample to confirm the diagnosis and then I'll prescribe some mebendazole syrup. Sister Jordaan can get it for you. We have it in the pharmacy. We're always running out, but I checked yesterday... or the day before."

"Doctor, will there be a problem? Will my first born get it too?"

"Yes, anyone can get it. But we can check for your first son if you want. Just drop off a stool sample here

46

with us and we can get it analysed. Also, everyone in your household must be very careful that your food is cleaned and cooked properly and that you wash your hands before eating. I think it won't be a problem for you after that. Now, Mrs Shabla if there is nothing else, I must see you out, as you know I am a bit behind with patients today. I do apologise..."

†

It had turned into a hot bustling day in central Cape Town despite the winter month. The area around the Caledon Square Police Station a particularly vibrant one as the imposing, four-storied, red-bricked building straddled the block between Buitenkant and Parade Street. The latter predictably leading to the city's Grand Parade, a vast open space bounded on the one side by Cape Town's five-pointed Castle; the other by the ornate Victorian turreted splendour of City Hall — both facing Table Bay in the direction of the grand Railway Station that brought commuters and the public to the Mother City from the Cape Flats, the Southern Suburbs, and as close as Simon's Town along the coast, or as far away as Johannesburg in the north.

Pieter had hoped to park within the Police Headquarters' courtyard but that was not to be. He was waved away by a police guard manning the high arched entrance way despite its black gleaming doors having been invitingly opened inwards, and so turned left at the corner of the building and felt lucky to find a motor car just exiting a parking space along the tree lined street that separated Cape Town's Magistrate Court from the police station. In a rush, Pieter was startled by Signal Hill's noon day gun booming out a single salute as he stepped out of the car, clutching his dark medical bag and looked down at his watch. Dam! It had stopped at 11.35. He had even less time than he thought: He shook his wrist and adjusted his watch to the correct time, hoping that it would restart by itself. He had planned to sandwich all his police work for the day into a lunch time visit. Now he might have to come back later in the afternoon and so couldn't go for the stress relieving windsurf he had planned. Pieter had patients scheduled for afternoon clinic starting at one p.m., and so increased his pace to walk around the building's corner, feeling the warmth of the sun on his sweating forehead, his safari suit sticky at his back. He stroked his trim beard to an imaginary point and strode past the six arched windows, trellised with white painted steel, on his way to the protruding stepped archway that announced the double oak doors fronting the police station.

Yanking the right door open, tensioned by the spring mechanism that hovered over-head, Pieter stepped into the cold interior, the waxy smell of Cobra floor polish rising to meet him.

"Good morning or should I say afternoon officer. Are you new here?" Pieter addressed the blue uniformed policeman behind the smart wooden counter that stretched across the back wall behind an iron barred grate.

"Good afternoon, you must be Doctor Marais, I called your office to ask you to visit. They told me that you would be coming in to see the sick prisoner. He is in the downstair cells."

"I know, I know, I, am no stranger here," Pieter saw that the gate that led to the basement cells had been left ajar, a bunch of keys hanging from the lock. "I'll find my own way down," he made a move towards the stairway.

"No, no Doctor Marais you must be accompanied by Officer Botha, I will call him up."

"Sorry, I haven't enough time," Pieter disappeared down the linoleum steps, neon lights overhead, the astringent smell of Sunlight soap strengthening as he descended, each footfall's slap echoing up the stairwell that centred the building. Although he visited the cells regularly; sometimes two or three times a week to check on prisoners', welfare, Pieter didn't like going downstairs to the double row of barred prison cells facing off across the first wide corridor, and especially not to the second far narrower corridor where the cells for solitary confinement and police interrogation were often noisy with the sounds of angry yelling, sobbing, or cries of pain, and the clanging closed of subterranean doors still reeked of repression and *kragdadigheid* — the *apartheid* government's term for the means of oppressing the blacks. Although that era was now past, Pieter far preferred seeing the newly admitted prisoners above ground in a holding cell before they were sent down; all prisoners needed a full medical examination, more especially if injured, under the rules of the Geneva Convention. Pieter shuddered despite the warmth, *he would have to have a look at those rules,* he was sure that the University of Cape Town's Medical Library, on Anzio Road, would have a copy.

"Yis, ja, Doctor Marais, you know you should not come down here unaccompanied, it is against the law," officer Botha tried to look stern but his pencil-moustached lips and piggie eyes crinkled with pleasure as he stood up from behind his desk and reached over to shake Pieter's hand with a firm clasp. "Let me take you to the patient, I mean prisoner. He was brought in last night, caught stealing a car in Victoria Street, along the Gardens for goodness sakes! He tried jimmying the lock and set off the alarm, just as a police van turned up from Adderley Street. You know there by the public toilets. I don't know about these guys. What a spot to choose. Anyway, ever since he has been here, he has been coughing and wheezing and crying bloody murder that he has asthma and is going to die if he doesn't see a doctor. He doesn't look too good. So we called you to come as soon as possible. And here you are." While saying all this Botha had put his arm around Pieter's shoulders and guided him to the end jail along the wide stoned alleyway between the barred cells.

Pieter had cringed and looked the other way as he observed the cells' inmates trying to catch his eye as the two walked past. He felt badly for them, no matter what their crime; he was responsible for his assigned patient's welfare and imprisonment was the antithesis of that.

The prisoner was a thin umber coloured man, clothed in a threadbare outfit and solid shoes without laces. He was sitting wedged in the corner on his grey-blanketed bed, his legs out in front of him. He bent forward to cough into his balled fist as the policeman unlocked the gate.

"Could you leave me alone with the patient please Officer Botha," Pieter had stepped into the jail cell and had pulled up the single wooden chair to sit down at the level of the patient, "I have all that I am likely to need to look after him."

"As you please, Doctor Marais, but I will have to lock you in and I will be just outside should you need me. Just yell."

"I am Doctor Marais. I hear that you have asthma," Pieter extended his hand to shake the prisoner's hand and then leant back, opened the bag he had put beside the chair and extracted his stethoscope.

"Doctor, I have an *asthma bors*. I don't have my pills or inhaler with me. I have been coughing and coughing; my bors feels tighter and tighter," he elbowed out his arms placing his hands on his pitching chest. "I had to go to Groote Schuur for it once. It got so bad. I was admitted to the hospital for an injection."

"Okay, tell me more while I take your blood pressure."

"I get so short of breath; I want to puke. No don't worry doc, I won't throw up now, but sometimes," a faint smile showed stained teeth, and a blue-tinged tongue.

Pieter put his first three fingers on the man's wrist and looked at his watch to count his heart rate: *at least the second hand still seemed to be working fine, although he couldn't be sure. He felt he had spent a lot more time with the patient than his wristwatch indicated,* 12:10.

"Well your breathing and heart rate are far too fast. Let me listen to your chest," Pieter stood up over the straining patient and listened from the front and at the back of his exhausted torso. In adult patients one listens for *inhalations* and *exhalations;* in asthma for the wheezes and crackles and the length of expiration to figure out its severity and what might have provoked the attack. Less breath sounds the more critical the situation. Pieter pulled the stethoscope's earpiece from his ears, letting them clasp his neck and sat back again in the chair. "Well I am glad you had them call me."

"I asked them early this morning... I've been suffering doc... and it's getting worse... I am getting tired of this asthma bors... I can tell you," the prisoner gasped, his hands on his knees and his black shoes planted firmly on the stone floor.

"Yes, we'll start treating you immediately. I will give you an injection of aminophylline over ten minutes. Nice and slow. You've got good veins; there won't be a problem. That will sort you out, and then I have some antibiotics and aminophylline tablets that will see you right. I'll telephone in tonight and see if you are okay. If not, we'll make a plan."

Doctor Marais occupied himself treating the patient, called Officer Botha to release him, grabbed his medical bag, his stethoscope still dangling from his neck, and rushed up the stairwell on his way to the second floor where the District Surgeons' had a shared desk in a communal office for police personnel; he had some paperwork that needed completion. He looked down at his wristwatch: 12:30, impossible. He would visit the second floor's tearoom, he knew there was a clock there, so quickened his pace, taking two steps at a time, and then lunged out of the stairwell and into the room. Momentarily distracted by looking down to arrest his swinging stethoscope, Pieter blindly crashed into a policewoman. The cup of coffee in her hand spilling its hot liquid over both of them, before splintering on the ground.

"Aai, jai, jai, watch where you are going, stupid. Now look at what you've done," the officer flapped her hands to try to shake the coffee droplets off her navy tunic and then spun around to the sink, grabbed a tea towel, wet it under the tap, and proceeded to wipe down her stained light-blue skirt before bending over further to clean her black shoes, all the time shaking her head upending the tawny braided ringlets that usually rested comfortably at her shoulders. Satisfied, she turned up to Pieter, saying, "Stupid... stupid..." until she saw who he was, "Aikona, I'm sorry Doctor Marais, I'm sorry, I didn't mean to say it. Oh," she put the tea-towel to her mouth, "you're covered in coffee!"

"Ja, it must have been a full cup. And I am in a rush," Pieter reached his hand out "could I please have that towel?" his pale suit looked like he had just been splashed with mud out on safari. "I am so sorry. It is all my fault. I am late. My watch stopped. I have to go and see patients," He looked up at the clock centring the tea-room: 1:30. "And now I am really late, I must go. How can I make this up to you. I am so sorry. It's Thembisa isn't it?

"Yes. You haven't seen me here before?" a coy smile, tipped generous lips, "I've seen you here, busy at that desk for the District Surgeons."

Pieter wiped the teacloth once over his face, stroked his beard clean of coffee, "yes, I must admit, I did notice you. Difficult not to. But I must go."

"Alright. You can make it up to me. By buying me a new cup of coffee... and lunch at Le Café across the road."

"Tomorrow?

"No. I have to be at the Truth Commission tomorrow. But the next day will be fine."

"It's a deal. Midday. I will see you there." Pieter looked down at his wristwatch; it seemed to be running again. He set the correct time.

"Hau, are you always so distracted?"

"Sometimes. I'm sorry. My watch wasn't keeping proper time, but it seems to be going again. I think it's a good omen. But now I must run."

†

4

Police Headquarters, 1996

Much earlier that day, Thembisa was woken by her insistent telephone, ringing. It was beckoning from the open plan kitchen in her rented flat. *What now!* She cast her eye at the electronic clock glowing red numbers in the dark: 4:05. *A.M!* she thought, *aikona, this cannot be good.* "I'm coming, shit, I'm coming." She peeled off her warm sheets, crimped her sheer nightie to her cooling skin, and stepped delicately on to the cold tiles, the bright moonlight falling through her uncurtained windows the only pilot to the adamant ringing.

"Detective Dlamini, Thembisa, is that you?"

"Yebo,"

"Plans have changed for your day."

"What do you mean?" Thembisa was trembling from the unseasonable cold, she hopped from one foot to the other, and pulled her free arm around her chest to conserve heat.

"You're not going to the Truth Commission today."

"Why?"

"You want to be a detective?" came the gruff voice, "well a detective you will be. We've heard that there is a body in the field alongside the car park on

Signal Hill. Some loving couple, who should have known better than to be out so late, called it in to the police station."

"But why me?"

"Your next in line for a case; Officer Vermeulen is sick in bed."

"Oh," Thembisa said, clenching her teeth against the cold. *She must remember to close the window.*

"Can you get there by yourself, or should we wait at the police station for you."

"No, I live in Tamboerskloof, so it will be quicker if I just ride there."

"Ride?"

"Yes, I have a scooter."

"Okay Thembisa. But don't let us down. You will have to present the case at police parade today. Nine o'clock sharp."

"Yes, sir," Thembisa, raised her hand in mock salute.

"And... Thembisa... I gather that Colonel Pieter Marais is doing the rounds today and wants to see our section in action at parade this morning."

"Who's he? His name sounds familiar," again hissed through clenched teeth.

"It better be. The colonel is the uber-Fuhrer, the officer in charge of Caledon Square, the whole bang-shoot... the whole operation. I'm sure you get my drift. We do *not* want to mess with him. And especially not you being a new detective. You'll see what I mean. Anyway, enough idle chatter. Get on with it."

Thembisa replaced the telephone in its cradle hanging on the kitchen wall, flipped on the electronic kettle, pulled open the fridge to get some milk, making her shiver all over again, and readied a cup of coffee for later. Then she stepped back into the bedroom, removed her nightie, and turned to access the bathroom. Bathed in moonlight, she paused to admire her trim shadow against the back wall; the side silhouette of a rounded buttock, flat stomach, pert breast, and angled face burnished by a bush of hair, before taking a quick shower (she remembered to put her shower cap on) and then shrugged semi-dry into her police uniform. Feeling much better now that she was warm again, Thembisa tied her shoelaces extra tight; she knew she was going to have to reconnoitre the veldt on Signal Hill, and then went into the lounge to have her coffee and a breakfast of Marie biscuits.

The room was sparsely furnished, but vibrant. A second hand couch, two higher purchase chairs from Bradlow's, their colours clashing vividly, were separated by a great leather travel trunk that had seen better days and was partially hidden under a springbok *velletjie.* Three clay circular coasters protected the scuffed leather from coffee and other spills. A series of African masks, fashioned with feathers, copper bangles, animal teeth and the like; and daubed with red ochre and white paint, lined both side walls.

During these standing breakfasts, Thembisa liked to gaze out of the wide spread of windows that fronted the room, out at the magnificent view over Cape Town and its harbour that the prime location on Woodside Road afforded. She munched her Marie biscuit and took a sip of coffee. This was Thembisa's second month on the job and her first case. She had studied the S.A.P. Policy and Procedures Manuals diligently and thought she could remember what had to be done with respect to securing and processing of a Murder Crime Scene, but she was a little nervous now. She chomped three more Marie biscuits wedged together as a wafer. She must hurry up. The manual had said, "the crime scene must be secured and the evidence found and noted as quickly as possible to guard against degradation of evidence." *Perhaps I should have gone to Caledon Square first, I could have picked up the manual and made sure I follow the right procedures. Oh well, let's get on with it. Upwards and onwards.* On thinking that her mood darkened and worry increased. *Signal Hill is certainly upwards, and Kloof Nek becomes terribly steep, will my little scooter make it. It's only 50cc?*

Thembisa grabbed her police satchel, stowed her hat under her arm, made sure she had a torch, locked up quickly, and descended the four flights of stairs from the top to the ground floor where her fire-red Vespa was kept under a communal aluminium awning. Gathering her navy raincoat around her tightly, Thembisa opened the scooter seat-well, removed her white helmet and replaced it with her police officer's hat. She attached her satchel on the back rack and sat down to crank the starter motor.

It cranked over and over — at first robust and then started to fade, but the engine didn't start. Thembisa looked down at the fuel gauge, the needle was at E. *Shit what now?* She continued sitting on the scooter, both hands on the rubber hand grips, her shoulders slumped over, and inspected her surroundings. Noting a coiled garden hose by the building's side and a vintage Beetle, two across, in the parking spaces in front of the building, Thembisa formulated a plan — *the end most certainly justified the means.* She got off her bike, took out her pen knife and cut off a good length of garden hose, then walked over to the Volkswagen to see if it was suitable. Yes, it had the 'old type' of fuelling system, eminently siphonable into her scooter's little tank. She brought the Vespa alongside, pushed the hose into the Beetle's tank, sucked hard on its other end, wary of not aspirating the petrol, but was unpractised in the art of thievery. *Shit,* Thembisa spat out the gasoline, "Shoo, shoo, shoo," she shook her head in disgust, her helmet felt heavy on her head as it rotated. *One more time, just one more time,* she got the petrol flowing without another mouth full and pushed the hose into the scooter's tank and watched the gauge rise beyond E towards F with satisfaction, when a dog's barking tested her nerves and she interrupted the transfusion, lifting the hose high to let the remaining fuel run back into its owner's tank and then secured the two petrol caps back in their respective places. Thembisa curled up the hose and put the evidence into the well under her police hat and closed the scooter seat with a crunch locking it in the process. She looked around again guiltily. *She would be in deep trouble if someone had seen her, but she would worry about that later. Now, upwards and onwards.*

Mercifully, the engine started and Thembisa maneuvered out of the driveway and on to Kloof Nek Road, reaching its peak far too slowly for her increasing sense of urgency; the 50cc engine had been just adequate to the task, but she could probably have *walked* faster. Thembisa turned right at the STOP sign and crossed on to Signal Hill road. The first part was excessively steep; the scooter's engine took a gulp and the bike a lurch underneath her, so she decided to get off to ease its burden, only getting on again, when the road that coursed beneath adjacent Lion's Head evened out into a less extreme slope, to curve round to the parking lot that topped Signal Hill, where she soon arrived, flustered, reeking of petrol, and inexcusably late.

†

Despite the brilliant moonshine playing over the stretch of veldt that gradually sloped down from the parking lot on Signal Hill that early morning, there was yet insufficient light to fully evaluate the crime scene, so the police van had been parked at its verge to train its headlights on the body lying collapsed in the sandy field, some one hundred paces on — Lion's Head a distant shadow across the void.

Thembisa could clearly smell the police van's

diesel exhaust fumes mixing in the salty air as she rode over the tarmac, past the public toilets that stretched underneath the gleaming signal tower, and over the deserted, paint-marked, parking spaces to come to a stop alongside the sputtering vehicle. The beam of her scooter headlight caught a glint of something in the underbrush as she parked. Thembisa had wanted to press the bikes' hooter in welcome but had pressed the 'beam' button instead, focusing everyone's attention on the light's trajectory as she settled the scooter.

A lean police officer, a flash of sideburns curling from under his cap and a cigarette burning at the corner of his mouth, opened the yellow vehicle's door and exited in one sliding motion.

"Good morning detective Dlamini we have been waiting for you. I am Jan du Plessis, Warrant Officer du Plessis." He glanced at his watch through slitted eyelashes and stroked down his tunic with the other hand. A puff of smoke passed his thin lips rimmed by an inadequate moustache.

"And I am Constable Thandi Matloapane at your service, pleased to meet you," a broad smile shone from a plump, coal coloured face and was accompanied by what looked to Thembisa like an ungainly cross between a curtsey and a bow, "and now it seems that you have found something that we must investigate."

Thembisa sat straddling the Vespa, her helmet still close on her head, keenly aware of the garden hose beneath her seat. "Good morning, sergeant and constable. Yebo," Thembisa adjusted the handlebars so that the scooter's headlight beam angled in the direction it had played, eliciting the flash again, barely visible through the distant scrabble of bush below a thicket of blue gum trees under what appeared to be a very large stone. "We must leave no stone unturned... Sergeant... I mean Warrant Officer du Plessis, no stone unturned. Now if you will excuse me for one minute, I will get out my hat, put away this helmet and we can get to business. Could you gather the team at that Port Jackson over there Jan?" Thembisa stretched out her left hand and used its malformed little finger as an indicator, "to the side, here by the curb. We can investigate that boulder later. We must survey the crime scene from a distance before we decide on a plan," Thembisa was pointing to the fledgling willow that stuck out from a small copse that lined a short section of the parking lot, its fallow leaves stirred in the slight breeze rising from the darkened sea, the distant horizon starting to edge with early morning light.

Suitably hatted, Thembisa felt a bit more in charge although keenly aware of the stink of petrol fumes that had leaked from the coiled hose and evaporated into her hat in the enclosed seat space. She walked over to the three police officers who stood clumped in front of the Port Jackson, surveying the wedge of veldt displayed by the headlights. They were stamping their feet in the rocky field to gain some warmth from the activity, interrupting, only for a brief instant, the annoying chirping of early morning birds, which were flittering about the brush.

Pleased to see a fellow policewoman, still a relative rarity on the force, on her investigating team, Thembisa waved her torch to light up her own face when she came to a stop in front them. "Colleagues, I am Thembisa, sorry for being a little tardy, engine trouble. Now fixed... I hope," she looked each in the eyes in turn, lighting on the third officer previously unmet.

"Constable Hans Smit, *goeie môre*," a sparse moustache outlined purple lips as the policeman raised a stocky hand to tuck a lock of hair under the cap perched askew on his head.

"And you other two, I know. Jan and Thandi, can we keep it to first names please; I don't want to stand on ceremony when there is work to be done," Thembisa returned the torch to the satchel hanging over her shoulder and pulled her coat a little tighter. "Hau it is too, too cold today. Too cold." She stamped her feet twice. "You all know that this is my first case, don't you? I will need all the help you can give me with this investigation. But... but the first order of business is that we must secure the crime scene and decide on only one access point to the victim," Thembisa raised her bent pinkie again and then swivelled to point it at Constable Matloapane, "could you do that Thandi? I have tape if you need it. Has anyone walked over to the victim yet?"

"No, we thought it best to wait," Jan du Plessis exhaled smoke from his seemingly perpetual cigarette, "but we have been observing the crime scene from the car with the headlights. The victim is dead for sure, it looks like his head has been stoved in and he is lying in a pool of blood," Du Plessis pinched his cigarette between finger and thumb and traced a glowing arc from the body to the police van's headlights at the tarmac's verge.

"I can see car track marks over there and it looks like there may have been a scuffle," Constable Hans Smit's meagre moustache was working out his observations, "you can see the grass is flattened there, and there... and then the victim was probably dragged from the motorcar to where he is lying now and killed on the spot. I think we should look under that rock over there in the distance under that thicket of trees — the one you pointed out with your headlight, Thembisa," the policeman indicated each site with a well-trained torch as he spoke.

"Nah, I think that stone is a red herring," Sergeant du Plessis re-joined, taking a final draw of his smouldering cigarette, the butt again pinched between finger and thumb; he then flicked it in the direction of the corpse.

"No, no, no... Du Plessis, nee, you are contaminating the crime scene with your cigarette, never do that," Thembisa plucked off her hat, shook her hair loose releasing a waft of petroleum, and then bunched it all back in place before continuing, "do you want to be implicated in the crime? That is totally against the Locard Principle of detective work. Every criminal leaves a trace, an *imprint*. We must find their tracks, find what they left behind.

That's how we can identify the perpetrators. We must take care *not* to leave our own trace. Cigarette butts are valuable sources of DNA evidence. Our lab can do DNA analysis can't they?" Thembisa took a deep breath but didn't wait for an answer. "But first we must photograph everything. Did you bring the cameras? We must take the wide angle scenes first and then focus down on every detail, especially those tracks," Thembisa, swivelled her hatted head in the general direction, releasing another whiff of fumes, "look to see if there were any tire marks left from a car. Will you do that please Hans? We'll go and look at the corpse when you're finished. I have my Polaroid here for extra closeups."

The police team employed themselves as requested, while Thembisa walked back across the tarmac, past the greying toilet block and on up to the signal tower looming behind it. She climbed up its funnel cage and observed the crime scene from above. *Observation distinguishes the good detective from the also rans. Powers of observation were the most important, but good notes, decent photographs, meticulous sketches, and appropriate collection, documentation and processing of evidence could help win the day,* Thembisa reflected, *attention to detail was the key point stressed in my training. And to be honest, I'm a little lacking in that department.* Thembisa gazed out over the 270° view that Signal Hill's steel tower afforded; the landscape emerging in the strengthening light. *I will just have to pay attention to EVERY detail if I am to establish the truth. To determine what actually happened here this past night. Who killed this man and why?* She was starting to rehearse already what she might have to say in court. *"Your Honour, we found the body..."*

"Detective, detective. Thembisa," Thandi was yelling through cupped hands from the parking lot below. "Yoo, hoo, we've got to get on with it. We've got two hours till shift change at eight o'clock."

Thembisa retraced her steps down from the tower back to her scooter and, feeling hot, took off her coat and draped it over its seat. "Alright, please follow me. Single file," and started walking towards the large stone in the thicket of blue gum trees. Once there she stopped to take a photograph and asked Hans to do the same before continuing. "What do you guys see?"

"Nothing," Jan had stopped while the photographs were being taken and was knocking another cigarette out of his Lucky Strike packet when he suddenly changed his mind and replaced the smokes in his top pocket. Looking a little chastened he continued, "maybe there are some footprints round the stone, it looks awfully heavy."

Constable Hans Smit bent down to look at the granite rock more closely, shining his torch around its perimeter, "just a gleam of something metal here, that's what we must have seen, maybe the silver lining from a cigarette packet squashed under there?" He looked up from the half-kneeling position he had adopted, one hand resting shoulder height on the boulder.

"Do you think we can lift it for Thembisa?" Hans

said, "I think it will take three of us at least, maybe four."

"No problem," said Thandi already crouching in position like the sumo wrestler she was built like. Thembisa could see that the policewoman was used to heavy work.

"Alright, said Hans Smit, pursing his lips, "but what do we do if there is indeed a weapon there Thembisa? Do we put the stone back in its place or try to move it to the side or what? I think that will be hardly possible. Too heavy. You're the detective. You decide."

Thembisa was a little unsure of what to do so she just took out her Polaroid camera and said, "If you guys can lift it, we will see what we find. If you can't, it is unlikely that there is anything there; after all the perps would have to have done the same thing to hide a weapon."

The three got into crouched positions around the rock and Thembisa counted down. She had taken off her hat, her hair again awash across her shoulders, and lay flat on the ground, crooked up on both elbows, camera poised, "One, two, three, lift! Lift!"

Thandi grunted, Hans groaned, and Jan roared as they overcame gravity and the stone slowly lifted, just enough for Thembisa to trigger the Polaroid which she had placed flat in the dirt, after which the three relented, and the stone dropped back to the ground with a heavy thud, a spurt of dust causing Thembisa to start coughing. She stood up to try and get away from the dust, the camera jiggling in both hands in front of her as the hacking dissipated. The breathless officers had clustered round to watch as the developing film emerged from the camera's front slit; the outlines of a knife blade materializing as the photograph took shape — the ambient morning light was now more than sufficient to dispense with the need for torches and continue their investigations at pace.

"Aitsa, we've got it. We've got the murder weapon," Thandi was pumping her arms in jubilation.

"Well almost," Thembisa said. "If you can lift the stone one more time I can reach under and pull it out."

"No, you must use a stick to sweep it out. It is too dangerous otherwise; you might lose your arm if we drop the stone on it, Thandi said.

"And, here Thembisa, wear these gloves. There is lots of HIV around."

The possible murder weapon — a blood encrusted dagger with an ivory handle — duly retrieved, photographed, numbered and bagged, the process of finding clues and processing evidence was repeated, until Detective Dlamini was completely satisfied that they had done the crime scene justice so that the body could be carried to the police van and transported to the Salt River Mortuary for forensic analysis. Pleased with a job well done, Thembisa thanked the officers, and finished scribbling her notes.

Keenly aware that she had to be back at Caledon Square Police Station for the all-important police parade at nine o'clock, she walked over to the Vespa, the only remaining vehicle in the desolate parking lot. She unlocked the scooter's seat with the ignition key and placed it in her top tunic pocket and then folded back the seat on its hinge to angle it up against the handlebars, bent over to retrieve her helmet, exchanged it for the hat, and wondered what to do about the garden hose still coiled at the bottom of the plastic seat-well; lasting evidence of her recent crime. She could feel the perspiration cooling underneath her helmet; her brow formed three v's involuntarily. Thembisa stood back and looked about and listened carefully for any sounds of approach. No one. Nothing. Just a few birds chirping and the rumble of the city's traffic coming up in little waves. She leant over the scooter again, winced at the petrol damp, pulled out the garden hose and rolled it into a tight coil and placed it into her hat lying upturned in the scooter's seat-well, noting with dismay that a few drops of petrol had stained the hat's felt lining. Leaving her hat where it lay, Thembisa stood up again, and twirled around slowly on one heel, her shoe point circling the car park to check again that no-one had observed her, then stopped to study Signal Hill's gleaming tower reflecting the rising sun's light above the black-roofed toilet building, now an off-colour white in the broadening daylight. Satisfied that no one else was present, Thembisa leant over her scooter again, retrieved the hat, bundled it under her arm, completely unaware that her ignition/seat-lock key had fallen into the padded seat-well, and so slammed the seat closed, and marched off across the tarmac in the direction of the toilet block beyond which she had spied a clump of bushy trees underneath the signal tower.

Thembisa's plans were rudely interrupted. A peloton of multi-hued cyclists breeched Signal Hill road's apex, heaving into view, their breathing punctuated by exhilarated gasps as they shot around the policewoman and came to rest in a line next to her scooter. They settled down to take in the vast view of Lion's Head and the deep-blue Atlantic beyond, leaving Thembisa little option but to dart into the *Female* side of the restroom, from where she observed proceedings through an envelope sized, grate covered, venthole that had been fashioned into the concrete wall; a less than successful contrivance to purge the stench of urine that saturated the tight space. Observing that the cyclists seemed to be having a leisurely break; they had dismounted, propped up their bikes against perimeter posts, and were walking around the triangle of police tape that Constable Matloapane had erected, Thembisa closed the stall door, and the latrine seat, pulled the hose pipe out of her hat and got up on to the toilet cover. Knocking her helmet on the close ceiling, Thembisa crouched, bit the hose between her teeth to free her hands, and lifted the top of the lavatory's cistern, set it back ajar, leaving just enough room for her to feed the pipe into the tank, replace the cover, and get down again, in a surprisingly fluid manoeuvre, that spread a sweaty smile across her taut face. Pleased, Thembisa nevertheless checked her work. *Attention to every detail,* she thought, and pulled the toilet's chain to make sure that the hidden hose pipe would not impair the good functioning of the latrine. She was dismayed to find the truth: the toilet wouldn't flush — there was no water in the tank. *No wonder the smell of urine had been so ripe.* She looked down at her watch as she considered what to do next: 8:30, there wasn't time for another plan, she wanted to get back to her flat, freshen up for the all-important parade, and get herself down to Caledon Square all in good time.

Thembisa left the privy at a pace. Police hat in hand, she trotted over to her scooter, her helmet strap tugging at her neck with every bounce, as she reached into her top pocket for the bike's ignition key. "Shit." Thembisa turned around and retraced her steps back into the *Female* section. Finding nothing she ran back to the scooter, the peloton of cyclists now attuning to Thembisa's increasing agitation.

"What's the matter officer?" called a blonde man, shiny in bright red lycra.

"I have lost my key; I think it may have dropped into the scooter seat and that's locked now. I must be at Caledon Square at nine... for an important meeting," Thembisa started to unstrap her helmet, having put down her satchel.

"No problem. You can keep that helmet on," a thickset muscular man wheeled his bike forward. "My mates here are always ragging me about my back carrier. Now we can put it to good use. If it's a little too hard you can sit on your police hat, it already looks bent out of shape," he grinned. "I'll get you down the hill in no time. No time at all. Get on."

†

Nine o'clock sharp. The parade proceedings were just getting underway, when Detective Thembisa Dlamini entered through the back door of the assembly room, styled to accommodate the wide range of police meetings necessary to the good functioning of the Police Headquarters of Cape Town. Today, around thirty police officers were mustered on hard wooden chairs in four arcs around a central, slightly elevated podium, back dropped, to the one side by a silver screen used regularly for slide shows, and to the other by a green board penned with fading white chalk. Slow-moving fans overhead blended mixtures of tobacco smoke; the one above the podium stirring the South African flag on the left and the South African Police flag to the right, both standing sentinel to events.

The burly officer in charge of the parade — his voice sounded like the one on the telephone that had awakened Thembisa earlier in the morning — was welcoming those marshalled from behind a lectern: "Good morning, *goeie môre, môlo,* we must greet you in *three* official languages these days in the new South Africa." He wiped a dark brow with a white handkerchief pushing back his navy police service cap, its eight-starred medallion lustrous as he looked over at the second lectern. "Today we have a special

72

guest... ah... ah... better to say... ah... a visit from our boss," a stretch of perfect white teeth, "Colonel Pieter Marais, who actually needs no introduction," another dab with the handkerchief, "he will be auditing, I mean to say, *observing*, today's case discussions, to see if we are doing a good jobp."

"No, I will not, I will be *conducting* the parade."

Thembisa observed a very tall, gaunt, leathery, almost skeletal man with a tight square jaw and curved down mouth that lined a tobacco stained, grey-stippled moustache, clipped precisely to the edges of his pressed lips. The colonel seemed to enlarge as he spoke, filling out his splendid police uniform, the multi-coloured decorations at his breast pocket gleaming as his barrel chest expanded. His brown eyes were hooded *like a snake's* and enlarged by broad horn-rimmed glasses *the size of goggles,* that pushed back a mane of greying hair combed behind his too-large ears and pressed tightly beneath his S.A.P. senior officers cap, festooned with gold braid over its black rim to reflect the commander's senior status in the police hierarchy.

The hefty officer of the day recanted, "Yebo, I understand Colonel Marais. I understand. I see that Detective Dlamini, has just come in from our freshest case. Would you like to start with her."

Thembisa shrunk into one of the back seats at the prospect. Her tunic was dusty, her light blue dress creased beyond decency and her black shoes scuffed and dirty from the frosty veldt. But more unforgiveable was that her policewomen's cap was ruined; its starred medallion lost, its navy felt misshapen and its black hatband was coming loose at a seam — never mind the petroleum smell she couldn't seem to escape from.

"Yes. Please call her forward to sketch the outlines of the case." Smack. Colonel Marais emphasized his points with the flat of his hand hitting the resonant lectern. "I don't want a longwinded presentation." Smack. "Just the facts. Come forward, come forward, and please put on your hat like the rest of us."

Once ensconced behind the vacated lectern on the podium, Thembisa first stretched to hold both of its varnished sides and then gazed to her left at Colonel Marais fixing him with hazel eyes now fully encircled by white, and then turned to her fellow detectives, searching for a flicker of recognition for the predicament she found herself in. Finding only blank stares across the smoky room, she started, her throat emitting a low rumble she was unused to. "Sir, I am sorry for my appearance. As you can see, I have just come back from a job. I would have tidied up and been in time for this presentation but my scooter broke down."

"Your scooter?" Marais' hand slapped down, "you don't ride in an official police car, DETECTIVE?"

"No sir, it was expedient to efficiency in the middle of the night."

"It does not look like it to me. Does it look like it to your fellow detectives?" Marais, gestured with a bony hand into the room.

But for a few shifting chairs, coughs and smoke

exhalations, no coherent response answered what became a rhetorical question.

"If I may sir?" Thembisa unlatched the flap of her satchel still hanging from her shoulder, "refer to my notes here," and pulled out a ring-bound pad to place it on the lectern, "I will be able to present a better case."

"Yes. That is all very well, but I am most interested in your *process*. The process you used to cordon off the crime scene. Did you avoid contamination of the crime scene?" Marais's hooded eyes, magnified through his glasses bored into Thembisa's, "did you or any of your team introduce foreign objects to the scene or its surroundings, that might be attributed to the perpetrators?"

"I... I... I... don't thi-i-ink so," Thembisa looked down, to get underneath Marais' stare, the crescent of white above her flashing irises almost a half-moon. "I followed the Locard Principles."

"The Locard principle... hah... that text-book rubbish... did you follow process. I ask, and you quote the textbook at me?"

"If I may sir? If I may?" A sturdily built Zulu policewoman rose from a back row, holding up a pink palm for attention.

"And who are you? I haven't seen you here before."

"I am Constable Thandi Matloapane. I have only recently joined the South African Police Service," she rested her ample arms across a wide bust, "I was there on Signal Hill, on duty with Detective Dlamini, early this morning. I can attest to her utmost efficiency at the crime scene. In fact she found the murder weapon because of the scooter's headlight... "

"That's enough, that's enough" Marais interjected, causing the policewoman to regain her seat with an exasperated snort and Thembisa to thank her with a glance, before fixing Marais in her sights; she was getting cross with the Colonel. *I am not sure what this man's case is.*

"Yes, Detective Dlamini. You can be angry with me," the colonel looked across at Thembisa, having parted his moustache with a downward stroke of his pincered finger and thumb. "I don't care. Police procedure must be followed at all times. I am still not sure that I got a straight answer from you. That big officer over there," the Colonel pointed his purple nose in Thandi's general direction, "interrupted my question. Did you or any of your fellow officer's contaminate the crime scene in any way?" Marais smacked the lectern, and his bushy eyebrows flared at Thembisa above his spectacles.

"No."

"No, what?" a further upwards flare of the eyebrows.

"No, Colonel."

"That's better," Marais seemed to deflate a bit, but then returned to the attack, "did you measure off the site properly. I saw your shoes were muddy. I hope you didn't use shoe-lengths for measurement?" He turned to his audience, where a few smiles at this question were playing on the assembled faces; Thandi's remained at a scowl.

"That was from the frost this morning, Thembisa replied. "No we don't use *shoe lengths* like you did in the past, we use modern methods; a tape measure of course. Thembisa rose on the balls of her feet, her flat hands on the podium, leaning towards Marais pugnaciously. "And we secured the whole perimeter with tape. We did everything exactly according to S.A.P.S. Policy five, and captured each and every event of the process."

"Each and every event of the process? Hah" Marais answered Dlamini's stance with yet another blow to the lectern, this time with his fist. You say you follow the Locard Principle, the crux of detective work. What do you mean?"

"Sir, every perp, or perps, in this case leave imprints of their presence; this must be found, photographed, documented, labelled and subjected to strict continuity of custody should the prosecution be successful... "

"You say perps. Plural. Why?" Marais lifted his hat, stroked back a v-line of greying hair and replaced it, before looking again at Thembisa, his grooming complete.

"It took three of us to lift the stone to find the murder weapon... "

"Okay. Okay, Detective Dlamini? Is that your name? Dlamini, a common Xhosa name, I know. Your birth name?" Marais looked at Thembisa as if he wanted to plumb the depths of her being, to turn her inside out and examine her.

Thembisa felt it almost as a questing look, like a

shy dog looking up at you. She was unsure how to answer, but she didn't want to put any further feet wrong: "Yes, my birth name," although she had had recurring doubts about the truth of that statement.

At that, Marais seemed to surface from the plunge into the personal and became the commanding officer once again.

"Okay, detective, so you secured the crime scene and located the murder weapon... what was it?"

"A dagger."

"Ja, don't interrupt my train of thought. So you secured the crime scene but did you examine the close vicinity? The car park and the block of toilets alongside. Did you ascertain that there was no evidence left there?"

"Hau," Thembisa put three fingers in front of her mouth and thought of the garden hose, "I... ah... I... we didn't examine the toilets" and turned to Constable Matloapane for help from the back row. Noting just a shake of the head, Thembisa turned to her persecutor, but this time her long eyelashes and dark eyebrows had sunk downwards; she could not meet Marais's irritated eyes.

"Very well. I thought as much. That's why I do these rounds. Dismissed," Marais turned fully towards the police gathered in the auditorium, as Thembisa stepped off the podium, waiting for the rotund presiding officer to laboriously regain the vacated place behind the lectern underneath the faintly moving South African flag, before continuing.

"Detective Xebo, please send another team, as

soon as possible, to scour the vicinity of the crime. I want those toilets checked, and fingerprinted and anything suspicious like saliva, blood etc. must be sent for DNA testing. We must leave no stones unturned when we investigate. None. My job is finished here. I will be on my way. Good morning to you all." Marais saluted, stepped down from the podium as the police rose to stand at attention, and left through a side exit, a rising commotion of voices contained by the thump of the closing door.

Thembisa made her way to sit forlornly next to Thandi, who put her heavy hand on the detective's satchel strapped shoulder.

"*Toe maar,* no matter, here take this hanky. That Marais is a bastard. I bet he came today just to show who is boss. To belittle us. You did a good job Thembisa, I know it. That's why I came to support you, past my shift."

Thembisa slid her hat over her face; her shoulders trembled.

"Hau, that hat is a mess. Here take mine, I will get you a replacement, the correct size, mine is a little big for you," Thandi's round face became rounder. "I'm sure you have paperwork to do and this meeting is going to take till lunch time, I think, given all the to-do with Colonel Marais."

"Thanks," Thembisa had put down her hat on an open chair next to her, blown her nose and swiped her face, a smear of grime imprinting the white handkerchief. She was unsure whether to give it back, so she held it clenched in her fist. "Do you think they will find anything in the toilets Thandi?"

"Nah, I went for a pee in there with my torch before you arrived and I saw nothing. Should be okay."

Thembisa wasn't so sure but left it at that. She moved forward to sit in the second row of chairs where a place had opened and tried to focus on the litany of cases that were being presented from the podium; the crime scene often sketched out on the greenboard as she had been prepared to do but not been given a chance by Colonel Marais. Her head in turmoil, she tried to straighten her thoughts about her first case by re-writing it in her notebook, willing the interminable meeting to be over. One o'clock. One-fifteen. The meeting finally ended, Thembisa sheepishly bid her farewells and walked wearily into the tearoom to get a needed cup of coffee. Filling the porcelain mug to the brim and turning away from the sideboard where the kettle had come to the boil, Thembisa crashed into a tall thin man dressed in a pale safari suit. She caught the flash of a stethoscope swinging from his neck as they collided. The cup of coffee in her hand spilling its hot liquid over both of them, before splintering on the tiled floor.

†

5

Cape Town, 1996

Le Café, a restaurant across from Caledon Square Police Station, a little way up on Buitenkant Street, looked much as you might have expected. Fronted by doubled glass doors concertinaed wide open to admit the warmth of the midday sunlight, its foot-square alternating black and white floor tiles stretched the length and breadth of the bistro. Busied by Capetonians sitting in high backed chairs around circular mahogany tables of various size, the seating arrangements squared off to a central bar-come-service counter where tenders were serving food and drink at speed, while liveried waitresses cleared vacated tables readying them for the next round.

Sitting in the back corner, triangulated by mirrors that circumferenced the walls, Thembisa sat sipping a cappuccino. Comfortable in her freshly pressed police uniform, her eyes darted around in search of Doctor Marais. *The man is either interminably late or he's stood me up,* she thought. *Ah well, it wouldn't be the first time, but the first time with a whitey, and he was kind of cute with that beard. Hau, here he is, all rushed and flustered and shy, he hasn't seen me. Just too many people.* Thembisa got up and waved.

"Doctor Marais, doctor, I am over here, joo-hoo!"

"I am so sorry, so sorry Detective. I couldn't find parking."

"But you're here now and its Thembisa, Thembi-sa."

"Ja, ja and Pieter please. Can I get you some more coffee?"

"No need, no need, I'll call over a waiter you just *skop jou nes.*"

'Kick your nest' — settle down — that's impressive, she knows her Afrikaans, Pieter thought and sat down heavily on the chair he had pulled back from under the table for two. He could see both their reflections as he did so. *She looks nice and what a mess I look; my hair, my beard.* Pieter restrained from pulling out his comb tucked into his beige safari suit jacket pocket, and instead tented his hands over his forehead, pulled them back to shape his brown curly hair behind his sallow ears and then pushed them forward again to sharpen his beard, finishing the motion, with his hands in a prayerful formation over his hooked nose, his two thumbs jutting underneath his chin to hide his crooked front teeth making his speech more nasal than usual.

"Agh, ja, I have looked forward to sitting with you."

"Aikona," Thembisa moved her head in a circular motion repetitively, "I cannot hear what you are mumbling, and can't read your lips if you hide them from me."

"I'm sorry," Pieter placed his hands on the table, "I said, I was looking forward to seeing you."

"Yes, better late than never," Thembisa raised her crooked pinkie to summon a waitress and ordered two cappuccinos and a plate of samosas, having checked with Pieter whether he favoured, chicken, veg or mincemeat.

"Mince, my mother makes those best, but wasn't I the one who was to do the ordering?"

"Nah, nah, too, too late," shake of the head, "and I'm flush, I just got my pay check. But more to the point, your mother made mince samosas?"

Yes, she came from Indonesia, and lived in District Six before it was destroyed," Pieter steadied the table and repositioned it: he had detected imbalance.

"And your father? I met Colonel Marais yesterday in a police meeting. He scares me shitless. How did they meet?"

Pieter fiddled with the table, unbalancing it again, and then stretched back see-sawing on the hind paws of his chair. He put his hands behind his head flailing out his elbows, "I'm not really sure, they don't tell me much about it, but I gather it was during some police activity."

"You haven't looked in the family photograph album to find out? Aren't you a doctor, don't you diagnose the truth? That's what detectives do. Sort of. That's why I like it."

My oh my, she's like a tiger, I wouldn't want to cross swords with her, Pieter pursed his lips into the semblance of a smile, careful not to unbare his horse-like teeth.

"And you don't look like your father, I think; you

83

just seem much kinder and caring and, and... softer."

"Ja, ja, perhaps, from the border, in the army, before medical school, that wasn't... good, but let's change the subject, this was supposed to be fun."

"You are not having fun?"

"Yes, actually dit is *lekka om te gesels*. It's great to talk. So tell me about your parents."

Now it gets complicated, Thembisa thought. She was brought up in Soweto Township; Faith Dlamini and Mamie Dlamini had cared for her as if their own. And then the Soweto Riots forced the move to Cape Town for better schooling — on to another branch of the Dlamini's, headed by Uncle Goodwill, the reason for her wanting to become a detective in the first place. But she wasn't going to that complicated subject now — to early — so Thembisa just shook her head again, her braided ringlets rippling over her hunched shoulders and said, "it's too, too involved for light conversation, maybe we will get there. I grew up in Soweto, then moved to the Cape after the riots and have just finished at the Police College in Bishop Lavis. I have a complicated case to solve."

"Truth tends to reveal its highest wisdom in the guise of simplicity," Pieter took a corner bite from one of the steaming samosas that had been placed on the table between them, two golden pastry flakes flecking his moustache.

"What? Are you a philosopher *and* a doctor?"

"A bit. I like Nietzsche best. *Thus Spake Zarathustra* — more or less a prose-poem; have you read it?"

"No, that stuff gets you nowhere, just plain navel

gazing. So what is that quote supposed to mean? You've got samosa all over your beard." Thembisa bent forward to pick up a napkin that fringed the plate of triangular pastries, dislodging one that skittered off the table and on to the floor.

"Now look what you made me do. When I see you, seemingly, accidents must happen." Thembisa, stroked the flakes out of Pieter's beard with two deft dabs, ignored the distant samosa, having observed that it had headed under a counter in a corner, angled her shoulders back to push out her breasts and took a prolonged sip of cappuccino, before placing the cup back in her saucer slowly, all the while observing Willem's response: *And he's a thoughtful fellow on top of it all, but he is a little weird; there must be something behind that, he looks frightened, and jittery.*

A wail of police sirens dopplered past, intensifying and when receded allowed conversation in the bustling restaurant to resume. Thembisa watched Pieter at first tensing, his fingers trembled, and then when the cacophony abated, relaxing and the tremor faded.

"Well, I think it means, and certainly that is often the case in medicine, that there is one explanation for multiple symptoms and signs. You know, the plethora of complaints and physical findings that a patient brings tells the story leading to a diagnosis of only one disease. That is the difficulty and the simplicity. Take for example Tuberculosis: TB. The patient can present with any number of symptoms — like coughing, or night sweats or weight loss, and signs — like wasting or lung pathology or even brain or heart problems that can be confused with other diseases like rheumatic fever, or an auto-immune disease. And then you have the one simple finding or test that clinches it all together."

"Yes, it sounds like the one piece of evidence, the puzzle-piece, that I must find in my first case," Thembisa said.

"Why don't you tell me about it," Pieter leaned forward into the prayerful position again.

"Can I? Its privileged information."

"Well, I'm a District Surgeon, aren't I? Perhaps I can help you piece it together. I have to present forensic evidence in court all the time."

"Yes, as I will have to, when I figure it out... But I am afraid, I'll screw it up."

"You screw it up? Nooit. You'll do a fine job, especially with a little help from your friends."

"You like that song by the Beatles?"

"Yes, but the Joe Cocker version; the one on the Woodstock album, that's the best. But back to business, go on, tell me."

"It was a murder case we found on Signal Hill, two days ago, when you ran into me, literally."

"You are too funny Thembisa, but that case I know. Was it the man with a stabbed chest? Did you take the Polaroids? They were actually very good. We can definitely talk about it. I did the autopsy. That and a few other things made me late and rushed the day I bumped into you; I usually take my time over things."

"Bumped? Aikona, that was a crash. Yebo, a crash."

"Oorait, a crash, but tell me how you found the murder weapon? I saw a Polaroid of a dagger underneath a stone."

"Yes, that was a bit of a business; just blind luck, my scooter... "

"You, you ride a scooter?"

"Yebo, cheap and cheerful, I have to watch the mullah. Not like you, Mister, Doctor.

"Agh, I have lots of expenses and overdrafts on my practice and a bursary to pay back to the state, that's one of the reasons I do the police work. My father, you know who?" Pieter looked up from jiggling the coffee spoon, stirring an emptied cup.

"Yes, I do, and hope that next time he is more friendly... but seemingly we are on the same case. Can you help me? Become my coach; you must have seen many detectives presenting their cases in court."

"Yes, ja, I will; but we have time, about two to three months, I would think."

"Will you excuse me for a moment Pieter, I must visit the Ladies?"

"Of course," Pieter giraffed his long neck to watch Thembisa recede in the mirror checking to ascertain whether she was moving in the correct direction. He reflected on the almost instantaneous affinity he had developed for this girl. *From the first moment, he had taken to her, despite their colour difference. Wait! Why was he wondering about that? Was it only in this country, that a difference in skin pigmentation would pose as a question around attraction?"* Pieter pursed his lips into a snout. *The colour difference that would have made criminal congress between them, as short as ten years ago, under apartheid. The concept of colour difference distorted perception. Like Immanuel Kant's rose tinted glasses. Nietzsche must have something to say about that,* but all Pieter could think of was '*That for which we find words is already dead in our hearts*' and ever hopeful of finding a compatible partner, he was glad when his brooding was interrupted by the splash of gaiety that Thembisa brought back to the table. She plunged him back to reality with her next question.

"And so what where *you* doing at the Truth and Reconciliation Commission in Bellville? As a whitey you stuck out like a sore thumb. I spied you trying to hide away from the cameras; the way you were skulking around in the back corner behind the organ. That was the first time I got to attend such a meeting and I must say I was impressed with the security preparations as well as the proceedings. Did you see that woman, Miss Promise Madiba? Such dignity, so empowering. The cruelty of apartheid. Like Miss Madiba, my head was turned to hate against you whites by the violence of the State against us. Those in power, not, people like you. The stinking NATs. Shoo, the stench. And after Soweto, I could not be the same, but I can tell you about that sometime." Thembisa had turned her brown-veined palms upwards and laid her hands on the table, while peering intently into Pieter's eyes, her dark eyebrows and thick eyelashes widening, her brilliant irises ablaze. She waited and sat still; a breath exhaled prodded Pieter to respond.

"I... I...," Pieter broke the line of sight and looked down at the varnished surface, his hands clenched tight, underneath the table, "I... I... have been following the TRC on television and wanted to see the situation first hand."

"Are you telling the truth? I'm a detective remember, trained... "

"Ja, ja," Pieter's eyes flicked back to Thembisa, "but not the whole truth... "

"Alright, but kind of the truth?" Thembisa's surprisingly low voice pitched up.

"But it may have to wait, until we know each other better," Pieter leaned in to Thembisa, but she leant back.

Can I trust her with my dilemma? Whether to apply to the TRC for amnesty for what I did or face criminal prosecution after the application deadline has passed. Afterall, the applicants for amnesty must ask for forgiveness from the victim's family. The perpetrator must do so at a TRC meeting. It could be a family just like Thembisa's. I know precious little about how the 'other' side lives. I've never been into Soweto nor any other township for that matter. Perhaps I can learn from her, and then in time ask her what she thinks I should do, and whether a black family would forgive me, or seek imprisonment.

"Doctor Marais? Earth calling Doctor Marais, you've gone into prayer mode again, a penny for your thoughts?"

"No, no, sorry, I was just looking at you. You are beautiful."

"Not so fast. I like you too, but lunch is over and I have to get back to work."

"Yes, me too. I have a prisoner to see."

They both stood up, a little awkwardly, and shook hands; Thembisa involuntarily clutching Pieter's a little longer and tighter than she had intended. They both said:

"When do we meet again?" And "snap." And then Thembisa started to giggle while Pieter provided a rare smile and said, "well what do you like to do?"

"I swim at the Longmarket Street Baths or at Muizenberg when I have time... and like to walk."

"Oorait then, come out to my place at Bloubergstrand. I have a flat across from the beach."

"But that water is too, too cold. Too cold."

"But we can walk along the beach and there is a nice restaurant, Ons Huisie, I can take you to."

"Then we must go Dutch."

"Oh no. If you tell me your life story, I pay for lunch."

"Well then you must tell me yours, and I pay for the desert. And you must provide coaching for my first case?"

"Okay, but that will no doubt require a series of meetings."

"Too clever, too, too clever," Thembisa put on her brand new police hat and exited Le Café, leaving Pieter to settle the bill.

†

6

Angola, 1980

"Pa my train ticket arrived today," Pieter said as he handed his plate over the table to his mother for another helping of the coriander spiced bobotie that was her special dish.

"For what? Call up?" The threesome were sitting in their habitual positions around the stinkhout dining room table that Pieter senior had made in his spare time in the woodwork section that backed their single garaged house in Parowvallei.

"Agh, ja. I should have volunteered for the police force as a conscientious objector."

"Never. We have spoken about this many times. My only son is not going to forsake his duty to his country," the police captain, still dressed in uniform, but for his tunic which now lay draped over the back rest of the flower-patterned couch furnishing the adjacent lounge, almost levitated from his riempie seat, only barely restrained by Marja's calming touch on his taut upper arm. "We've had this out before, I don't want to hear any more of it. DO YOU UNDERSTAND!"

"No. I still don't. I don't want to fight and kill. That's what's going on up there on the border. We're killing SWAPO soldiers and even civilians, I read."

Pieter ran his fingers through his increasingly long curls; school haircut rules were no longer in force now that he had matriculated. "You are always telling me to follow God's Word; forcing me to go to church," Pieter glared at his father. "Though shall not kill etc. That's why I want to be a conscientious objector. I don't want to kill anyone. I wouldn't have minded doing the three years of service for the police instead. Much better than two years in the army."

"Well, whose going to go to the army in your place? Tell me that? The Blacks? The Coloureds? Nooit, we can't trust them." Pieter senior had stopped eating, his fork and knife hovering over his plate. "The country is short of conscripts as it is, and there is a total onslaught against us. Why do you think military service has been extended to two years? Why? There's a *communist* onslaught. That's why. Inside the country, with the blacks causing all sorts of kak that the police force must contend with, and outside, with the Cubans. We are the final backstop for America. I read in *Die Burger,* that Fidel Castro has committed Cuban troops to fight us in Angola. And Russia is supplying weapons. They are arming the ANC's Umkhonto we Sizwe. Bah! I cannot pronounce that bloody name. The Spear of the Nation. What shit. The ANC is bloody well banned. But still they are killing our people." Pieter senior's handle bar moustache quavered and his brown eyes distended behind his thick glasses. "As a police officer, I deal with this kak every day. And the blacks are crafty. But we have informers, but still our people are getting killed. Not just on the border but here... here... at... at... home." The police officer removed and polished his bifocals, they had become soiled. "Inside the country. Pieter, if you only knew what I know, you would sing a different song my son. The armed forces and the police are fighting a total war — here and abroad, to keep us all safe."

"Yes, but we are doing the killing too. It's our boys on the border that are doing the fighting on the side of UNITA, and against SWAPO in South West."

"OKAY, Pieter, but I don't want you to shame our family, with this conscientious objection shit. Dit is NIE wat 'n man doen nie, to forsake the fatherland. You must be obedient to it. Like the good Book says. We must honour our country. When you join the army, you will get a Bible with an inscription from the State President. It is your holy duty to defend us against the enemy."

"Oraait, oraait, oraa-i-i-i-t that is now enough boys," Marja still dressed in her habitual yellow (she had forsaken saris for western dresses when she married Pieter) now connected father and son by patting their balled fists, both clenched on the batik tablecloth in front of her. "Pieter what are you called up for?"

Pieter reached back to the yellow-wood cabinet where he had left the ticket on top of the letter, he had received some time back, and read it out in a strained voice.

"P Marais, 10 Plein Road, Parow, Cape Town" and looked up and swallowed, "Burgermag-Citizen Force. 1 SA Battalion. 8 Jan '80 to 5 Jan '82. Bloemfontein.

"What date is the train ticket for?" Pieter senior pulled out his diary from his back pocket where it rested next to his comb.

"January 7th"

"That's a Monday, I can't make it. Mom will have to take you."

"Will you mom?" Pieter junior reached across and patted Marja's wrist lightly. She had been wringing it with her other hand.

"Of course. Now I am going to do the dishes so that you two can have a father and son chat."

"Marja, can you bring the brandy? The ten year old KWV, it's a special occasion, our son has got his marching orders." Pieter loosened his top pocket button and took out his red and white packet of Winstons and tapped out two cigarettes. Handing one to Pieter, he lit his own with a Lion match after which he passed the match box to his son. "Have you started to smoke yet?"

"No."

"Well best to start before you go to the army. Gives you something to look forward to in the breaks. It's going to be pretty rough, but I'm confident you will do us proud."

Pieter broke the first match, but on the second attempt it flared to life and ignited the tip, provoking the inevitable cough that accompanies the first draw, his face coloured and his eyes ran. His father clapped his back.

"There, there, 'taste America', that's what the advert says in the bioscope. Taste America."

"Have you thought what you want to do after the army? I want you to follow me in the police force."

"Agh nee, Pa. I'm thinking of medicine, if my matric results are good enough."

"That will be a pity; I think you will make a fine police officer."

"Yes, I know Pa, like you, but I want to help people. I don't like guns; I hated shooting practice during cadets. I've been reading a lot of philosophy, particularly Nietzsche. I'm trying to find out the meaning of life and what my role should be. So far, I have concluded that there is no meaning. God is just a man-made creation to soothe our conscience... provide visions of an afterlife or hell. Ever since I read *The Origin of the Species,* Darwin's book, it's clear. God did not create the world in seven days, natural selection did over billions. So, life is what you make of it. We create our own meaning and purpose. That's why I want to study medicine. To help cure people. I think that's meaningful. And... doctors don't take sides; they treat everyone equally."

"Nee, nee, you need a tot of brandy, that will set you straight. Of course there is a God, Our Father, and *no* other, and that is the first and most important commandment," the captain took a slug from his brandy glass, refilled it, clinked it against his son's, said "cheers" and then watched Pieter down the amber liquid, his prominent Adam's apple rising to the occasion.

"Yes, and I honour my father and my mother," Pieter junior raised his emptied glass, "I really do, but the Bible also says thou shall not steal, commit adultery, and not kill. And I see this happening around me... all the time. Especially the latter. We've just been talking about killing. I want to do the opposite; to heal. To follow the Hippocratic Oath, a *healthy* moral code," Pieter smiled at his own joke, "Nietzsche said. God is dead. He says so in a parable in *The Gay Science*." Pieter tipped his head back and downed the second brandy glass and shivered, drawing his lips downwards, "Nietzsche means that we must create our own moral code. Not rely on religion, for we have failed. Look around us pa. In the name of religion... of the Bible, we are killing people. We have no morals."

"Yes, Pieter, but we must. They are terrorists. They are trying to destroy our way of life here in South Africa. We have to act; we must root them out."

"Agh, nee pa, is there not another way; a political solution? *Apartheid* is clearly wrong minded. This whole contention that we are 'separate but equal' is never going to fly. Throughout history the oppressed have risen up. Look at what's just happened in Rhodesia. Mugabe will probably be named prime minister."

"It's exactly because of that we must fight, Pieter. Don't you understand? Mugabe is a bloody terrorist. If we don't kill them. They will kill us. Steal our farms, ruin the country. The blacks can't run anything. Look at the rest of Africa, what a mess that is. Corruption, looters, coups, that will happen here if we don't fight against it. Tell me of one country that has done well after colonial rule? One. No," the captain jutted out his square chin, "I must follow my orders. That is my job... as far as Nietzsche is concerned, I know only one of his quotes: 'What doesn't kill me makes me stronger,' I have it stuck on my wall in my office, to remind me of what I must do to survive. For *us* to survive. You and mom and me. As far as the rest; philosophy is *maar* nonsense. Too much thinking, too little action, I say." The captain downed his umpteenth glass of brandy, sat back in the chair, stretched out his arms, his light blue shirt cuffs rode up above his hairy wrists, "And I am sad to say, as to the question of studying medicine; we can't afford the medical school fees. Not on a police captain's salary. Maybe if I become a commander. But perhaps we can work on a police bursary for you... that's for another day. What I wanted to talk to you about, is your mother."

"What about her?" Pieter lowered his voice, looked around and then focused on his father.

"You know that I love her, don't you?"

"Yes, I think so... "

"And you too... don't ever forget it. Even though I give you a hard time sometimes it's for your own good; that's how I was brought up. From the first time I met mom, she shone. She was beautiful... still is, but she was angry at me at the beginning..."

"What for ?"

"No, that I can't tell you. But what I can tell you is that it took quite some time for Marja to come round to my way of thinking, but after that... you,

Pieter," the captain placed his non-smoking hand over his son's and squeezed, "have made that love run stronger. I took a chance with you and Marja and it has worked out for the better."

"What do you mean dad? You are speaking in riddles."

Captain Marais took a deep suck on his cigarette, exhaled the smoke slowly through mouth and nose, and continued.

"She's got cancer."

"Agh, no."

"Yes, of the female parts. She needs an operation. When you're away. She didn't want me to tell you, but I thought I should. She thinks we are talking about the 'birds and the bees.'"

†

Cape Town's Victorian train station pulsed with sounds of departure. Marja had parked her car in the adjacent parking grounds and accompanied Pieter into its vast foyer leading on to the trainlines running to the hinterland of South Africa and beyond. Now more acutely aware of the preciousness of life because of the cancer diagnosis, she was greatly afraid of what the army might visit on her timid teenager. She had fussed and faffed over him, to hide her disquiet. Ironing his white shirt, pressing his navy blazer and grey trousers so he could join the army in good style, despite his protestations that he wanted to wear jeans.

Marja had thought of Promise as she performed

the ironing, as she so often did when she saw hints of Promise in Pieter's face as he grew up. Marja was filled with sadness at the loss and missed Promise's love deeply. She could still not fully understand what had impelled Promise to abandon her only son, to her care. Marja had made peace with the fact that Promise had said she needed to keep her self-respect by opposing the destruction of her house, but could not imagine that she, Marja, could ever do such a thing. Especially, because his true father, Doctor Willem Jansen, was not there for Pieter. Perhaps, Promise had felt abandoned by Doctor Willem's suicide. Because that is what it was, Marja thought. Doctor Willem could not find a way out of the trap that was the Immorality Act. Even if the prosecution against them was unsuccessful as it turned out to be; he could not live with Promise in South Africa with the Act threatening their love, making it illegal. So he must have jumped, not fallen off Devil's Peak, the day before the Supreme Court hearing exonerated them. Willem had thought that there was no way forward for Promise and him. He had said as much, when the three of them were picnicking beside DeVilliers Dam on Table Mountain, back in 1960. The day Marja remembered so well, because that was the day Promise's and Marja's relationship started; Marja had been teaching Promise how to swim! They had both been naked because they had forgotten their swim suits. And that night there was a great rain storm, that broke over the house in District Six, and Promise came into her bedroom... and...

The smell of burning had interrupted Marja's thought stream. She had held the iron too long in one place on the ironing board. Marja raised it on its side and pulled out the wall plug to let it cool. And then continued thinking back.

She had taken up Pieter's offer of marriage, without any qualms. Afterall, she knew how to manipulate men. After being forced to train as a Geisha and become a comfort woman for the Japanese in Java, she had wanted to move to Holland after the War but was captured into prostitution when her ship docked in Cape Town. Here things went from bad to worse, until she married Henry Plaatjies to get out of the prostitution ring he controlled and became beholden to just one man. She had been quite happy with Henry and had lived a life of civic responsibility, but then he was killed standing right next to her during the Langa Riots, when she was stabbed in the heart with a bayonet and her life was saved by Promise and Willem at the Groote Schuur Hospital. And, having nowhere to go, Promise had taken Marja into her house in District Six and through a twist of fate, during the police raid that Pieter Marais conducted to catch Promise and Willem contravening the Immorality Act, Promise had escaped out the back window, and instead Marja and Willem had been prosecuted.

Marja picked up the iron, plugged it back into the wall plug again and with the other hand tested it for warmth, before starting on another of Pieter junior's shirts.

She smiled to herself as she thought back to the

Indonesian days when Willem and her had been teenage sweet-hearts before the terrible War separated them in 1942, only to be re-united in 1960, when Willem and Promise had saved her and given her a new life.

None of this was Pieter Marais' fault of course; he had had to follow orders. Pieter had been ordered to conduct the police raid on Promise's house to catch her contravening the Immorality Act with Doctor Willem in 1960, and again in 1966, to destroy the section of houses in District Six. He was not to blame, nevertheless his offer of marriage had been quite a shock. What would a God-fearing man like him want with a Coloured prostitute?

"Colourblind, Pieter Marais had said. I'm colourblind, I love you for *who* you are not *what* you are. I will look after you and the boy to the best of my abilities." And he had. Despite his brusque ways; Pieter had been loving, kind and tender. It was I who failed him; I could not give him another son. I was barren; an ex-prostitute all worn out. I blame all the sex I endured for the cervical cancer I now have to contend with. So what started as a marriage of convenience has worked out well for Pieter and me. I just wish I could see Promise again. I've no idea what has become of her. At least I have a part of her with me, though... but that too is now leaving; I hope nothing happens to Willem, I mean Pieter, in the army.

Marja had packed Pieter's kit bag with his civvies, a toothbrush, and the other bare essentials the army had mandated they bring, for they were soon to be clothed by the South African Defence Force and were not in need of more than a spare set of clothes — unlikely to be used during the next 6 weeks of basic training, with no earlier relief in sight.

"Mom, you can go now, I have my ticket and am all set."

"I want to see the train leave."

"No, mom, you don't look so well. You should go home. I am oorait."

Marja, dressed in a white blouse, yellow skirt and sandals against the summer heat had to reach up to put her hands on each of her tall son's shoulders, her long silky black hair dangling as a ponytail between her shoulder blades.

She regarded him, her cheeks puffing up pulling her scarlet lips into a feint of a smile and saw the spirit of the man he might become, dressed in the clothes she had prepared, his brown hair curled like a cauliflower over his ears. She moved a hand to feel the fuzz of his first beard.

"Stop that mom."

And then gave him a big hug, both arms around his midriff, which he reciprocated warmly, and then turned outwards, tripling away across the station's flagstone floor like a Geisha and out into the sunshine baked Adderley Street, where Pieter could see her turn a corner, stop, turn back to give a wave, and then disappear before he himself turned towards the trainline designated for Bloemfontein.

†

"You're sitting in my seat!"

Pieter had just got semi-comfortable at one of the two window seats of the leather and mahogany finished train compartment. His kitbag and blazer placed carefully on the aluminium rack overhead, his long legs folded sideways so as not to cross the imaginary line that protruded from the common basin that separated the two large outside windows, both slid down to refresh the concentrated air. The six occupancy space was full. Filled with anxious males from all walks of life. Some holding their army-issued tickets, others starting conversations, while yet another offered a freshly opened cigarette packet around the compartment.

"Yes you, *lang derm* you are sitting in my seat," a globular red face, already shorn of all hair, jutted through the glass sliding doors wedged open by a bulbous torso, followed immediately by a stubby, nail-bitten finger which pointed directly at Pieter, "6B, by the window."

"Let me have a look," Pieter got up, retrieved his blazer, and excused his way into the narrow corridor, wobbling as the train started haltingly, gathering steam, and rolled out of Cape Town station, out across the Cape Flats. "Yes, 6B is my seat. Here is the ticket."

"Let me see. By the way I'm Cornelius van Wyk, Corli for short," he held the tickets side by side between two equally fat thumbs and index fingers — the teenagers inspected the evidence. They had wedged their backs against the steel corridor wall,

Pieter at least a head taller than Corli,

"I'm Pieter Marais, I have no, *for short.*"

"That's because you are long! Ha, funny. But they're both 6B tickets. "*Dis nou mooi, dis nou fokkin mooi*" just like the army to fuck things up. And I'll bet the train's *stamp vol.*

Just then a navy-uniformed conductor, his cap crammed down on untidy grey hair, swayed into view between the interlocking carriage doors; the snapping of his ticket punch getting louder as he closed in.

"*Troepe,* what seems to be the problem boys. You are not supposed to be in the corridors, obstructing traffic. You must be in your seats for ticket collection."

"Jis, ja, well here's the problem conductor. The Army has issued us with the same ticket, 6B. Only one of us can sit in the seat. Are there any others?" Corli held up the tickets to demonstrate his point.

"Let me see... you're right," he snapped both tickets as one and gave them back, "trains full, not my problem, sort it out. But no obstructing the corridors, stand next to the lavatory, if you must. Get used to it, there will be plenty more of that where you're going. Hah." The conductor shoved past them and went into compartment six, to complete his rounds.

"Possession, is 9/10ths' of the law," Pieter said, "and I've got the seat."

"No you haven't. Youse out here, and I'm much heavier, I need the seat more."

Ja, kort, dik en ongeskik, short, fat and unruly,

Pieter thought, but said, "do you want a smoke?" and offered Corli a Winston, glad that he had followed his father's advice on the matter.

"A peace offering?"

"Sort of."

They each inhaled America after lighting up using a single match cupped in Pieter's hand; the quandary briefly at bay as the shared nicotine hit home.

"Let's share. Let's take turns," Corli offered, exhaling a stream of smoke through his nose.

"Like sentries."

"Yes, two hours on; two hours off. I'll go first, youse already been sitting for a while."

"No, I haven't. I just got there when you accosted me."

"Accosted? That's a big word. I merely begged the question. But still, I must rest. I've been travelling from Simon's Town to get here."

"That's only about an hour by train."

"There were unforeseen delays; wake me up in two hours' time," and with that Corli pushed past Pieter, his kitbag weighing down his left shoulder, heaved it on to the rack, and collapsed in seat 6B, almost immediately asleep, contained by comfy green leather.

†

"Uit, uit, uit. Troepe uit. Troepe get out and form a straight stripe in front of your carriage. Yes, I said your carriage. Get on with it, get on with it."

The overnight troop train had pulled into a siding to offload. Its locomotive, black with coal, releasing unspent steam, had hissed to a halt and stood clanking as the iron vehicle contracted; adding heat and the smell of oil to the concrete platform already warming in the early morning summer sunshine. Disturbed birds tweeted in competition.

"Welcome to Bloem. Line up. Line up. Put your kitbags at your feet and stand straight. I am Kaptein Odendaal." A thin ramrod of a man dressed in khaki, his brown boots capped by white spats, a purple beret slouched perfectly on his bald head, where a thin moustache pointed to a snout of a nose, making the officer look like a ferret who continued the strafing.

"No crying for your mommies now, boys. We will make men of you in short order. Riflemen. *Skutters*." He raised his swagger stick, before putting it back in his left armpit. "Six weeks, under my command. Ja, six weeks of basic training. That is all. Should be enough. We will make you into fighting men. Proud members of the South African Defence Force," the captain rolled his shoulders, causing the stars on his epaulets to shimmer, and moved his hand across his chest to clasp the brown stick.

"There is method to our madness. You have been grouped in carriages, so if you took the wrong one. You are in shit already. You don't want trouble with the SADF. We don't like shirkers. Check your carriage letter on the outside, and that will be your company."

There was a rustle as each *skutter* turned to note their carriage letter, Pieter and Corli having taken position next to each other on the platform — their obvious differential in height and weight caught the Kaptein's unwanted attention; he beckoned at them with his swagger stick.

"You two, Laurel and Hardy, what's your company letter?"

"Company C!" Corli rang out.

"Company C, Kaptein!" is what you say to me skutter, "and stand at attention."

"Yes Kaptein!" Corli and everyone else in the long line ranged across the platform became more erect, their average height increasing by several inches.

"Now select a buddy. Laurel and Hardy over there are already paired. Your buddy will be your compadré during basics, your wing man, your confidante. You are responsible for each other. Got that boys?

"YES, KAPTEIN.

†

Over the next six weeks, the new *troepies* learnt why it was called *basic* training. Everything was basic and basically shit: *af-kak* was the modus operandi and the rite of passage.

Accommodations were basic: a muddy tent and a hard bed that had to be tended to perfection. Ablutions were cold showers and toilets were unspeakable 'long drops': tin sheds erected around wells of reeking excrement that had to be cleaned regularly by an unlucky few, while nourishment was an oxymoron: an indigestible slop delivered morning, noon and night, by a series of cooks unversed in the need for taste and edibility to sustain the famished riflemen.

Training was hell and geared for maximum af-kak, especially if you were slow or fat or both, like Corli was.

"See that hill, Hardy."

"Ja corporal."

"Why are you not running yet? You'll run twice round if you are not back in seven minutes."

"Laurel," the corporal turned to Pieter already panting from the last excursion, "beat your buddy back or you're going round twice with extra bricks in your backpack."

"Check them out manne," the corporal continued his harangue egging on the race between the two buddies, "whose of you are volunteering next? You there," he pointed to a rifleman who had started giggling, "*Jy lag soos 'n meisie*, shit-face, we will have no girls here. You're next. Whose your buddy? Go, go, go at the double, whoever is back last of youse runs again."

Pieter could see that Corli couldn't take much more as he hurtled up to the top of the hill, fast on his friend's heels. Corli had sagged to a walk, was sweating profusely, and looked red in the face under his bush hat. (Pieter had heard of servicemen dying of kidney failure from such exercises in the heat of the day.) They disappeared from the corporal's view behind a kakie-bos at the top of the kopie.

"Corli, stop. Let me take those extra rocks out of your backpack. I'll put them in mine. You don't look good."

"I don't feel good. I'm exhausted, Pieter."

Pieter looked at Corli's eyes: they were sun-setting; the boy could barely stand upright.

"Can we swop packs instead, mine has more bricks? It will be quicker. Here behind the bush. And give me a sip of water? I'm parched," Corli cowered.

"Okay, go. We'll jog back at your speed and cross the finish line together.

"Playing tricks hey, for laughs Laurel and Hardy? You think I don't see things. I have eyes in the back of my head. Laurel you were ordered to *beat* Hardy back here. Not pussy foot along together like two Siamese twins. Take twenty push ups now, here," He stamped his foot, "up to the height of my stick. Nou gaan julle *af-kak*. You're going to shit-off for the Engelse that don't understand Afrikaans. No one fucks with Corporal Venter. V-e-n-t-e-r, verstaan jy? Do you understand?"

This time it was Corli who came to Pieter's rescue: he carried fewer bricks on his back and was built like a bulldog — structured for such an activity, so when Pieter collapsed after the third repetition, his left arm in spasm unable to lift himself any longer, Corli stood up and confronted Venter.

"*Korporaal*," Corli put both his fists in the small of his back underneath the backpack and pushed his stomach out, "that is enough. My buddy can't do any more. If you carry on, I will report you to the authorities. *Ek gaan jou aan kla!*"

"You want to play with me Hardy?" The corporal had returned from doing battle with other recalcitrant troops and now glared Corli in the face. "Very well," he looked down at Pieter lying prostrate in the dust: his chest heaving, spittle leaking from the side of his mouth as his breath puffed the sand next to his cheek, "but I won't forget it. I never do. Now... Manne! You look ready. So stand up. And fall in."

The twenty rifleman rose, or helped their buddies do so, dusted off their khakis and quickly formed a squad: Venter standing erect to one side yelled the orders.

"Right Dress!"

Right arms shot out to measure the distance between adjacent shoulders. The shuffling of boots scraping the sand increased and then quietened.

"Eyes front. Forward march. Hut two three four... Hut two three four...

†

"ATTENTION."

The ten squads of two hundred newly ordained rifleman stood squarely and neat; straight as a stripe on the parade ground. Kaptein Odendaal looked well pleased with himself; at least his upturned moustache seemed to indicate so to the men standing closest to the wooden platform from which he was addressing them.

"AT EASE."

There was the sound of hard boots scrapping tar made molten by the unrelenting sun. A slight breeze threatened to unfurl the orange, white and blue South African flag rising above the Kaptein as he continued the announcements.

"Skutters. This is not a passing *out* parade. It is a passing *on* parade.

"Now that you have completed basics, this company will be transferred to Oudtshoorn for border training. South Africa needs you on the Angolan border to combat the terrorists attacking our outposts on the Caprivi Strip. That's where the Oudtshoorn service men are usually deployed, but only when you are needed. You may spend three months or... even six months... getting prepared until you are *reg en klaar.* That is up to high command in Pretoria. Not up to me."

The Kaptein tugged at his purple beret, touched the tip of the polished swagger stick protruding from his armpit and then raised his index finger above his balled hand to hover in front of him.

"Today is selection parade. We will select you for special training at Oudtshoorn. We need only a few skutters for Intelligence and Signals and to be drivers, machine gunners, or mortar men, so most of youse who are not selected will serve as infantry for border patrols. Hence, if you want to stick with your buddy, I need make no further suggestions. Now... STAND AT EASE. You can discuss this amongst yourselves and we will start selection in ten minutes."

"Hey Pieter," Corli had walked over from an adjacent squad, "Kaptein Odendaal will never select me as a driver or intelligence man — one of the cushy jobs; I am sure Corporal Venter must have informed the Kaptein that I was going to report him if he didn't stop torturing you."

"So?" Pieter asked.

"I want to be an infantry man with you. We've got each other's backs. Haven't we?"

"I think so. But I don't want to be in the field. To carry a gun and have to shoot someone. I want to be in Intelligence. I hear Intelligence never go out of camp on patrol. You just sit in the camp and radio messages to the other camps and co-ordinate patrols via their signal man's radio. That's what I am going to try for. Otherwise a driver."

"You can only volunteer once. So you'd leave me to my own lot, even though we're buddies?"

"I am afraid so. I never wanted to be in the army. But my father wouldn't let me become a C.O."

"A what?"

"A conscientious objector."

"Shame on you. You would let all the other boys fight in your place and get killed," Corli wiped his index and second finger under his nose and walked away.

"OKAY SCUTTERS, FALL IN," Kaptein Odendaal held up the end of his swagger stick at four o'clock like a conductor, paused, and then brought it down to six o'clock, "ATTEN--SHUN. Rifleman, observe on the right, three tables with three corporals

112

ready to sign you up. First come first served till there are no more places.

If you have a first class matric go to Intelligence and Signals: Table 1, with Corporal Smith.

Rifleman with driver's licenses for more than two years: Table 2, with Corporal du Toit.

High school sport heroes: Machine Guns and Mortars: Table 3, with Corporal Venter.

The rest of you. Oil your weapons; you will serve as riflemen. Good luck.

AT EASE. DIS--MISSED."

†

The army camp on the Caprivi Strip in the South West African bush abutting the Angolan border was well protected. Similar to the other three outposts set like dash marks to the east of the frontier projecting South African Defence Force power north, bulldozers had fashioned three-meter-thick sand walls to create a rectangular encampment — about the span of one street block — and thus sufficient in size to house a two-hundred man company well provisioned with the most up to date weaponry that ARMSCOR could provide.

The base enclosed trucks, mine-prepared-vehicles, Casspirs (landmine proof troop carriers with machine gun turrets), and a scatter of artillery cannon and mortars, while a machine gun nest held watch at each corner point. Protected by circular corrugated iron roofs, held down by sandbags, the nests put one in mind of a rondavel camouflaged against mortar attacks.

An extensive area around the fort had been cleared of surrounding bush, exposing the snow white sand to the overbearing heat — to the one side of which was an encircled perimeter marked with a large H; an orange windsock directing helicopter pilots as to the safest approach when Casualty Evacuations, labelled CASEVACS, were called for to extricate injured troops from the bush with French built Alouette helicopters. And, although doctors and medics were stationed at each base and often went out on the Alos, they could only give immediate life-sustaining attention to casualties: major emergency operations required transport to the Military Base Hospital at Rundu, 160 kilometers due west.

Communications between the four outpost stations, the helicopters, the vehicles in the field and the all-important foot patrols used to flush out the enemy trying to cross the border into South West Africa, were co-ordinated by the Intelligence operators situated in the Signals and Intelligence room that formed part of the administrative offices, again protected in a bunker by a sandbagged corrugated iron roof.

Foot patrols were three days in duration and could vary in size but routinely constituted ten members headed by a corporal and nine infantry men, one carrying the essential B25 radio on his back. The skutters were secreted into the tangled bush and conveyed there by Casspir to protect them from the land-mined bush paths that had recently claimed both local Hereros and army casualties alike as the Angolan incursions had amplified. Armed with automatic rifles, and grenades, a heavy backpack weighing them down further, the *infantryman often crossed the border, to search and destroy insurgents, returning to a predetermined rendezvous point at the end of the harrowing experience. Reports of recent deadly interactions with insurgents from a squad who had sallied from the adjacent Caprivi Strip encampment some forty kilometers to the east had heightened the rifleman's terror of serving on the patrols and amped up the anxiety level considerably.*

"One zero, this is five zero, establishing contact. We have just been dropped off and are heading into the bush. Over," Pieter was speaking through the microphone tethered to the uncomfortable back-pack-radio that he was responsible for.

"This is one zero. Is that you Marais? Its David, you should have volunteered for Intelligence; much better than being in the bush. Over."

"I know, I know. I'm here for a friend, out." Pieter, dressed in beige canvas fatigues specked with dashes of green and brown, looked Corli in the eyes, lit up by the bright sunlight filtering through the dark sunglasses that wrapped around his plump, sunburned face like a protective shield under his olive bush hat. Corli had heard the clipped radio conversation and turned away to gaze across the vast veld yellowed by hip height grass stretching into the distance. The squad had been dropped off in the open and was exposed.

"We must get out of here manne. Too bloody dangerous. Single file. Radio silence until I say so. Follow me," Corporal Venter, a rifle clasped in both hands, its butt hard against his shoulder and the muzzle pointing downwards in the low ready position, followed words with action, and headed towards a distant brush of trees, arid from the unforgiving sun; he had proved to be a damned good soldier, despite Pieter and Corli's earlier experiences of the man during basics training.

Once they had reached the cover of the thicket, the tweet of birds and koer-koer of turtle doves providing a welcome sense of normalcy, the patrol regrouped and in muted tones Venter outlined their briefing plan.

"Manne, I know that this is your first patrol. You guys must be wide awake! Altyd! Always! There is no protection out here. The enemy can be anywhere. And they are good. They're black, quiet as lions, difficult to see, highly trained and know this bush like the back of their hands." Venter lowered his voice for the next; eighteen anxious eyes rimmed by sweat trained on his. "If you see one. Shoot to kill. No pussyfooting around here. Kill them no matter what your conscience says. This is war. Either they're dead, or you are. Finished and klaar." Venter moved his palms over each other with a dusting motion, having shouldered his rifle on its sling. "They will do the same to you or me. Do not hesitate. He who hesitates is what?"

"Lost," some said.

"Correct. We'll advance now, in formation, for about three or four hours, then find a place to camp overnight. Rifles at the low ready. Move out."

Pieter and Corli trudged a safe distance from each

other swaying their cocked rifles from left to right and back again; hyper alert to their surroundings, their basic and subsequent training at Oudtshoorn, consolidating their fractious relationship to a bond of friendship despite their obvious differences. They had laughed about, and were glad of, the fact that they had shared the same train ticket: otherwise this friendship would never have taken place. They had supported each other through *thick* and *thin*. (They had laughed about that saying too, over a few necessary beers when they were finally out on their first leave pass after basics. And Corporal Venter had long ago stopped calling them Laurel and Hardy: he had grudging respect for their camaraderie.)

They were now well trained and much stronger and fitter and had pledged to look after each other — blood brothers. And now here they were on their first three day patrol.

"I'm nervous," Corli whispered when they sat together during a short break and talking quietly was allowed.

"Me too," Pieter said "but that's what we trained for. We better get used to it."

After the short break, and an uneventful march had helped gain their shaky confidence, they encamped that first night and at dawn continued a march across yet another wide open veldt, the sun crimsoning the golden grass as it cleared the mist and slowly rose to its zenith and then arced down again; the promise of a sweaty day fulfilled, as they entered the shade of a desiccated brush of trees, thrumming with birdsong, ready for a rest and rations from their chafing backpacks. Finding a gully fed by a meagre stream, but surrounded by intermittent rocks that could provide cover, Corporal Venter marched deep down, all the while turning his head from left to right, his rifle at his shoulder, keenly aware of the danger of such a position, but attracted by the promise of extra water for his men, nonetheless. The damp smell of it, and the coolness, a welcome relief from the burdensome heat.

"*Oorait manne ons kan hier uitspan*. Okay men, we can decamp. Pieter radio our position, I have it here on the field map. Rifleman Jooste?" Venter had undone his backpack and rested his rifle against a massive boulder and now pointed to the skutter in question, "no eating now. Climb on to that rock and stand guard."

"Yes corporal, but I need to pee first."

"Dis oorait, but then get on it, at the double."

After radioing through their position, Pieter had joined Corli in taking off his radio and backpack in the lee of another creviced boulder and pulled out some biltong to squat next to his friend who was sitting on a ledge, legs swinging in rhythm to the crunching sounds of the rations he was demolishing with evident gusto.

"Well here we are. Half way, on our first patrol. Kind of exciting, isn't it?" Pieter had placed his rifle on the ground in front of him, just in case, and was looking up and back at his friend, when, as — in — slow — motion, he heard the *crack* of a rifle shot and saw the back of Corli's skull explode bright red against the grey stone. The impact of the bullet knocking his friend's head back against the boulder imprinting a dark welt of blood. Corli's sun glasses shattered, and his bush hat was blown away, after which Corli crumpled forwards, his slack body falling on to the ground, a fine sand spray settling around him after the impact — a spreading pool of blood reddening the bone-white earth where his head had come to a rest.

Not thinking, but reacting, as he had been trained to — Pieter grabbed the microphone still hooked on to his fatigue pocket and pressed it to his lips.

"Contact, contact, we're under attack. My God, my God, Corli's got a bullet in his head, CASSEVAC get us out, get us out!" And then, stood up, grabbed his automatic rifle and went beserk.

The South Africans had been ambushed by insurgents who were pouring down into the gulley from the surrounding rocks. A huge black man in a khaki uniform, leaping down to confront Pieter who surprised them both. Pieter started screaming. "You fucker, you fucker, you fucker" and shot point blank into the man's chest, continuing the firing despite the certain knowledge that his opponent was already dead, until his rifle magazine was empty — his rapid gunfire ricocheting sharply off the surrounding rocks. Its reports' echoes fading to zero as the distant chopping sounds of a dispatched helicopter's rotor increased, compelling the remaining ambushers to retreat.

Corporal Venter found Pieter later, weeping, craning over his dead friend; Corli's blood spattered skull, cradled in the cross-legged lap, Pieter had made for him.

†

7

Soweto, 1976

"It's your turn to take out the pot Thembisa," Zindiswe said, bending down to strike a match to light the coal stove in the sparse kitchen that served as dining room and overnight bedroom for the sisters.

"No, it's not, it's his," Thembisa untangled from her rolled out bed clothes and thrust her tawny head beyond her grey blanket to point through the doorless frame into the adjacent living room, doubling as sleeping quarters in the four roomed Soweto house they called home.

"You can see there's no waking him, and anyway he's a boarder so we can't force him. You better do it, before Outa or Mamie kick it over," Zindiswe inhaled deeply, pursed her lips and blew into the stoke-chamber, enflaming the newspaper and kindling meant to ignite the charcoal, sending a stream of sharp smelling smoke into the room and out the black chimney pipe to merge with the grey-brown mist overhead, fed by one hundred thousand similar fires, expelled from row upon row of the red-brick houses that comprised South Western Townships. The monotone shoe-box-sized-homes were only occasionally differentiated by their faded multi-coloured asbestos roofs or their little fenced off gardens; some carefully husbanded from the single tap on the plot, connected to the outhouse, where Thembisa aimed to dump last night's leavings from the malodorous chamber pot in question.

Zindiswe, four years Thembisa's senior, felt empowered to order around, especially at this untimely hour of four a.m. when the locations' adults and children arose.

The adults in most families, to ensure food on the home table and to feed the maw of adjacent Johannesburg's work force needs, had to get up early to be transported to the big city by four hundred daily trains — their rumble and clatter a constant backdrop from the nearby tracks that busied the vast location's landscape — or to catch a Putco bus. For taxis were unbearably expensive, while personal cars were out of the question; their rare owners, fearing breakdown in the city, and the penury of parking and petrol, reserved their vehicles only for special occasions, like family visits, funerals and weddings.

While the children had to get ready for school, or, if too young, ferried off to a neighbouring house to be minded for the day by a willing *goggo*. A long suffering grandmother — yet another scarcity in the township — who welcomed a cluster of children into her home having not been forced back to the 'homelands' at the death of her working husband.

Today, Thembisa and Zindiswe were both excited about going to school. It was the last day before a long weekend at the Naledi School, and the headmaster had promised to screen a film after assembly.

"Alright, I'll do it," Thembisa hissed, furling back the blanket from where she lay crooked on one elbow, a shadow playing out on the white pictureless wall behind her illuminated by the guttering kindling that had produced a fitful fire.

"Not a drop, Thembisa. If you spill the pot like last time, we're in heavy doo-doos."

"You just keep that fire burning so I can see something," Thembisa arose and tip-toed into the darkened room, the lone flickering street light visible through its bare window unhelpful to her task; she could hear a faint whispering, as a train's racket receded, and so she froze.

"What? No job?

"Yes, today is the last. They will pay me off today," Mamie replied to Outa's question.

"What are we going to do? I've promised both the girls new school blazers; they deserve them, they're good children."

"Faith, we'll see. God will provide; we'll make a plan."

Thembisa's face fell as she rose, the pot held in front of her. She tried to steady her trembling hand but had to return to the kitchen by stepping over the boarder who had turned in his sleep wedging her in the corner in the process. She stretched over him in a V-step in the semi-dark, when he twisted yet again, his arm flailing against the bed pan. Its urine no longer constrained, awoke the man with a splash in the face; he sat up in bewilderment colliding with Thembisa in mid-stride above him, sending the white enamelled utensil clashing to the concrete floor, and its contents no longer in need of emptying in the outhouse.

"What the hell is going on?" Faith Dlamini, a man of outsize proportions, crowned with a dense nest of dark hair topping a no-nonsense face, had appeared in the interjoining doorway that centred the four rooms. Dressed only in a sagging white and blue striped pyjama bottom, he had to step back so that his bare feet were not wetted by the urine seeping towards him.

Thembisa began to cry. She folded her chin to her breastbone, her thin chest heaving with every gulp making her pink nightie quiver. Zindiswe came over to the rescue and put her arm around her smaller sister.

"Not your fault. Not your fault. This stupid," Zindiswe gestured in the direction of the boarder who had stood up, taken off his T-shirt and was trying to rid himself of remaining urine by mopping it off his body. "He should watch where he sleeps!"

†

That evening, after Faith and Eugenia Dlamini had returned from Johannesburg by train and Zindiswe and Thembisa had walked back from school, played hopscotch in the scrabble street outside and finished their homework, both being diligent and well regarded pupils — Zindiswe, thin but wound taut like a rope, kept her hair close-cropped and was a junior prefect in standard eight; while, Thembisa was a foot shorter and in standard four — the family had sat down to dinner, as usual, by the light of a paraffin lamp hanging from the ceiling, its flame swaying slightly from the gusts of wind that filtered under the gaps in the roof seams circulating the distinctive fuel's smell around the room.

"Girls," Dlamini stretched back on his chair, positioned around the small square table that consumed the kitchen's limited space, his back rest leaning at a precarious angle against a white-washed wall to give his torso breathing space, "Mamie and I have to tell you something. Mamie has lost her job at the clothing factory and they're not hiring anywhere else... that we know of at least. No don't interrupt please Thembisa," he held up his hand, the brass Dlamini ring flashed in his palm. "I had promised you new uniforms and Zindiswe a red scarf for your birthday. That will not be possible, unless mom gets another job," he rested his head against the wall with finality.

"Why don't you set up on your own as a dress maker Mamie. You've got the Singer machine and your good at fixing our clothes," Thembisa said, "and we don't really need new uniforms; we'll just carry the blazers over our shoulders and no one will know their too short."

"Maybe you can go into the school uniform business... compete with Rex Trueform," Zindiswe reached an arm across the table and patted her mom on her generous shoulder.

Eugenia, a person of abundance like her husband, with a broad chest, placid, settled face, underneath wiry hair always neatly strung in a headwrap of dark coloured cotton, adjusted her capacious bottom to be more comfortable in her seat and displayed her flawless teeth, "I could try my hand, try my hand. But I will have to get a hawker's license, otherwise they'll charge me with illegal dressmaking. That costs plenty."

"Yebo, Mamie, how much?" Thembisa encouraged.

"They cost fifteen Rands, but the other problem is *selling* the clothes. I can't just go to Jo-burg and hope for the best. We have to go door to door. I can do the dress making, but will be too, too tired for the selling. That I can't do."

"Well, we can. After school, we'll help, won't we Zindiswe?"

"Maybe, I'm worried about my prefect duties."

†

Naledi School was a beacon of learning. Built in 1963, the complex comprised a series of six yellow-face-bricked buildings housing one story of six to twelve class rooms each, some of which had verandas, but all protected by a red corrugated roof that fed white-painted gutters into downspouts positioned to weather the Highveld's heavy deluges. The rain storms that regularly flooded the red dirt pathways between the buildings and the car park that lead to the well-tended garden fronting the institution's single administrative building.

Dressed in their black, but white bordered blazers, often arm in arm or holding hands, with schoolbags hanging from opposing shoulders, Zindiswe and Thembisa would generally walk to school together, but today had decided not to.

"I've got an early meeting today," Zindiswe was cleaning crockery in a soapy pot of water she had warmed on the stove. The smell of carbolic ever present as she scrubbed.

"A prefect meeting?" Mamie had placed her Singer sewing machine on the table and was getting ready for a day's work.

"Nah, Mamie."

"What then? What then?"

"I'd rather not say."

"Out with it, there is no hiding from your mother."

"Yes, I want to know too," Thembisa had just put on her grey school skirt and was tamping it down, with the flats of her hands.

"But you mustn't tell anyone, okay?"

"Okay..." Thembisa, looked intently at her sister.

"There are a group of students who want to write a protest letter to the minister. About the Bantu Education Act."

"The what?"

"You don't know silly. Don't you know anything?" Zindiswe smirked at Thembisa. "They want to protest against the fact that the government has mandated that we are taught maths and geography in Afrikaans and aren't allowed to do that in English anymore."

"I thought it was always like that," Thembisa had bunched her hair on one side in a red elastic band and was combing her middle parting into place.

"No, not even the white children are forced to do that. They can study in either language, but Africans are being forced to learn in Afrikaans, by the Nats. Our students want to arrange a protest march and I should be part of that as a prefect."

"Aikona, aikona," Mamie's neck jiggled, "this will lead to trouble."

"Yes, Zindiswe, I agree with Mamie. I want nothing to do with politics. I just want to keep my head down and get ahead."

"In Afrikaans?" Zindiswe looked again at Thembisa, mopping her hands dry on her hair, having finished the clean up chore, "you want to be taught in that Boere taal?"

"I'll do what it takes, and anyway, I have deliveries to make this afternoon, so I have to get some homework done now... and it's your birthday soon..."

"Thembisa, just be careful out there, especially if you're delivering far from here. At the prefects meeting we were told by the headmaster that the urban councillor," Zindiswe continued her hand's motion each side of her glistening face leaving a few droplets on her long neck, "has ordered that the police pick up juveniles bunking school so better wear your school uniform. And look like you're on an errand or something."

"Not to worry, Zindiswe, I know what to do. You can be sure of that."

†

Later that afternoon, Thembisa was too vain to take her sister's advice but did, somewhat, heed her caution. She had returned home after school to pick up the clothes for delivery and put them in a big OK Bazaar's paper bag that she re-used for the purpose, and then changed into the warned-against street clothes — after all her mother *was* a dressmaker so she should look the part and advertise her mother's work to the best. But she tempered her enthusiasm, by wearing a rather plain black and white striped dress with a modest top, rather than the vibrant coloured smock she had had in mind. At least the outfit matched her black school lace-up's that were essential to navigate Soweto's potholed, dirt covered roads.

As Thembisa was about to leave though, lightning flickered a crackling rumble from a cordon of darkening clouds in the distance, contrasting the clear sky of her direction of intended travel, so she set a determined face, latched closed the shaky gate of the chicken-wire fence that enclosed their patch of thready grass, hitched the bulging bag over her shoulder and under winged arm, and took halting steps down Batswana Street, only increasing her pace when she turned up Matlala Street as her anxiousness abated and a feeling of purpose set in.

She knew the family was under severe financial strain, like everyone else around them, and realized how important it was that she help her mother. Only yesterday Outa had complained that he didn't have the money to buy the materials to fix the leak in the roof over the boarder's room. Reckoning, that if we didn't fix it soon, we would lose that source of funds too, "in a hurry," he had said.

As she ambled along, Thembisa wondered for the thousandth time who her real parents where. Thembisa had figured out she must be adopted, because she was so very different from the other Dlamini's; they were thoroughly dark, in fact, ebony in colour, and had the beautiful shiny skin that she had only encountered in Zulus. While she had the caramel skin of a blend. And she had a hooked shaped pinkie that no-one else had. So, one day, not so long ago now, she had collected all her courage, and, when she was sure that Zindiswe was nowhere within earshot had asked for an audience around the kitchen table with her parents.

"Outa and Mamie," Thembisa had pressed her hands together in the fold of her dress between her thighs, "I'm not sure how to ask this."

"Go on," Dlamini had rocked back against the wall in his customary position, while Mamie had put one hand up in front of her face.

"Are... are... you, my parents? I... I... mean, my real parents." She had not dared look them in the eyes, so Thembisa looked down instead, only looking up when they responded.

"Of... of... course," Dlamini cradled his hands behind his massive head, suddenly appearing to perspire more than usual, "why-ever would you ask that question? We are not going to throw you out because we're short of money. Don't worry about that."

"I... just thought. I'm a different colour."

"Aikona, aikona," Mamie seemed to awaken from a trance behind her hand, but did not remove it, and instead spoke through her fingers, "Thembisa, you must never, never worry about that," and got up slowly to turn towards the stove, bend down, and make some adjustments to the kindling.

Thembisa was getting hot from the walking. She had decided that she would start at the furthest drop off point and work her way back home even though that didn't make logical sense in terms of lightening her load. She just liked doing it that way; it seemed to be both faster and safer, because walking around with a bag full of clothing was a risky affair; not only could she be accosted by a *tsotsi,* one of the many murderous ne'r-do-wells that seeded Soweto, but also because of the range of mangy dogs that roamed its streets. (Thembisa thought she could outrun a tsotsi any day, but not a dog.) Accordingly, like any thoroughbred Sowetan, Thembisa was hyperaware of her surroundings; scanning in front, sideways and behind her for trouble and noting anything of interest or concern for her trip back. And so, she couldn't explain it to herself later when it became so important to do so afterwards — had she been thinking of Zindiswe's birthday present and the fact they couldn't afford it? — Thembisa suddenly became aware of it. A bright red scarf dangling from a clothes line in a back yard as she sped past. She stopped, turned around and retraced her steps. Yes, it looked just like the one they had seen in the O.K. Bazaars when she visited Johannesburg with her parents. She looked to her left and to her right and went into automatic pilot — *he who hesitates is lost* — and lunged towards the clothesline, ripped off the scarf, and plunged it out of sight into the OK Bazaar bag under her arm — *where it belongs*, she thought, sprinting out of the plot and back on to the dirt road to make up for lost time. Thembisa returned to the purpose of her journey with renewed energy before doubt and feelings of guilt arrested her. *But now it is too late,* Thembisa narrowed her steps, *if I return it, they'll catch me. And report me to the headmaster. They'll kick me out of school.* Thembisa surveyed ahead and saw an open plot: scraggly bushes, interspersed with old newspapers blowing in the developing breeze, and what looked like a timid dog, it's salmon coloured tongue out, panting under a blue gum tree. So, she stopped, put down the brown paper bag and thrust the scarf beneath the other clothes, and then, feeling only slightly better, returned to her duties; although her guilt had not been assuaged, at least its source was now hidden.

Arriving at the furthermost delivery address, Thembisa was pleased to find a wizened goggo, her grey hair tucked beneath a black wool-cap, sitting outside the front door on a kitchen chair. A few chickens pecked at the dust around her while a scruffy *brak* lay wagging its tail covering her feet. The crone was taking in what remained of the wintry sun and pointed in the direction Thembisa had come from, tenting up the drab blanket folded around her, as the schoolgirl approached the ten steps from the front gate.

"Kunjani, Thembisa, there, see... there... is a great storm brewing over the land. I fore-spell trouble... trouble... "

"Lungile Umamkulu," Thembisa's hazel flecked eyes showing more white than normal, as she turned to take stock of the imprecation. The old lady was correct, the brewing storm was almost upon them; the edge of dark clouds had caught up with her, threatening to dispel the sunlight with drenching rain.

"Come in my child, come in. It will be bad," the goggo had arisen from her plastic chair, picked it up and carried it inside with practiced care. She offered tea while they waited for the storm to spend. Its downpour a deafening roar that dissuaded talking, but enhanced intimacy; a humid peace enveloping them once the front had passed, and the dripping surroundings came back to life — the dog rising to nudge open the front door so that time could proceed: "Thank your mother for the beautiful work. Here one Rand owed. Tuck it away from the tsotsis. But you know that my dear. Where do you put it?"

"Umamkulu, I don't have a bra yet, so I put it here," Thembisa tapped the back of her dress."

"In your panties?"

"Yebo… but I must go, I have many more deliveries and many puddles to contend with on the way back. Oh, I almost forgot. Any other orders? My mother can make shirts too."

"No, no," the goggo said sadly, "times are not good. Money is short. But pop around at the end of next month and ask me again. And give my good regards to your mother, Eugenia, will you?"

As Thembisa hurried into Nyakale Street, the long street that eventually ran past the Naledi School, she encountered what she had hoped against hope to avoid: a uniformed police officer lounging by a parked police van.

"Yes, Miss. Yes, Miss, you," Thembisa had stopped walking when she heard the snapped address. The crumpled OK Bazaar's bag now empty — save for the scarf — hanging flat against her black and white smock. Her school shoes muddy beyond recognition and her white socks a wash of brown. "Shouldn't you be at school? Bunking eh!" the officer's burly lips curled his brown moustache into a scowl as he pushed back his blue cap, its medallion winking in the sunshine that had reappeared after the rainstorm.

"No, no, I… I… am doing deliveries for my mom."

"What kind?"

"Clothes, she is a dress maker."

"Let me see what's in that bag."

"I have finished my deliveries."

"Yes, but there is still something bulging in that bag."

Reluctantly, trying to show nothing in her face, Thembisa unhitched the brown paper bag and opened it for the officer to see into.

"Aha, what is this?" he plucked the pilfered scarf from the bag and inspected it.

"Your mother make this? I think not. It has a Wool Mark sign here... must have come from Joburg. There is no OK Bazaars here! Did you steal it? It smells new."

"No, it's my sister Zindiswe's, I just borrowed it against the cold." Thembisa looked down inspecting her shoes.

"Then why aren't you wearing it?"

"It's no longer cold!"

"Don't you be smart with me, young lady. I don't trust you, far too big for your boots. Where is your sister now, so I can verify the facts of the matter."

"At Naledi, she's a prefect. She has duties till late."

"Right, get in, there... in the front seat. We'll find out."

At least he hasn't put the siren on, although, I can see the blue light flashing, Thembisa thought as they raced towards the school, and then turned slowly into the front gate to park aside of the squat red bricked administrative building that, up till now, fortunately, she had never yet seen the inside of.

"You wait here. I will speak to the headmaster, I know him well," the officer exited the van in a smooth movement that belied his bulk and disappeared into the building, while Thembisa couldn't hold it in any longer, and so quickly alighted and ran around the offices and on into the school's toilet building behind it. Entering the *Female* side rapidly, she relieved herself, and returned to the car, just in time. The officer had come out and was beckoning her in.

Now I'm in for it.

Thembisa was shown into the principal's office and bade to sit down in one of the trio of chairs that had been set across from the teacher's gigantic oak desk. She had the foresight to take out the red scarf in question and place it on the bag folded on her knees, which she clamped primly together to best prepare for the inquisition which must surely follow. Thembisa hoped fervently that 'blood was thicker than water' a quote frequently bandied about by Outa when he was pontificating around the dinner table, and so Zindiswe would know what best to do.

"Miss Dlamini, Thembisa. Officer Jabulani has just informed me of the circumstances of your situation," the withered headmaster took a tug of smoke from the briar pipe angled at his lips, expanding the double-brass-buttoned navy jacket that encased his scrawny chest — by half — before exhaling, "he is very well-known and well-disposed to this school. Indeed, he is one of our most trusted allies in our fight against truancy. Against the 'pushouts' that you have heard me talk about." He stopped to measure the effect of his words on Thembisa and Officer Jabulani who had taken the seat furthest away from her, leaving the middle one open, which the principal now directed their collective attention too with the stem of his pipe, "I have intercommed for Zindiswe and I understand from my secretary that she will soon be here. Oh," the principal made to stand up from his seat, "please come in Miss Dlamini, please do, and sit down there," the pipe stem again. "Now Officer Jabulani, will you please conduct the proceedings? You can dispense with introductions. I am in a hurry. It's getting too late."

The officer rose at his seat, harrumphed once and then louder before starting to address Zindiswe, who was still in full uniform, her long legs elegantly displayed at an angle, her two ebony ankles touching above her white bobby socks. He explained his findings, of the new red scarf, in Thembisa's bag, and sought the truth of the matter.

"Of course, of course... Officer Jabulani," Zindiswe stroked the back of her hand along her short cut hair and continued the motion down her neck to close her hand in a fist over her heart, "that is my scarf, I try to never separate from it. But Thembisa, she is my sister. She had deliveries. It was cold today."

"Forgive me for thinking otherwise," Jabulani tried an ingratiating smile but failed, his moustache marring the effect from view, "but Mr Headmaster, I think we must address the push out problem. This truant, here, was outside selling merchandise when she should be doing schoolwork. Isn't that what our Urban Councillor wants the Police Force to address?"

"Yes, I agree," the headmaster had squared his elbows on the huge desk and was holding his pipe's stem between two sets of fingers, having again deeply inhaled, he puffed out a long stream of smoke like one of the locomotives, they could hear clattering past. "Thembisa, until the end of this school year you will have to report to the Naledi Police Station on the way to and from school." The headmaster pointed the pipe's tip at Thembisa. "You will have to sign the Police Register that we hold specifically for that purpose. Now if there is nothing else," he made an effort to rise, but didn't, "girls, please, you know the way out. I want to chat with Officer Jabulani alone."

†

Around a month later, although the dust had settled with respect to the scarf incident and Zindiswe had been most appreciative of the birthday present having never learned its true provenance ("I exchanged it... that is all you need to know"), Thembisa had not taken lightly to the enforced bi-daily visits to the Naledi Police Station to sign the police register for delinquents, even though it was just one block down from the school.

"They make me feel like a criminal. And all I was doing was helping us make ends meet. What do you think Mamie?" Thembisa had parsed the oily cabbage she was eating to the edge of her enamel plate, and looked up at her mother, the paraffin light's shadows playing across Eugenia's trouble-lined forehead.

"Ewe, it is true that you have helped. But sad that you were caught."

"And that… is the golden rule, girls… if you are to survive in this struggle. Don't get caught." Dlamini cranked forward tipping his chair back into place at the table.

"Hau! struggle? Faith this is not for the girls, they're too young for this."

"No, they 're not! What do you think is going on out there Eugenia? Are your eyes closed? Woman! Only yesterday, Naledi students stoned the police."

"Stoned the police? "Faith, shoo, shoo, aikona," Mamie swayed in her seat like a sow, "*do not* shout. You know there are spies everywhere."

"Yes, stoned the police, Mamie. They were coming to get Enos Ngutshane for writing that letter of protest to Minister Kruger, I told you about," Zindiswe had stood up, two fists on the table.

"Aikona."

"And then they set alight a white Beetle. They turned it over first, then lit the leaking petrol with a match."

"I hope you girls got away from the trouble…." Mamie turned her palms upwards and swivelled her wide eyes to her husband.

"Why are there so many police? Why are the students striking at Phefeni? I'll tell you why. They don't want to be taught in the oppressor's language," Dlamini rumbled. "They want English, the international language. Not Afrikaans. I hear of protest marches. I hear the army is mobilizing against us. What about the ANC!"

Just then the trundle of a passing train made all

but yelling in the close kitchen a waste of breath. Its energy dissipating in the distance, Dlamini continued at full steam, "do you girls even know what's going on; do they teach you anything at those schools? Do you know who Nelson Mandela is? Do you know about the armed Struggle? Do they tell you about the sickness of apartheid?"

"Shush now Faith, do not mention the ANC, or we'll all get into trouble. That's enough now, enough," Mamie kneaded his shoulder with her free hand, soothing him back to lean his chair against the wall.

"Yes, we know. But not from our school books," Zindiswe had sat down again, "in one of our meetings, someone showed us a picture of Mr Mandela. He is in prison on Robben Island."

"What?" Mamie raised her hand to her mouth, "Zindiswe you are playing with fire. All pictures of Mandela are banned. Anyone caught with one will surely be jailed. I want you to stop whatever you are doing. It is too, too dangerous and is going to get you killed. Do not march, stay away from such things."

"Yebo, but it must be done," Thembisa was tackling the cabbage again, "injustice must be dealt with. I feel it every time I step into that awful police station. Those officers are full of it. They make my blood broil."

"Boil silly, not broil," Zindiswe playfully mock-slapped Thembisa around the face, interrupting her chewing.

"No, I *mean* broil, I feel like a simmering piece of

meat on a braaivleis. I get hot under the collar, sweat and shake with anger, just at the sight of the police. I'm willing to help now, Zindiswe, when is your next meeting?"

†

The day of June 16th started with a sense of excitement at Naledi, as if they were just going on a school trip, not a protest march. Because of the cold, or just to celebrate the event, Zindiswe had put on her red scarf tucked around her neck and into her uniform's blazer, despite Thembisa's warning; you'll stick out like a rag to a raging bull.

"No, silly, it's a *flag* to a *charging* bull. I want to stick out, how else are the boys going to notice me."

Naledi's headmaster wanted to close that mornings' assembly with a hymn, but instead the students rose as one, downed their songbooks, some raising their fists, and shouted AMANDLA twice, and then broke into *Nkosi Sikelel' iAfrika,* the banned ANC's anthem, an African prayer song. Unfurling banners daubed with AFRIKAANS MUST BE ABOLISHED and VORSTER SHOULD STUDY ENGLISH, held aloft on white sheets, they continued singing and chanting as they headed en-mass, 10-20-30 abreast — whatever the pot-holed streets allowed — up on Nyakale Street and beyond in the direction of Morrison Isaacson High School, the planned rendezvous point for the school children coming from the west side of Soweto. The Student

Action Committee's plan — developed on June 13th — called for school students from across Soweto to stop off first at the Phefeni Junior Secondary School; there to sing a hymn in solidarity with the school's protest strike, and then travel on to Orlando Stadium beyond which were the offices of Bantu Education where the student leaders planned to deliver a memorandum reflecting their grievances — already clearly displayed on the ever-increasing white banners undulating to the rhythm of the toy-toying students, reflecting both their sympathies and the warming sunshine of the day's cloudless sky.

Zindiswe and Thembisa had started together one-third way deep in the Naledi throng, arm around blazered arm, their white shirts setting off nicely the black and white school colours against their grey dresses and black stockings. The whole school in step like a regiment reaching, in time, the various rendezvous points where the Naledi School students blended with the greys and greens, blues and browns, of the other schools' pupils, creating a hotchpotch of colour as they mingled and progressed. Yelps of joy on meeting old friends on the way, mixing with the early morning woodsmoke still fresh on the warming air; an assortment of dogs walked along with the crowds, often shooed back home by the passing children.

Zindiswe broke away from Thembisa and started jogging ahead when she thought she saw a friend from the Thomas Mofolo School. She had wound the bright scarf around her head in a sort of turban so that Thembisa could follow but was soon lost from sight as she joined with the hundreds of green and orange clothed Mofolo schoolchildren rolling into the mass of marchers that would eventually become ten thousand strong.

The first signs of trouble for the marching participants came from the air about an hour later. A South African Police helicopter thundered above, hovering every now and again for all the protestors to see, then disappeared, as the column of marchers advanced along Vilakazi Street. Cleared of traffic, they could advance forty abreast. Thembisa finally caught up to Zindiswe, and restrained her from advancing to the very front of the pack, pulling her back into the second row — she held her hand tightly to rein her in. "Stop, Zindiswe, come back, this is madness."

The crowd was forced to a stop. At the cross road, in the patch of veld in front of the Orlando West High School, a heavily armed wall of blue-coated police had cordoned off the street. A mechanical loud hailer came into play; a clipped voice skreiching, "Students you must disperse. You must return to your schools. Now. We give you three minutes to turn around."

A marcher had climbed into a tree and responded: "This is a peaceful protest. We don't want trouble!"

Upon which, at first with faltering hesitancy, but then with growing strength, *Nkosi Sikelel' iAfrika* was again rendered, the beautiful lilting lament of the African's quest for freedom, a rising force echoing along the streets of central Soweto.

The police were having none of it. The banned song was like a red flag to a bull; they loosed a snarling Alsatian from its chain at the crowd. Which, as it rose in flight to bite at a front ranker — the rest of the vanguard reeling back in fright — was clubbed to death by a tsotsi well-schooled in the use of a knobkierie, where upon a maelstrom of gunfire was let loose by the posse of policemen.

Thembisa, clasping Zindiswe's sweating hand in hers, heard the stutter of shots; the rifle volley recoiling off the surrounding buildings had found a mark. Zindiswe's turbaned head slapped around next to Thembisa, twisting the slender school girl unhurriedly — Zindiswe's life leaving the hand clasped between her sister's fingers like a fading shadow, both girls sinking to the ground. Kneeling over her stricken sister, Thembisa started wailing with grief, at one with the mayhem of shock, confusion, crying and teargas smoke that followed the first salvo let loose by the embattled South African Police. The first of many, many more such assaults. For that day, and many more days afterwards, would see pitched battles throughout Soweto and countless other townships across the nation, which left hundreds dead and thousands wounded. The Soweto Riots would become a political turning point for South Africa, and a pivot in Thembisa's life.

†

"Let us join hands around this dinner table. Our hearts are heavy with loss,"

Faith Dlamini had bowed his enormous head and clutched both Mamie's and Thembisa's hands ringing the table and enclosing within their circle an upstanding, framed photograph of Zindiswe in their midst, a candle left burning in front of it guttered weakly to fill her empty space.

Having released their hands after a little squeeze, Dlamini looked up, stroked his face clear of a tear with the flat of his hand, leaving a streak that glistened down his puffy cheek.

Thembisa sat with her face down watching the candle flicker against the dark wood, contemplating her crooked pinkie and whimpered, "I should never have given her that scarf. It was too beautiful. Just like her. I am sure that is why she was shot. It was all my fault," Thembisa looked up, squeezed her eyelids tightly closed, and put both index fingers either side of her nose to part the moistness as she looked at Mamie and then Outa in turn. "I tried to warn her, pull her back from the front of the crowd... "

"It's alright, it's alright, it's not your fault. Not your fault," Mammie covered Thembisa's outstretched hand laid bare on the table in front of them.

"Yes, it is. It is all because of the scarf. The scarf..."

"Aikona, aikona... you didn't pull the trigger..." Mamie cradled her forehead in her hand lowering over the table, before righting herself and again locking her hand tightly over Thembisa's, "but now we want to talk to you about your future."

"Yes... yes...your future, this is no longer a good place to be for you. You cannot go back to that school and Soweto is unsafe with these riots everywhere. We must send you away," Dlamini's downturned eyes reflected the shimmer of candlelight.

"Away... away... where is away? I don't want to go away. I want to stay here with my friends and with you," Thembisa wailed.

"Aikona, aikona, it is no longer safe, and the schools are being burnt. We want you to go to the Cape, to Cape Town," Mamie's stout hand firmly applied pressure to Thembisa's arm.

"Yes... yes...," Dlamini said, "you have an uncle there, Goodwill, my elder brother. He lives in Langa Township, you must complete your schooling there.

†

8

Bloubergstrand, 1996

There is a lovely beach that lines the curve of Table Bay. Stretching from the mouth of the Salt River at Paarden Eiland, just beyond Cape Town's Duncan Docks, the shoreline travels some thirty kilometres up the coast to Melkbosstrand, the panoply of the Table Mountain range a majestic backdrop to the treacherous sea — the salty graveyard for forty-one shipwrecks since the day Captain Jan van Riebeeck anchored his three jagts to establish a victualing station at the Cape for the Dutch East Indies Company, in 1652.

Walkable for its full length, depending on the state of the tides, due to the continuity of coarse granular sand interrupted only by an easily breached estuary at Woodbridge Island south of Milnerton Beach, the coastline extends via a promontory of rocks on to the Klein and Groote Baai of Bloubergstrand. The location of a small fishing village that nestles in the shelter of a low-slung hill which hues blueish when the blanket of morning sea mists are breached by the winter sun — the site of a defining battle that saw the British take-over of the Dutch Cape Colony, in 1806.

Pieter, having completed his Sunday morning flat cleaning, had exited Zeezicht, walked across Marine Drive, and sat waiting for Thembisa on a bench between a breach in the low sand dunes that divided Blouberg Beach from the strip of sand-streaked tarmac that served as both a pedestrian walkway and held poorly marked parking spaces to provide access to the sea for the length of the two-kilometre road that stretched from Marine Circle into Bloubergstrand.

Thembisa and Pieter had decided to meet on neutral ground. *Although this is hardly neutral,* Pieter thought, having moved into the flat seven years earlier, when he became a Medical Officer at Tygerberg Hospital after completing medical school there and was finally earning some money. On searching for a place to stay, he had marvelled at the fantastic view the fifth floor flat afforded.

Everchanging as the weather and state of the Atlantic ocean dictated, the small apartment's two wall-spanning windows, allowed a stunning vista — it was as if a winter storm could unleash its massive waves right through the glass, or, on a tranquil summer day, the wind breathless, as if the whole of vast Table Bay and its backdrop of granite layered mountain range, flowed through the opened window, the sounds and salty smell of lapping waves on the beach below, ebbing and flowing with the passing traffic.

The other big attraction of the place was that Pieter could learn to windsurf— the new water sport which had blown over from Hawaii. Here an enterprising surfer had planted a mast on a surfboard, attached a sail, and started riding the sea, combining wind and waterpower to navigate the enormous waves that the Island was known for and were surely equalled here, during a Cape summer south-easter storm, right in front of where Pieter now sat, waiting for Thembisa. She was late. He imagined himself windsurfing in a howling, thirty-five knot gale, to pass the time.

Dressed in a grey wetsuit, with a red and white biking helmet protecting his head, Pieter stepped with one foot on to the bright yellow board, balanced in the broiling sea-foam, and pointed in the direction of travel by the fulcrum of the mast pushed down with one gloved hand while the other hand angled the bright coloured sail's boom to keep its surface flat to the wind until Pieter was ready to be shot headlong into the oncoming waves, his speed of propulsion adjusted by the extent Pieter opened up the sail to the wind whose power brushed all before it; his feet were still smarting from the runnels of sand that raced across the beach, only somewhat anesthetized now by the ice-cold water he was readying to meet. In his imagination, Pieter read the oncoming wave-sets' size, and shape, looking for the sites of their peaks through slitted eyes and calibrated the gusts of wind strength with his taut body: the tenor of the wind against the flat of his ear, the play of the sail in his hands at the angle he set for it; and the extent of the sea-spray that hissed off the thunderous waves collapsing to foam in front of him. Pieter readied himself for the sheer joy of streaking out over the roiling sea, and measuring his skill against its great power. And, when he judged it right, took off — his left foot positioned in the board strap, he pivoted the sail out to gain the wind, repositioning and adjusting its slant, as the board started plying through the water. At first at a slope but then gathering speed flattening, allowing Pieter to position his right foot into the back-strap while, in the split seconds he was afforded, attaching his harness via a hook to the loop of waxed rope that stood out from the boom, relieving the toll on the precious reserves of arm-strength required for the exhausting *water-starts* that would inevitably follow, should he travel out for one or two kilometres into the tumultuous bay. Gaining speed, Pieter made it safely over the first two waves that had not fully broken, rising in the water to meet them and then gliding off their backs; he looked for the next wave, now towering, searching for the point where he could sail up and over it — where it was peaking but had not yet broken, anticipating the rate of their mutual approach and the point of collision, all his senses afloat as he sped along, adjusting his sail for the slight lull in the wind strength, in the lee of the wave, as he coursed up its three meter water-wall, and shot up beyond it — ecstatically free — and not a milli-second too soon.

As he sat their waiting, Pieter could almost feel the sea cresting at his feet — stuck firmly in their straps — as he caught the draft of wind coursing over the wave's back and flew through the air adjusting his sail to become a kite to prolong the flight until he touched down with a splash, the black skeg beneath the board, cleaving the water as Pieter steadied himself against the aft-coming hurtle of wind that could catapult him into the seething sea, spreadeagled, still tethered by the harness hook, to the boom that encircled the toppled mask.

"Earth to Pieter, earth to Pieter," he felt a tap on his straw boater and smelt a whiff of intoxicating perfume when he looked round to see Thembisa, who had stepped back and was standing next to her fire-red scooter. White helmet still on her head, she wore a slight turquoise dress patterned with white and pink roses and had wrapped a thin white shawl twice around her neck. She held its two long ends out towards him and struck a pose; one cyan sandaled foot in front and the other aft like a marching drummy, her shiny nail-polish coloured like her scooter, showing herself off to good effect. "Shall we?"

"Aren't you forgetting something?" Pieter had stepped from the dune on to the tarmac and was trying to kick the sand out of his tan clogs, he took them off instead, tapped them out against each other and put them in the bag hanging off his green shirted shoulder, a streak of sand settling on his white shorts.

"What? Smarty-pants."

"Your helmet."

"Hau yes, that reminds me. I brought the Polaroid."

"The police one?"

"It's in the seat-well, let me get it."

Thembisa extricated the camera, whipped around, and took a photo of Pieter with the Table Mountain range as backdrop.

"Hey, I didn't give you permission for that."

"I know," Thembisa tore the developed photo from the camera's front slot, compared it to its subject, and then thrust both into her upturned helmet, which she placed into the scooter's seat-well, taking special care to hold the Vespa's key in her hand as she did so, "but it's police property now. Let's go." Thembisa marched off over the dunes and down to the water's edge holding a plastic water bottle; the becalmed sea spreading salty foam in cold curves on the beach, her sunglasses sparking in the almost cloudless sky of the near perfect day that Cape Town sometimes offers its citizens in autumn.

Thembisa, having kicked off her sandals, stepped on into the sea, bending over to catch water in the opened bottle just as a wavelet curled over bathing her calves to just below the knee. She twirled round and ran back clutching the half-filled bottle and stamping her feet in the silt leaving slight impressions in her wake, "Hau, hau, hau," she giggled, "it's just too, too cold."

"You'll adapt, just do it again. You're body gets used to the cold."

"That's alright for you, whitey, you Europeans, you're used to the cold, we Africans need the sun!"

"What do you mean? I'm an African too. I was born here too."

"An Afrikaner! Aikona, it's not the same," Thembisa cast back her head, her ringlets sliding back over the thin strap of her dress on to her shoulders, pursed her red tinted lips, and took a delicate sip of seawater from the bottle.

"Nooit," Pieter said, "seawater is poison to drink."

"See, you make my point for me," Thembisa took another slight sip and swallowed slowly against the burn, while Pieter looked on fiddling with his shoulder bag. "Did you not know that for us water is the source of creation, we must collect some of its spirit whenever we are at the seaside. That's what my Mamie told me."

"Where was that?"

"In Soweto... I told you."

"You lived there? I thought you were from the Cape."

"No." They had both turned, north, Pieter closer to the water than Thembisa, and started walking along the stretch of beach that played out in front of them, mirroring each other's step, and splashing through the foamy sea water whenever the slowly ebbing tide breached their planned pathway.

"Tell me about Soweto, I have never been there."

Thembisa, sluggishly at first, but then almost as a stream of conscience, blurted out her history, adding how guilty she still felt about the scarf she had given to her sister. The scarf that Thembisa was sure had unleashed the kill shot that had changed her life, bringing about the break with Outa and Mamie Dlamini; the abandonment that forced her to take up here in Cape Town with extended family.

"What changed?" Pieter had picked up a seashell and sent it skimming out to sea. They had stopped to look back at the view across Table Bay and turned to look out at the brown contour of Robben Island.

"I was activated after the Soweto riots. At first, I felt so helpless and lonely and at a loss for what to do. But then after Steve Biko was killed by the police the next year, I became active in the Black Consciousness movement. He was the father of BC and we became it's daughters."

"And," Pieter looked down at Thembisa, "did you blame us?"

"Before the riots, I had hardly seen a white man. Your people never came to Soweto, too dangerous, but after Zindiswe was shot by a white officer, my feelings changed. I started hating the white government. Not specific whites. Black Consciousness was *not* about hating, but about *not* feeling inferior to whites. Being proud of being black, instead. And especially not being called a *non-white*. So when the UDF came along, I supported them."

"With Alan Boesak, in '83?"

"Yes, I had just finished matric in Langa." Thembisa pressed her foot deep into the silty sand letting a front of water cover her foot. "But with Black Consciousness, we were not *against*, we were *for*. We were *pro* black. We became proud to be black. Black is beautiful. What do you think?"

"Nietzsche said, 'It is not the strength, but duration, of great sentiments that is important,' or something like that."

"Nietzsche, again?" Thembisa pulled her foot out of the sand puddle and took a long drawn out step to catch up.

"You know he went mad?"

"I can see why, with such statements."

"No he had neurosyphilis; General Paralysis of the Insane we call it. GPI."

"That's all very well, but do *you* think black is beautiful?"

"Yes, I have told you that before," Pieter glanced down at Thembisa who was standing two paces aside of him but returned the look nonetheless holding his eye until he looked away and she pointed to Robben Island.

"Yebo, you're right," Thembisa added, "that was at the time when Nelson Mandela was still imprisoned over there. It is amazing to see the island so close up."

"It's the closest point from here. Eight kilometres. People swim across. But it's dangerous because of the sharks," Pieter said. "By the way, where were you when Nelson was freed from prison?"

"Oh that's easy. But when was it again?"

"1990."

"Yes, yes, just after... " Thembisa turned away, took two steps and turned back making a little skipping movement, "I was on the Grand Parade waiting in front of City Hall. We waited for hours in the sun until he arrived. But then when Mandela got out on the balcony and raised his hand in a fist and spoke into the microphone, and shouted AMANDLA, and the crowd roared back NGWETHU, NGWETHU — it was all worth it. Shoo, shoo, shoo that was something else. And you, where were you. In hiding?"

"Agh, far from it. I remember it well. It was a beautiful Sunday afternoon. I had just started my practice in Tamboerskloof but a group of my friends from Tygerberg Hospital and I watched Mandela's entourage go by from the Brackenfell Bridge over the Paarl Highway, on his way to you guys at the Parade. I remember thinking. I hope we don't have a revolution now. A civil war, between white and black. A bloodbath. We were scared, but also in a funny way, filled with hope. Of course we knew nothing about Nelson Mandela."

"Ja, we didn't either. I had seen a picture once though. Hey, look there, is that a seal bodysurfing in the wave?" Thembisa pointed to a dark torpedo shaped shadow just beneath the surface of a breaking wave, "she's having fun."

"How do you know it's a she?"

"I don't. But its black and it's doing what I like to do, but not here, rather at Muizenberg in the warm water. Shouldn't we be walking though; I get hot when I'm standing still."

Upon resuming walking, now just a tad closer to each other, with Thembisa on the seaside this time, she returned to the conversation, "Now, it's your turn."

"To do what?"

"To tell me about yourself. Why you're so strange."

"Strange?"

"Yes, and kind of strained, and distracted."

"Ag, ja," Pieter seemed to stoop a little more, "it was the border, that got to me, the fighting on the border," and he told Thembisa what had happened in a voice alien to himself.

"I blame my father. I could have been a conscientious objector, but he wouldn't let me. It would bring shame on the family."

Pieter and Thembisa stopped to allow a fisherman on the beach to cast a line deep into the ocean, the rod's reel whining as it released the bowing nylon pulled by the lead weights hurled into the distance, released by the tall pole's whiplash. There was a loud plop as it broke the water's surface despite the constant churn of the restless waves; the man held his rod high and beckoned that they could pass underneath.

"My father taught me to fish, just like that. But we would go off the beach at Paarden Eiland. After school, or on Sundays. When he was out of uniform, he was a totally different person, kind and patient and caring. I respected my father. He was always good to me, but after the border and what happened later, that all changed."

"What happened later?" Thembisa had picked up some sand in the palm of her hand and was trickling it back on to the beach through spread out fingers.

"No, I can't tell you. 'Even the bravest of us seldom has the courage for what he really knows.'"

"The syphilitic philosopher?"

"Yes."

"What about your mother? Is she nice?"

"Ja, but... there is always something sad about her, I think. I started noticing when I came back from the border. She was treated for cervical cancer, while I was away, a big operation. But it seems that ever since then she has lost something, or maybe she had lost something or *someone* long before, and I only started seeing the signs when I was studying psychiatry at medical school."

"Why do you think it's someone?"

"Well, I catch her looking at old photographs and when I ask what she's looking for, she gets all secretive and teary eyed."

"Shoo, shoo, we are getting too, too heavy. Not that I don't want to hear but we need a break," Thembisa had stopped to look at a pool of sea water lining the craggy promontory that jutted out into Table Bay, which signalled the start of Bloubergstrand proper. Reams of dark brown, tuberous, kelp lay criss-cross along the beach. Like heavy duty rubber hoses, they lined the multiple pools cradled by the rocks left by the receding tide, giving off the malodour of salty, rotting seaweed — rankly familiar to any who knew the tidal beach path that reached around the promontory and on to Klein Baai beyond.

"Why don't we rest here, there's a nice place over there, on that big boulder," Pieter pointed and made his way on to the warm surface of an enormous outcrop, long dried of the surf that had pounded its shape. He settled down on a smooth section of rock, opened the catch of his shoulder bag and pulled out his thermos flask, unscrewed its two plastic cups, and filled them each with a shot of rich black coffee, offering one to Thembisa as she sank down on her haunches, her flowery dress's rise catching his eye; he stayed there longer than was perhaps seemly, because

Thembisa pulled down the crimplene cloth with her free-hand and attempted to redirect his attention.

"Wow. This is a beautiful view. I've never seen Table Mountain like this before. Cheers by the way, I like it black," she tapped her cup to Pieter's after taking a sip, "I hope I am going to be able to finish this without mishap."

Pieter studied her silhouette; Tembisa had removed her sunglasses, the shock of bushy hair swept back from her high forehead, angled narrow eyebrows, and prominent eyelashes, all one of a piece with her hazel-flecked eyes, slightly pointy nose and fawn cheekbones that produced the impression of an impala absent the horns.

"Stop staring at me. You can take a photograph if you like."

"With what?"

"My Polaroid."

"You mean the police Polaroid that you left in the scooter. I'd rather do a sketch if you'll sit still enough. Do you mind?" Pieter pulled out a pencil and paper that had already been loaded on to a clip board and deftly sketched her outline. The profile capturing nicely Thembisa's key features and frame of mind — her heightened senses accentuated by a darker shade here and a lighter line there. Pieter was learning to leave an open white space to represent the sparkle in his subject's eye. He had taught himself to complete a satisfactory rendition in five to ten minutes like a pavement artist, but never sold his work. Instead he kept the drawings in a binder and hung the best ones in his study.

Pieter flipped the clip board round and held it up for Thembisa to see.

"Can I have it?"

"No, it's not finished yet. Just an outline," Pieter had stood up and was holding out his hand to help Thembisa up from her crouched position. But, instead, she got up, swivelled out towards Robben Island and turned back to speak over her shoulder, the shadow of her long legs visible through the shear dress, a slight beach wind defining her womanly shape.

"Seemingly then, we will keep our pictures to ourselves," Thembisa rucked her hair together, enwrapped it in her shawl and fashioned a white turban, before turning round to follow Pieter off the boulder and down to the tidal path which clung round the pebbled promontory and angled up against the concrete seawall protecting a string of ocean-facing cottages. Parts of the pathway were perilous and slippery; the sharp craggy outcrops that jutted the curvature off the point were slick with still wet seaweed, green moss, or obstructed by frank smelling kelp, requiring either climbing with two hands or the assistance of a helping one — Pieter held up his, this time tentatively, having just climbed down into a sandy cove and turned around to help Thembisa navigate the particularly treacherous section that he was so familiar with. She was perched on a half-way rock, her painted toes clutching the edge ready to jump by herself, but instead, arrested her flight for a moment to accept the offer, grasped Pieter's hand in both of hers and launched, pulling them both down on to the sand — they tumbled to a rest still clinging on to each other's hand, one of Thembisa's feet stretched submerged in the inlets water, the other, under her haunches, while Pieter crouched beside her.

"Hau, hau, hau, you are too much Pieter."

"Me?"

"Yes, you."

"No, it was you who unbalanced us, you threw yourself at me. *Van die wal in die sloot.* From the wall into the ditch."

"Aikona, it wasn't, you pulled me down. Anyway here we are, trouble seems to follow you around doctor," Thembisa studied the sand covered hand that she was still holding tightly and stroked away a few pebbles imprinting his arm. "You know, your arm, is not very different from mine."

"Of course it isn't we're 'Human, All Too Human'"

"Nietzsche again? But I mean, more than that, you don't have the skin of a totally white man."

"Agh, ja, people tell me that all the time. I'm swarthy, whatever that is supposed to mean, and I tan easily. But it says 'white' in my book of life. What more do you want?"

"Aikona, aikona, I don't want to be white, I'm proud to be black. Nothing more. Where to now?"

"There," Pieter pointed north, "round there is Kleinbaai. *Ons Huise* is there."

"Our House?"

"Yes, that's the restaurant's name where I have booked for us. We should be right on time."

They made their way to the Cape Dutch styled converted farmstead, that abutted the south-side of Klein Baai's sickle-shaped beach. Harking back to the Battle of Blaauwberg, its darkly thatched roof covered the single gable of the main building and was attached to a small outhouse from which protruded an equally white plastered chimney signalling the site of the terracotta tiled kitchen within. The restaurant was fronted by a freshly cut lawn, with an array of tables providing a grand view of the bay. The smell of grass and sea made for a surf and turf mix as Thembisa and Pieter took their seats at a table.

Thembisa was keen to get the promised courtroom coaching session underway as soon as they had ordered a glass of wine each. Red for Pieter; white for Thembisa, "with ice."

"We've broken a lead on my first case you're supposed to be tutoring me on," Thembisa had undone her turban and had twirled her shawl to fashion a ragged ponytail, leaving the ends splayed over her bosom. She was resting on her elbows and took another sip by manipulating the wineglass held between both hands.

"How so?"

"We believe there was only one getaway car and it may have been a police van."

"Why?"

"Your father wasn't very nice to me. He interrogated me that day we first crashed into each other and, he

162

wasn't satisfied with my work. He ordered another team to go and investigate the crime site on Signal Hill. He thought I had done a shoddy job, despite the fact that I found the murder weapon."

"And?"

"The team took a tracker dog, gave him the scent from a sample of the victim's clothing and it led them to a spot under a bushy tree. They found tire marks in the dirt and oil on some loose stones. And, also, they found hanging in a branch of the tree — it must have been shorn off — part of the canvas cover used to close the van's back section. Standard police issue!"

"Oorait, that is suspicious, but there could have been more than one car."

"There was only one set of tracks on the veldt, leading to the parking area."

"Yes, but there could have been a second car parked there, that left no tracks, so I would not make that assumption. And I would not make such a strident statement in court."

"Alright," Thembisa was pointing at the menu, I'm going to have the calamari; what will you have?"

"The steak looks great... or should I have fish... but was there any forensic evidence that points to the police," Pieter looked around to see if no one was within earshot, "I think I told you he was tortured."

"No, you didn't."

"I must have thought it; by the helicopter method."

"Hau, too terrible. So painful. Awful," Thembisa opened her mouth wide and clucked her tongue.

Having placed their order, the waiter safely away in the direction of the kitchen, Thembisa leaned forward to within two feet of Pieter.

"Yes, apart from forensic analysis of all the standard items, there were also a number of cigarette *stompies* at the crime site. Three matched the saliva of Warrant Officer Jan du Plessis, who I had warned not to contaminate the scene. He together with two others had been waiting at Signal Hill for me; I was delayed because my scooter wouldn't start."

"Go on," Pieter could see Thembisa hesitate.

"They found a length of garden hose stuck in the cistern of the *Female* toilet," Thembisa reclined and tugged at the two ends of her shawl, aligning them within the crease between her breasts. "Forensics is testing the hose for finger print analysis."

"The key to success," Pieter bowed closer, enjoining Thembisa's bright eyes, "is to speak the truth."

"Yes, but what is the truth? Is it what you have seen and documented at the crime scene or what you believe happened. Can you project what you think happened when you present in the court room?"

Pieter watched Thembisa's shiny irises thin.

"No, I don't think you can. Nietzsche says, 'Convictions are more dangerous enemies of truth than lies.' I think therein lies the path to mistakes; you will bend what you find to make the situation fit your projection, your conjecture. And so convict the wrong person and have that on your conscience. You must present only the facts."

"And what about omissions? The things that you know but don't mention," Thembisa's pupils dilated further.

"For example?" Pieter asked, but thought, *this is getting distressingly close to my own quandary.*

"Contamination of the crime scene, I told you about... potentially incriminating someone that you know had nothing to do with the murder," Thembisa took a long draught of wine and asked for another glass from a passing attendant.

"How do you know that to be true? Could officer Du Plessis have been there much earlier as a perpetrator? I'm telling you, just say what you know to be true. Just mention that you saw Du Plessis flick his cigarette butt if that is what he did. Nothing more and nothing less," Pieter studied the glass cupped in his hand, swirling it round and round to release the wine's bouquet, "Only then, by your words in court, will I know I can trust you."

"And why is that important?" Thembisa re-fixed her eyes on Pieter's.

"Because I want your advice... from a black family's perspective."

"On what?"

"The Truth and Reconciliation Commission," Pieter looked around again, bent still nearer, his face reddening, a drop of sweat trickled down his ear's crease alongside his beard-line, "whether I should bring my case to the Amnesty Committee, to ask for clemency from the affected family."

"Aikona, tsk, tsk, what case?" Thembisa lunged

back in her seat hissing, "that is too, too much responsibility."

"But I am helping you, so you must help me."

"Aikona, aikona, you are meeting me under false pretences," Thembisa, pushed back her seat, bent under the table to pull her sandals back on, and rose, just as the two lunches had been placed on the table. "False pretences," she placed her palms astride her hips. "I won't have anything to do with it. There's your surf and turf, I'll find my own way home," and with that Thembisa descended the lawn, her shawl trailing from her ponytail as she disappeared in a southerly direction, taking a left turn on to Stadler Street.

†

9

Becoming a Doctor,
1982-1990

"What is the name of this nerve?" the anatomy docent, Prof de Jager, had pulled the cadaver's eyeball out of its socket, squashing its glazed surface with a stainless steel forceps, and was pointing to the glistening nerve at its back with his equally shiny tweezers. Gowned in a starched lab coat covering his grey suit, the bald, black-bearded professor, who reminded Pieter of a boiled egg settled in a wooden eggcup, had bent forward and was sitting on a raised stool at the head of the dissecting table. He had placed his elbows on the rim of the table's steel frame, one to each side of the corpse's shrivelled head, its death mask shrunken further by the formalin, the odour of which was ever present in the large dissection hall in the anatomy section of the Stellenbosch Medical School. De Jager rested there, winced at the rancid smell that his demonstration had released, and looked up at Pieter, similarly clothed to his fellow second year medical student colleagues: Cherise, Lance and Tinie, in yellow-smudged lab coats.

"I ask again, Meneer Marais, *wat is dit?* All four students were standing over the table, two to each side, following the Prof's anatomy quiz intently —

the *viva voce* examination a culmination of four weeks of head and neck dissection they had pursued using the worn Gray's Anatomy Atlas which lay alongside a tray of dissecting instruments, many still encrusted with globules of fat tissue that was the inevitable by-product of the endeavour.

Cherise knew that Pieter did not take well to such confrontations. He had shared with her his fear of dealing with the dead — of studying anatomy, the after effect of the shooting of his friend on the border, but she had helped him navigate this essential step in advancing through medical school, despite the obvious psychological trauma now again playing out before them.

Pieter had frozen, but for his head, which waggled eccentrically like a spun rugby ball, slowly coming to rest, his eyes deviated upwards, his pupils unfocussed, "I...I...don't know. I can't see what you are holding."

"It must be patently clear. A policeman could tell me what this is. How can a budding doctor not."

"Perhaps, I can help Prof," Cherise provided a pretty smile to help things along, her lips curved arterial red, her face powdered white, eyes bright blue, while her flaxen hair, plaited into a ponytail, lay fetchingly over her shoulder obscuring her name embroidered above her jacket pocket.

"No you can't, he must," De Jager pointed with a varicose nose; his hands displaying a slight tremor were otherwise occupied, "or he will fail and have to do *a hereksamen.*"

"Pieter... Pieter," Cherise was looking upwards at him as were both Tinie and Lance; he was at least a head taller than his fellow students, "look into my eyes," and then mouthed silently "my optics," providing the essential clue which seemed to refocus him.

"Prof... I am sorry, the optic nerve."

"And this one?" de Jager was pinching a slight nerve running along one of the eyeball muscles. "The abducens nerve."

†

The four medical student friends wanted to stick together for their forthcoming clinical rotations. Having successfully concluded their second year by passing stringent examinations in anatomy, physiology and pharmacology, after attending innumerable lectures, performing lab experiments, and dissecting their shared cadaver in the Fisika Building, they applied jointly to serve on the same medical firms at the adjacent Tygerberg Hospital, Stellenbosch University's new teaching hospital. Completed in 1976, the eleven story, square, brown-bricked behemoth, dwarfed all around it and dominated the Cape Flats, like a fortress against disease, having the capacity for over two thousand in-patients. Built alongside the Medical School's Administrative and Fisika buildings, the University of Stellenbosch's satellite campus included two student residences: the recently completed *Huis Hippokrates* and the much older, *Huis*

Francie van Zyl, both named after prominent doctors: a Greek who was considered the Father of medicine and an Afrikaner, joined together across two millennia of medical practice.

But first the foursome had to complete six months of histology and pathology as well as a litany of minor subjects to get them fully prepared for the three and a half years of clinical training needed to complete the six-year MB ChB degree they all strived so hard to attain. Strived, because the demanding degree was for many an unrealizable goal. The first two years had been overwhelming; a flood of basic sciences — physics, chemistry, biology, and mathematics — at the main University campus in Stellenbosch, and then the tsunami of anatomy, physiology and pharmacology they had just survived at the Tygerberg Campus: many had sunk and either *opgeskop* to go to other fields or had just left university altogether.

Pieter, to his surprise, found pathology to his liking. He had the treasured ability to convert the two-D image of the histology slide he slipped into place under the binocular microscopes, to a three-D perspective, adding texture and depth to the tissues from what he had learnt through performing dissections of their cadaver, and loved the fact that pathologists were the ones who made the final diagnosis; who determined the truth behind what was ailing the patients or had killed them. He didn't like the autopsies though, and especially not the forensic ones. In fact they made him nauseous. And the dread of performing one kept him sleepless the night before, until he learnt to control his anxiety and was slowly overcoming his fear. He was striving to become Nietzsche's *Uber mensch.* Pieter, like Nietzsche, had no faith in God. *After all how could there be a loving God who looked away at Corli's wanton death.* But Pieter had read the philosopher's *Thus Spake Zarathustra* and concluded that overcoming the self, to achieve self-mastery, conquering one's own worst fears, gave one the will to power, to become the *Superman* that set you apart from the herd: The *Uber mensch* concept that underpinned the German's powerful philosophy and motivated Pieter to become the best he could be, despite the mental stress this unlocked.

†

On the wards, Pieter, Cherise, Tinie and Lance started finding their clinical feet. As this was during the apartheid era, Tygerberg Hospital had been built with separate but equal in mind. There was a *White* side and a *Non-White* side to each floor of the massive building, euphemistically termed *West* or *East,* a designation still very much in practice in 1984.

At first they went on a six week surgery rotation, receiving lectures in the mornings, attending surgical ward rounds in the afternoons on Doctor van Zyl's *diensgroep,* and if their firm was on *spoed,* they helped out with emergent surgical cases that had been admitted in C1D-Oos or C1D-Wes, the casualty admission wards that stretched the length of the ground floor of the hospital and were connected to the ambulance ramps which fed patients from as close as Kayeltisha Township or as far as Worcester in the interior — for Tygerberg was the largest referral hospital in the Cape Province.

Next came the six week obstetric rotation, starting with a series of lectures in one of the tiered auditoriums at the Medical School complex, followed by instruction by the midwives and obstetric registrars in the obstetric unit on the second floor of the hospital. Cherise and Pieter had been paired off to observe their first labour case by the presiding matron of the busy maternity unit.

"You two. Yes, you two," a corpulent midwife clothed in a dark-blue dress, her flight of black hair barely retained by a white nurse's cap, her wide neck at one with purple epalet crowned shoulders, "you... *Handsome* and... you... *Blondie*, tighten your scrubs and follow me." The matron led the way into a close, green tiled room; a shocking scene for virginal eyes. A woman lay bellowing in labour, screaming at the top of her voice, "Aii, aii, aii, my poes is seer, aii, los my, los my." Already propped up on white crumpled sheets, her legs flexed at the hip and splayed wide apart, held up by stirrups around her ankles attached to inverted j-shaped stainless steel poles; the patient's private parts bulged — a trickle of blood and syruplike fluid slipping from her vagina had coiled around her pouting anus. A silver bucket beneath the delivery berth was heavy with strong smelling excrement.

"Push, mama, push," the midwife advanced into the room to the head of the bed and was addressing the patient, who was pulling herself into a ball by hooking her thighs with clenched fingers, blanching her brown flesh, sweat beading frizz cut hair, her tight face contorted as she panted. She looked like a life size version of the curled foetus Pieter had seen floating in formalin in the anatomy lab, curved around the bulge she was trying to expel. *The life within that must come out... alive,* he thought, and looked at the nurse accoucheur, a slight stringy woman, who had been sponging the patient's forehead with a white and blue *Tygerberg Hospital* towel and was in the process of taking her blood pressure by inflating the grey cuff wound tightly around her outstretched arm using an orange rubber bulb. Pieter watched the deflection of the silver mercury column as it fell in the thin glass tube attached inside the lid of the L-shaped blood pressure apparatus set up on the bed.

The nurse called it out: "220 over 110," shook her head and looked up at the midwife, who, standing alongside the patient, went into sergeant major mode, completely forgetting the experience level of the two medical students who had entered the crisis with her.

"Much too high, pre-eclampsia. She'll convulse next. We must get the baby out. Now. You," the midwife pointed at the nurse, "go get a registrar, and some magnesium from the pharmacy. And you, Mr Handsome, get some gloves on and get ready to deliver. And you, Blondie, come and take the blood pressure again," she gesticulated in Cherise's direction.

Pieter had studied obstetrics avidly. He had read about the rotation of the baby's cranium as it traversed the birth canal; about the need to pull down the head once it was out through the vagina, to avoid the baby's aftercoming shoulder from hooking under the symphysis pubis; perhaps to swipe a finger up into its axilla to help lift the baby out. He knew all these things and had watched a film once about delivery techniques. But that was all. He had never touched an obstetric patient.

"Do a PV, tell me what you feel, is there still a lip of cervix? Or is the head crowning?" The midwife bent down with a black plastic tube clutched at her ear and placed it on the patient's heaving abdomen to listen for the foetal heartbeat, "Fifty-five. Shoo. Too slow. Too, too slow," she stirred her head, her heavy earlobes moving in tandem and looked up at Pieter who was standing over the patient performing the prescribed per-vaginum examination as the midwife tried to listen again balancing the foetal stethoscope between her ear and holding up her wrist watch to count the baby's heart rate. "Well, report you two, report."

"I can't take a blood pressure. The patient is unwell. She's starting to jerk," Cherise had bent down, and was trying to restrain the patient's convulsions by pressing down on both her shoulders.

"Eclampsia, shoo, shoo," the midwife had abandoned trying to listen for heart sounds, unbent her back, and turned her head to look at Cherise, who was crying. "Stop your sobbing, try taking the blood pressure again!"

The patient's shaking had stopped, her face was still and just a drool of spittle extended from her slackened mouth on to the pillow beneath. Cherise stood up and with her two index fingers curled her matted hair behind her ears, repetitively and then seeming to regain control of herself, started pumping the blood pressure bulb, and placed her stethoscope at the patient's brachial artery at the elbow to listen for the change in Korotkov sounds that signalled the systolic and diastolic blood pressures.

"She's fully dilated," Pieter had not felt a lip of cervix and so assumed he was correct in his pronouncement and so said the magic words which should allow an unobstructed delivery to take place.

But there was a problem. The midwife identified it immediately. "She can't push, she's unconscious."

Cherise called out the blood pressure, "230 over 110, no better," and then reached down to place her hand on the mother's belly. She could feel an involuntary contraction, the swollen uterine muscle hardened through the stretched skin, and so offered a solution, "Perhaps I can push from above."

"Yes, you can, but where is the registrar? The baby is stuck. We have to pull from below with a forceps to get the baby out." The midwife had hauled a tray of delivery apparatus, stationed on a side cart, and was folding back the green cloth covering the implements. She took out the foot-long forceps that consisted of two parts: two cupped stainless steel clamps that crossed each other like an X to join into a Y- shaped device — the 'V' placed around the baby's head in the birth canal, and the 'I' the handle used to manage the extraction. The midwife conducted the delivery as she had done countless times before, "Handsome, you are going to have to do it. Can you feel the orientation of the head? Feel for the fontanelle."

"Yes, its vertical," Pieter, was sweating all over, his armpits were soaked, producing dark green blotches on his scrubs.

"Good, now cup your hand around the right blade, and insert it carefully into the vagina. Wait. Wait. After this contraction is over. Now."

Pieter felt thumping in his dry throat and with a slight tremor palmed the forceps and pushed it around the baby's head feeling the patient's body pulsing against the back of his gloved hand. "It's in."

"Good, now the same with your left hand..."

.....

"It's in."

"Now... carefully... very carefully, manipulate the forceps, until they lock to form the Y."

Pieter mustered everything he had learnt from his studies, took a deep breath to calm himself; his heart was racing, perspiration dripped from his forehead into his right eye clouding his vision, forcing him to shake his head to clear it. But he nonetheless managed to ease the forceps into the correct shape locking the device around the baby's head. He felt terrible. Was he injuring the child with this clamp? Crushing it to death?

"Good! Blondie, when you feel the contractions tell us and push. And you pull when the contraction is at its height, I'll help you."

And so they pushed and pulled with every uterine contraction until Pieter and Cherise's first delivery was executed: the baby was delivered, lifeless, from its mother, encaged in the forceps, passing in a whoosh of bloodstained amniotic fluid, the placenta following soon after.

The registrar, retained at another emergency, arriving far too late to help salvage the dead child. He battled instead to save the comatose woman, and positioned her on her side, administered magnesium intravenously and having started the infusion, turned to the two students who stood abjectly in the corner, holding each other's hand. Pieter had hung his head, his upper scrubs stained with blood, loose above his matching pants, while Cherise stood erect, having flicked her hair behind her ears over and over again she moved her hand over her face. Her mascara had leaked black across her pale cheeks.

"This is your first death?" the registrar asked.

"Yes," Cherise said. "No," Pieter narrowed his eyes.

"You'll never get used to it. But know this. We had to get the baby out to save the mother. Matron and the two of you did that," the registrar said.

"We know," Pieter said catching the look in Cherise's eyes, and holding her returned gaze steady, till her eye lids compressed; little line marks puckering her tightened skin, *the orbicularis oculi muscle contracting in sympathy,* Pieter thought and increased his hold on Cherise's hand. And feeling reciprocation, tugged lightly, excused himself, and guided his colleague out of the labour room and into the busy corridor.

†

As a condition of moving out of the family home in Parowvallei to stay in Huis Hippokrates, the all-male residence at the Tygerberg Campus, Pieter's father had insisted that he join his parents for Sunday lunch after they had returned from the church service at the local Dutch Reformed Church, where the police officer was an alderman. Pieter didn't mind the routine; he got on very well with his mother, Marja, and loved her cooking; it was so much better than the food at Huis Francie van Zyl, the female residence across the way from Hippokrates where all boarders took their meals because the male residence didn't have its own kitchen.

In fact, Pieter thought, *the communal meals were the source of countless courtships.* He was sitting at the origin of many such liaisons; a slatted bench situated to one side of the glass paned front doors, recessed on a polished terracotta patio, backdropped by red brick walls. A large scarlet bougainvillea housed in a faux marble cistern lent a semblance of romance to the busy thoroughfare. Pieter didn't want Cherise to suffer alone after the terrible event they both felt responsible for, and if he were honest with himself, he quite liked her. So he had got himself dressed in his navy medical school blazer and maroon Stellenbosch

University tie and bought five red and white roses now lying wrapped in thick brown paper on the dark green painted slats beside him, their subtle perfume reminding him of Cherise when he purchased the bunch at the corner café, just down the road, hoping that she would be free and willing to join him at the Sunday lunch. Pieter was staging an ambush of sorts; he had not actually invited Cherise yet.

Pieter looked up expectantly each time a new student exited the Huis Francie doors, and looked down as new arrivals from nearby Hippokrates entered; he didn't like the banter, nor the exposed position that the prominent seat put him in.

"Howzit. Who's the lucky girl?"

"I hope she says yes!"

Pieter just semi-smiled and thought through the situation. *I'm sure mom won't mind. But dad? He might... he's very formal about such things. But he'll relent when we tell him about what happened on labour and delivery.*

Pieter looked up for the tenth time, no go. He knew Cherise was still in the rez because he recognized her car parked to the right and had established from one of her friends that she was free and had no fixed plans for the day — rather hoping the friend might reveal his interest, despite forswearing any mention of it, when he asked her about the state of affairs.

But what would happen if I brought a Coloured girl home? Pieter suddenly thought. *There are lots of Coloured nurses at the hospital, and they joke with me all the time. 'Why don't you come over to our side? You'll enjoy it!' And I guess, I would. I've always liked them. The way they move. The way they smile. Their easy way with others; it reminds me a bit of mom's mannerisms.*

The door banged closed, a breeze had overpowered the restraining mechanism, shattering Pieter's reverie; he slipped back to the colour question — only white girls came out of the doors at Huis Francie van Zyl.

It's illegal. It's against the Immorality Act. And I never meet blacks socially anyway. Except for going into Bishop Lavis to do a clinic; I've never even been into a township. I wouldn't dream of it and... it's not allowed. As a White I would need a pass to go into a location.

"Pieter, what are you doing out here?" Cherise, her blond hair snugged back into a ponytail pinching her face, had emerged and was floating overhead interrupting the daydream.

"I... brought you these, they match your skirt... too cheer you up," Pieter had grabbed the bouquet in one hand and used the other to lever himself up from the bench, "And" he fixed her light blue eyes, "will you come to lunch with my parents... they will be most gratified."

"And you? Will you be gratified?" Cherise grasped her ponytail and brought it forward to lie just short of her modest violet-coloured bodice, and then took the flowers, sniffed their scent in deeply, exhaled, and held out a winged arm for him to engage, having nestled the brown paper packet gingerly under her other arm, wary of embedded thorns.

†

"Have you seen what's in the Sunday Paper?" Pieter couldn't help but have, as he introduced Cherise to his mother and father at the front door, because the headlines were clearly visible on the newspaper held clenched under his father's black-suited arm. Marja had not needed to set another placing at the Sunday table; she always held a seat open, a tradition from her past that remained unexplained, so they had seated around the table and started the meal of gravied sheep shank, roast potatoes, and assorted steamed vegetables. A second bottle of Nederburg Pinotage hovered over each glass in turn, as Pieter senior asked the question.

"Fourteen killed in rioting," Pieter junior said.

"In a number of townships round Johannesburg. It's the worst rioting since Soweto. Black on black violence again. They're killing their own," Pieter senior had risen, picked up the paper from the lounge table where he had left it and returned with the broadsheet to the dining table and was pointing to the article and read it out loud.

"Rioters hacked the deputy mayor of the township, Sam Dlamini, to death in the street and then put his body in his car and set it ablaze."

"There were also three bomb explosions in downtown Joburg," Cherise took a delicate sip of wine, "they say it's the ANC."

"Probably, but at least no one was killed," Marja said.

"It's all a protest against the Tricameral Parliament. That idea is never going to work. Excluding the

Africans from power is madness. Pushing them into homelands where they must vote is worse. Alan Boesak and the UDF are right. We need power-sharing with *all* the peoples of South Africa if there is to be a future for us. The alternative is bloodshed. Civil war," Pieter junior chewed on a tough piece of meat.

His father poured himself another glass of Neder-burg, downed it in one draught and sucked his teeth, jutting his cheeks up against the frame of his spectacles; he concentrated to avoid slurring, his dulled eyes magnified for all to see, "And the Afs want to run the country? They'll run it alright... into the ground. We must keep that Mandela locked up on Robben Island. And the ANC from bombing our people. It's my job to keep the place safe. To get the commies to talk. To tell us what they are planning. Who we must capture to put down the '*Armed Struggle*,'" he raised his two index fingers and flicked them down twice, "*Umkhonto we Zizwe*," he flicked his fingers again, "What kak, if you'll excuse my French. The only good k....r. is a dead k....r,", the captain refilled his glass and pushed back his chair releasing a shriek from the wounded parquet floor.

Marja got up and left the table.

Cherise looked down at her plate.

Pieter adopted his prayerful position, elbows on the batik tablecloth, and glanced at his father, speaking from behind his hands, "the problem dad is that you think the ends justify the means. I don't think they do. We are really all the same; we have one common humanity. We should be colourblind. That's why I went into medicine. To care for all people no matter who they are. To save them; not destroy them. Everyone bleeds red. In fact we don't ask whose blood it is when we transfuse a patient. Just their blood group, not their race."

"Did I not show my humanity, in bringing you up as my son? Did I not take you fishing and spend time with you? Marja please come back," Pieter senior turned his head in the direction of the kitchen. "Your son doesn't appreciate what I have done for him."

"Oh, I think he does," Marja had returned to the table and spread her fingers like two wayang fans on the brown and tan patterned surface, "don't you Pieter?"

"Of course I do, it's not about that at all."

"Cherise, let me explain," Pieter senior turned to the medical student who had diminished in her chair, "I got Pieter a police bursary, and so he will have to pay it back. One day, I *will* be in charge of Caledon Square Police Station."

"I expect you will," Marja closed the gaps between her fingers, "you've spent enough time there."

"And when that day arrives, I want Pieter to come and work with me as a District Surgeon to help with the prisoners. You see, I am very proud of my son, even though he gives me no end of grief," Pieter senior turned from looking at Cherise, got up from the table, picked up a glass brimming with Pinotage and continued, "come outside onto the stoep Pieter, grab a glass and we can settle the world's problems in

183

peace. Let the girls clean up; I can see they want to talk too, but without us interfering."

Pieter glanced at Cherise, who provided an encouraging smile, filled his glass, and followed his father out onto the stoep, closing the heavy glass paned door carefully, a strong wind had come up.

Marja reached over and, lightly, between finger and thumb, touched the diamond that protruded from a gold band around Cherise's middle finger. The medical student had rested her hand on the table, and leant forwards again, when the two Pieters had exited the room.

"What a lovely ring."

"Yes, it was my mother's wedding ring. She left it to me in her will."

"Do you miss her?"

"Yes, for five years now and you, may I ask? Have you lost people that you love."

"Ja, of course you may ask. I miss my parents in Indonesia. They were killed during the second world war by the Japanese. It was after that, that I came to Cape Town. It was too dangerous for Indo's to remain."

"I didn't know you were from there, Pieter never told me. You look a bit sad to me. I hope you don't mind me saying that?"

"Do I?" Marja lifted her hand from where she had let it rest on Cherise's and splayed it across her bosom, covering the brown birthmark and the edge of the scar that peeped above the yellow bodice of her dress. "Can I trust you with this?"

"Yes. Yes. Of course you can. Professional secret," the tips of Cherise's lips edged upwards.

"I miss Willem Jansen, my childhood sweetheart, and Promise Madiba, my girlfriend, very much. They saved my life together when I was stabbed in the heart during the Langa Riots. He was a doctor and she a nurse."

"Was?"

"Agh ja, Willem fell climbing on Devil's Peak."

"How awful. How long ago was that?" Cherise placed her ringed hand on Marja's bare shoulder, the gold glinting in the sunlight slanting through a window pane from the stoep outside. They could hear the slow thud of a helicopter droning off in the distance accentuating the quietness that had settled between them. Marja seemed to go into a trance and then answered.

"Before Willem was born... ah..."

"Willem?"

"Cherise, sorry, I got carried away, this is not of your concern..." Marja, put her hand over her face, bowed her head, and continued, "I just wanted to tell you that Pieter's father is a good man. A very good man. I know he can be harsh and crass as today, but he really loves our son and wants the very best for him. I must apologize."

"No need to apologise, Mrs Marais, I hear this kind of talk all around me."

"Please do call me Marja, Cherise, that is much better. Now... do you... like Pieter?"

"Mrs Marais... I can't say Marja yet... I am sorry,"

Cherise deflected her pale eyelashes over her blue eyes, "yes, I must admit I do. He is so brave, and bright, despite what happened on the border. But he does suffer as a result of it. I want to help him."

"Ja, he is a wonderful son, I am so proud of him. And although he hasn't told me much about you, I can see in his eyes that he likes you. A lot. I can tell. But, please Cherise, what I have just said must *please* remain between us. Can you promise me that," Marja palmed Cherise's ringed hand once again and gripped tightly.

"I promise. It will go with me to my grave."

†

Notwithstanding the contentious nature of their first date at the hands of Pieter's belligerent father, by their sixth year of medical school the two were a well-established *item*; Tinie and Lance had started speculating as to the date of the wedding — before or after finishing medical school. The couple had decided that they wanted to be earning before making that commitment but were greatly pleased to keep working on the same firm together, especially in the penultimate internal medicine rotation on *intake* rounds at C1D-Oos.

This is where the rubber meets the road, Pieter thought. The four friends were now the Student Interns, SI's, on the Watterman Firm. They had spent the previous night together with lower order medical students and the supervising internal medicine registrar as well as two medical officers on spoed — triaging incoming medical patients and then performing anamneses, physical examinations, side room tests (urine, blood), ordering x-rays and special investigations, collecting results, starting emergency treatment, and generally getting ready for the morning rounds conducted by Professor Bok Watterman.

Pieter had found the intricacies of arriving at the correct diagnosis for a particular patient's condition, the most elusive and yet thrilling aspect of medicine. He discovered that the meshwork of patient *symptoms*, be that their complaints, feelings, or pain-points and the elicited *signs* determined from a thorough head to toe examination of all the systems — neuro, cardiac, thoracic, urogenital, abdominal, autonomic and skin — using all one's senses, often enhanced by *diagnostic aids* such as the ophthalmoscope, stethoscope and patella hammer, were a fascinating puzzle to solve.

All had to be painstakingly gathered in the service of developing a working stratagem for *side room and special investigations* that would help to include or exclude a specific disease entity for the all-important differential diagnosis list that the Student Interns had to draw up and then present at the professor's rounds the next day.

In that presentation at the patient's bedside lay glory or abject defeat, Pieter thought. *With an easy patient, correctly diagnosed and treated, you were fine. With a difficult diagnosis in a complex patient that you got wrong it was embarrassing. But if it was a complicated patient and one could make the correct diagnosis, your reputation soared.* Pieter wanted his reputation to soar; he was certain he could clinch the diagnosis from his reading of Nietzsche — all the signs were there, but he had to wait his turn till they got to his patient.

"Miss Cherise, please present your findings," Professor Bok Watterman, a short doctor, in a wide coat, with a determined chin pushed his namesake bok-beard out in the direction of the diffident medical student, while scuffing back what little hair was left on his wrinkled pate with the flat of his hand.

"Prof," Cherise glanced down at the crumpled note stretched out with two hands in front of her, "we think Mr Sassman has an asthmatic exacerbation. I mean attack. An asthma attack."

"Any background information?"

"Yes, he has DOPS Prof."

"DOPS?"

"Can I say it in Afrikaans Prof?"

"Of course you can, this is an Afrikaans Medical School, but you can study in English, Afrikaans, even Dutch did you know that?"

"No, Prof," Cherise consulted her notes while trying to put her stethoscope back into her doctor's coat; it was hanging half out. "Diffuse Obstruktieve Pulmonêre Siekte."

"Correct. How did you treat it?"

"Prof. I didn't."

"Why not?"

"I wasn't feeling well, and the registrar sent me

188

upstairs to get some sleep. I've just come down to present."

"Juffrouw, I am sorry for you. Is the patient, okay?"

"Mr Sassman is Prof, and I'm a little better, yes."

And so it went. The Firm of around twelve, all dressed in white coats, their stethoscopes across their necks, in their hands, or confined to pockets, trouped from patient to patient stopping at each bedside. Here the students were habitually asked to demonstrate their findings, listen to a cardiac murmur, palpate an abdomen to feel the border of an enlarged liver, or tap a flexed ankle tendon to make a neurological diagnosis. Often the most difficult diagnosis to make was when several of the systems of the body were involved. For then it could be one of the innumerable forms of cancer, infection or autoimmune disease that had tormented humankind from well before Hippocrates' day and would continue to do so in perpetuity despite the inexorable advances of modern medicine — the correct diagnosis remaining ever crucial to contrive the best possible treatment regimen, to cure the patient. And, whenever a cure was not possible, to allay suffering and heal the patient's spirit as best as one could to prepare the patient for the hereafter.

Professor Watterman waited till the entourage had crowded around the next patient: a brown coloured man of 56 years of age, sitting up in bed, his over-laundered hospital pyjamas dishevelled around his thin frame. He had a beetled forehead —

the furrows frozen upwards — pushing back wavy hair, and a snub nose with an expressionless, almost sad face. His left eye was deviated upwards, and yet he appeared happy in himself, "*Môre allemaal*, good morning, *volk*. Are all the doctors in good health? It is a lovely day! *Ek sê,*" the patient pulled his lame left arm across his midriff with his right.

"Mr Marais, do you have a diagnosis or a differential?"

"Yes, the gentleman has General Paralysis of the Insane caused by syphilis."

"That's a brave statement Pieter, how did you get to that?"

"Frederick Nietzsche had it. I like to read his work."

Prof Watterman directed his attention to the patient, "May I ask who you are?"

"I am the President of South Africa," the overhead light accentuated a crinkled smile.

"No, no, that is P.W. Botha, why are you here?"

"I'm not sure. My arm went dead, it wouldn't work, so my wife brought me in. She say's I'm *mal* too," the patient adjusted his arm and looked up at Prof Watterman with his good eye.

"Beyond the delusions of grandeur that I have just demonstrated Mr Marais, what else do you have to support your diagnosis. Is there Tabes Dorsalis as well?"

"Prof, the patient has Argyll Robertson pupils which are pathognomonic of General Paralysis of the Insane and his sad facies points to Tabes; he also has some ataxia when standing and absent vibration and position sense."

"Well done. Have you started treatment Mr Marais? Where is your registrar?" the head of the firm, smoothed his crinkled scalp with one hand and grabbed his grey beard with the other.

"The reg has taken a telephone call; his beeper went off. No we haven't started penicillin yet until we're sure of the VDRL test."

"I think you can start, but warn the patient about the Herxheimer reaction first," then turning again to look at the patient, "Sir, you're in good hands with SI Marais, he'll explain everything in detail to you," and then turned to face Pieter who was standing across the bed, summoning him to lean closer as he bent forward towards him "and please look after your girlfriend; Miss Cherise does not look well today," the Professor regained his former erect state and gruff voice, scanning his firm, "let's have a tea break; we'll restart in one half hour at the next patient."

†

"Cherise, what's wrong?" Pieter asked when he found her in the small laboratory that centred between C1D-Oos and C1D-Wes, crying. The students often congregated in the space for tea breaks, and performed the essential side room investigations there indicated for their patients.

Cherise was perched on a lab stool and rested her elbows on the counter that stretched across its back wall, her forehead yoked in the flats of her hands. Daylight streamed through the glazed windows that lined the opposing wall, making her features appear ashen and showing a line of tears on both sides of her face.

Anaemia, Pieter thought.

"Pieter, I feel so sad and weak and my heart is racing. I thought it would be better this morning, but I feel worse."

"Agh, my dear... do you have any pain, any nausea?"

"A little in both knee joints, I'm scared. Please have a look at me," Cherise sniffed.

"Oorait, let me close the door... give us some privacy... I can lock it from the inside. Take off your jacket and lie on the counter. We can do a finger prick HB with the hemoglobinometer, I think you're anaemic."

"Yes," Pieter was looking into the eyepiece of the handheld device, adjusting the slide mechanism on its side, while Cherise had disrobed and was positioning herself on the hard surface. "I'm afraid it's low."

"How low?" Cherise sat up.

"Six."

"Are you sure? That's really low," she lay back again, wiping both sides of her face with a paper towel that she had retrieved from the aluminium washbasin as Pieter started the examination.

"*Bekyk, betas, beklop, beluister,*" she said in Afrikaans.

"Yes, peruse, palpate, percuss, and perform auscultation, I will call out the positives only." Beginning the examination, he ran his hands down her neck and then felt in both her axilla's.

"That tickles," Cherise giggled.

"I'm sorry, but it's not funny Cherise, you've got enlarged lymph glands, and..." Pieter palpated her abdomen gently on the right, "and an enlarged liver," and then moved to her left side, "I can feel a spleen."

Cherise's face faded as the possible diagnosis dawned on her, "leukaemia, Pieter, I've got leukaemia. That's a death sentence."

†

"Captain of the men of death" was how Sir William Osler had put it at the turn of the century when describing the bacteria that overwhelmed Cherise's weakened immune system on C6D-West, the ward where the sixth year medical student died. Modern medicine had failed to contain the rampant streptococcal pneumonia that had killed her, and Pieter felt responsible; he should have picked up the signs that Cherise was sick earlier. Only then the medicines that might have cured the smouldering leukaemia could have stood a chance. Instead, Pieter had been blind to her problems; too involved in himself. Cherise's blighted white blood cells had failed her. What good was all Pieter's medical training if he couldn't help the one's he loved?

Pieter had been banned from any direct medical

involvement once the diagnosis of Cherise's terminal illness had been confirmed but had been allowed into the ward by Prof Watterman at the end. Pieter looked down at her wilted figure. Cherise's once beautiful face was frozen like candlewax, her lips now venous in colour, her hair a tangle of straw on the pillow. A rumpled sheet was drawn up to her chin; redundant medical apparatus and infusion devices had been removed or pushed to one side. Half-light played across her hospital bed, filtered through adjacent drawn-down shades against the glaring Cape sun. A vase of browning red and white roses remained on the night stand. It was a desolate afternoon.

Tinie and Lance had come into the ward to say their goodbyes and came and stood across Cherise's bed from where Pieter stood looking miserable.

"I feel as if I am the kiss of death; whenever I love someone or make a friend, I lose them — there's just no point," Pieter trailed off, his eyes strayed repetitively rightwards, demonstrating the nystagmus that caused his eyes to flick repeatedly in the direction he was trying to look that developed when he became stressed. He tapped the sleeve of his white coat against his nostrils, his fingers tightened into a fist and then Pieter bent over Cherise's unmoving chest and rested his bearded face against her sheet-covered shoulder, caressing her neckline with his curly hair, "It's such a waste, such a waste."

"Yes," said Tinie sniffling.

Lance bent over and put his hand on Pieter's where it curved over Cherise's thorax and pressed softly.

"Did you make a sketch of her?"

"One of my best," Pieter said looking up at Lance, their faces close.

"Well... then her beauty will be with you to treasure always."

"Yes, but not her future. You know we were going to get married? Next year."

"I know... I know, won't you come... come with us... we can take you to the beach she loved," Lance said. After which he and Tinie stepped around the bed to embrace their colleague.

"No, I just want to sit here with Cherise for a while. My mother will come and join me. She said she wanted to," Pieter sank into the uncomfortable chair at the head of the bed and waited for Marja; Tinie and Lance had left, leaving a fresh red and white rose on the sheet next to their classmate.

Pieter wondered about a future without Cherise. With her he had learnt to cope with the after-effects of the border killing. The nightmares of being back in Angola; the pathological agitation he experienced when stressed. She had calmed him by reframing each new stressful situation for him, adding a dose of reality and humour to temper his catastrophizing. *Even after we killed that child at our first delivery together, she helped me get over it,* he thought.

"It wasn't our fault. We did our best. What more could we do. At least we saved the mother" *Cherise had said.* Pieter got up and went to lay next to her on the bed, under the sheet. He nuzzled Cherise's neck and fell asleep.

Until his mother, dressed in black, awakened him and Pieter returned to his chair. "I've been sitting here awhile, you looked so peaceful and happy, just like when you were a little boy," Marja rearranged the matching black hairpins in her jet-black hair restoring its pile. "Don't you want to come and stay with us, until you finish medical school? Leave Huis Hippokrates behind."

"Mom," Pieter reached over and rested his hand lightly on his mother's thigh. She was sitting askew on Cherise's bed facing her son in the corner chair. "I can't stay at home because of dad: every time there is a fight."

"Pieter, he hasn't changed, but you have. He doesn't think you respect him for the work he has to do. When you were younger, he fought for you, that was our deal."

"Deal?"

"The... understanding between us, and now you have to pay back as far as he is concerned."

"Yes, but I don't have to stay with him."

"No you don't but where will you live after you finish... " Marja's words were extinguished by a fire alarm, the wah-wah-wah, filling the room from the hushed corridor till a metallic voice announced the all-clear over the hospital's public address system and they could resume.

Pieter's eyes flicked as he spoke: "Cherise and I were going to do our internship and medical officers' year here at Tygerberg and then go into private practice together, in Durbanville, but now I think

196

I'll go to Cape Town instead."

"Pieter, you like the sea, I saw an advertisement in *Die Burger* for a flat in Table View; I'll help you pay the rent till you're making your own money."

"Mom, I go there all the time. It's only thirty minutes from here. I've been learning to windsurf at Rietvlei, I'll go and have a look. But first, I have to get over this."

"You never will, my son. Not fully. Cherise will always be with you, always remain part of you. I know... That will never be lost, even if she has gone away."

†

By 1990, Pieter had opened his one man general practice in Tamboerskloof on the rising slope common to Lions Head and Table Mountain. Although considered good looking, he was nervy, reserved, and stand-offish and so branded a loner. Not that he cared. He had a great passion for medicine and was learning to distance himself from his patient's personal problems while still demonstrating empathy for their clinical condition; Doctor Marais was regarded as having a good bed-side manner.

To stem the inevitable stresses of practicing medicine, he found antidotes in extreme physical activity, sketched, and read widely, focusing particularly on the world's great philosophers to attempt to understand the meaning of the lives that he worked so diligently to preserve.

One day, in January, in his first month of practice, his secretary answered a telephone call from his father. Pieter was in the treatment room performing a procedure under local anaesthesia and could not be disturbed. Colonel Marais had finally become the officer in charge of Caledon Square Police Station the previous year.

"Did he say what it was about Suzanne?" Doctor Marais asked as he pulled off his surgical gloves and approached the front desk where she was sitting.

"No, he just said that today's District Surgeon was not available so you must come to Caledon Square immediately. To the 4ᵗʰ floor office. He stressed that you <u>must</u> check in with the secretary first. Drop everything, he said," Suzanne jammed the scribbled note she had consulted back on to the spike of her pin-pad.

Pieter parked his car perfectly between the newly whitened lines of Caledon Square's courtyard parking space. He had gained access through the police headquarters marble arched portal when the officer at the gate recognized who he was. In a rush, Pieter decided to use the enclosed fire-escape stairs rather than the normal access via the lift that centred the building. He had grown very fit from windsurfing and only needed to catch his breath, stopping to do so, as he rounded the pitch dark, concrete stairwell's shaft, a half-flight below the fourth floor. His further climb was suddenly arrested by his father's snarl in clipped Afrikaans:

"K....r, we must have the truth or we will kill

you." Followed by the sound of a slap, and gasped, moist grunting.

Pieter crept up the darkened stair to the bare stone landing, his eyes flickering left and right like a cat's. The air was thick with dampness and smelled of cigarette smoke and blood in the poorly lit passage. A ceiling light fizzed on, then off. Further down a steel door stood ajar; a slice of light fading to black across the passageway was like a magnet. Pieter reverted to his army training. He crouched low, although his brain sought flight, and edged along the rough wall — streaking his safari suit with dirt — so he could peer into the room unseen.

An overhead light bulb revealed the ghastly scene unfolding in the dank jail. At the centre of it a large naked black man was suspended upside down in a ball. A broomstick thrust between the crook of his arms and legs rested between two stout tables providing the fulcrum for the helicopter technique of torture.

"He won't talk so spin him again," Colonel Marais said turning to a gorilla of a police officer, stripped down to his waist, his black sweat-run paunch tightening with the effort of propulsion.

The prisoner was spun round vertically once more. The police officer grunted with great effort and tried to avoid being covered with the blood and snot and excrement that leaked from the man as he was turned, adding to the mess of fetid effluent collecting on the floor beneath him.

He came to rest upside down again, his shaved

head a foot off the floor. Pieter could not judge his age but could see the sjambok stripes on his back and the massive scalp laceration, puffed bloodied face, damaged left ear, and one eye extruding from its socket. The other, open, darted around like a frightened animal, until it stopped and the prisoner's mouth opened and he retched.

"Bloody k....r, *hulle will mos nie praat nie*" Pieter's father said and emptied half a bucket of water over the prostrate man and then kicked him full length in the face.

Pieter burst through the door, "no, no stop. You'll kill him."

"That's all he's good for, no bloody use to us isn't that so Officer Ndlovu?"

"Yes, baas."

The torture victim had swung back from the impact, dribbling blood, saliva, vomit and water, and returned to the vertical position like the pendulum of a clock, leaving a streak of discharge on the sluiced concrete floor, when the colonel kicked him once again. This time with the point of his shoe, breaking the bridge of his nose with a crack before, turning to accost Pieter.

"And you," he pointed his finger, "you were supposed to go to my secretary to sign the papers and not come barging in here where you have no business."

Pieter was decompensating. The terrible facial injuries and the bleeding reminded him of Corli in the bush. He started shaking uncontrollably, *like an allergic reaction from a wasp sting* he thought and then bent over and vomited into the just emptied bucket left standing to one side. *I have to get out, I have to get out,* he could not focus, his eyesight blurred from the frantic motion of his nystagmus.

The hanging prisoner had not moved after he stopped swaying from the final kick. Blood and saliva continued to expand the pool below his head but his breathing had stopped.

The colonel had left the room and returned with a form attached to a clipboard; he had pulled a ball-point pen from the array stashed in the top pocket of his police tunic. His trousers and spit polished shoe were still marked by evidence of the death kick.

Officer Ndlovu had put on a T-shirt and having refreshed the bucket with water was sluicing away the evidence of the torture with a mop, adding humidity to the smell of bloodied death in the sweltering room.

Pieter felt ambushed again as he was in Angola, his father's voice only just breaking through.

"Pieter, PIETER, DOCTOR MARAIS, sign the Death Certificate."

"What does it say? I can't stop my eyes, I can't focus."

"That the prisoner fell down the stairs, isn't that right Officer Ndlovu?"

"Yes, baas, he slipped while trying to escape. That's the cause of death."

"I can't," Pieter's eyes danced around and he felt bilious. He clenched his teeth to stem the judder

201

of his jaw, "it's against the Hippocratic Oath, false testimony."

"Nonsense, look at the prisoner's face, it's an obvious cause of death. And *I'm* your father, not Hippocrates. Here," the colonel held the clipboard out to Pieter and offered the pen, "it's your duty to your father after all I've done for you. Now it's your time to bring your part."

All Pieter wanted was to get away from the threat; he wanted it to be over. To be away from his dad. Away from death. Away, away. He scrawled down his elongated signature, above his typed name, struggled to put the ball-point in the clamp of the clipboard and so threw both on the floor instead, and then fled through the steel door, turning only once to look back into the torture chamber. His father had stooped to pick up the clipboard; Officer Ndlovu had resumed his mopping, and the prisoner hung lifeless on the broomstick. Pieter walked rapidly away along the corridor to turn down the stairwell. Once there, and as he was quickly descending the stairs, he attempted to wipe away the smudges of dirt on his safari-suit, well aware that the stain on his character was not so easily removed; in fact, it was as indelible as the signature that would seal his fate.

†

10

Becoming a Police Detective, 1976-1990

"Sawubona my daughter, welcome." An abundant Goodwill Dlamini, his face broad and lips protuberant, spread out his arms like a latter day Jesus, tenting the multi-coloured Dashiki shirt that extended down to his stolid calves and grimy feet, "what took you so long?"

Thembisa, tired after a two day train-trip from Johannesburg to Cape Town, had struggled to pick the right Putco bus to Langa township from the confusion of motor vehicles that radiated out from the waterfront's Victorian style train station. She felt lucky when a conductor indicated she could go up the rubbish strewn stairs of the double-decker bus to find a front seat free and so occupied it immediately, stacking her meagre belongings next to her so she could keep the double seat to herself. Sweat trickled down the nape of her neck. She removed her pullover, added it to the pile, smoothed down her grey school dress and white short-sleeved shirt and twisted her hair into a knot with a red rubber band, an array of which she kept on her wrist; she had broken quite a few on the trip and there were only two left, green and blue.

Thembisa could feel the reverberation of the bus; its great engine had been revved up by an impatient bus driver. She could smell the fresh petroleum as the smoke from the exhaust rose; Thembisa had pulled down the dust-streaked side window to get some fresh air and a better view — one she had only seen in a picture book in the Library at Naledi School.

It was overwhelming. The bus had been parked facing the Grand Parade bustling with commerce. To the left she could see car choked streets, and the dark grey walls and turrets of what must be Cape Town's Castle. In front, the golden coloured City Hall buildings rose elegantly, topped by a clocktower (around the back of which was the Caledon Square Police Station, but Thembisa was not to know now that the forbidding building would hold her future) and behind that, beyond a sprawl of city buildings, rose to a horizontal top, the grand magnificence of Table Mountain. It seemed to Thembisa like the city traffic sounds echoed back from its granite slopes as if from a gigantic loudspeaker. She was startled by the report of a cannon-shot and saw a puff of smoke rising from half-way up a peaked hill topped by multi-hued flags aligning in the stiff breeze.

"Aitsa! Dis nou lekka! Die noon day gun! A wiry man of walnut complexion, wearing a tattered tweed cap tilted to one side, had taken the other front seat and pointed in the general direction with his pinkie and index finger, "from Signal Hill. Always on time. See, look at the clock there." He took a draw from an evil smelling cigarette clenched between his teeth and angled his prong shaped hand a shade higher to the right, "there is Lion's Head. You see its head there, the same granite as Table Mountain, with the tree sticking out of its side like a lollipop? And then the lion's flank, there... curving behind Signal Hill."

"Yebo, I do."

"You look Xhosa, perhaps half Xhosa, not dark enough to be full. Where did you come from?"

"Soweto, Sir," Thembisa picked at the elastic bands, rolling her wrist.

"S-o-w-e-t-o, bad, bad," the man took another drag, "Where are you going?"

Thembisa uncrumpled the paper note clinched in her hand, "Harlem Street, Langa, Cape Town."

"That's easy, the bus stops at Washington Street and it's not far from there. I'll point you in the right direction."

Thembisa settled in the green vinyl seat, bending forward to grasp the aluminium railing that jutted up from the front windowsill to steady herself against the bump of the bus as it exited Cape Town's railway station, rattled along the Grand Parade, turned past the Castle and ground up on to Eastern Boulevard to pass over the plexus of railway lines that had brought her to the Mother City.

Sitting on the right side, *in the pound seats* she thought, Thembisa cast a wary eye at her neighbour and then turned around to look behind her, to make doubly sure that her fellow passengers were all *non-White* and she was not sitting in the wrong place.

205

"I know what you're thinking Miss. Not to worry. This is a *non-European* bus, youse won't see any whitey's here. Not on your life. The only whites you'll see in the townships are the cops and there's plenty of them since the riots started."

Thus somewhat reassured, Thembisa started enjoying the ride punctuated by her guide. They were driving out of the City Bowl up the lower slopes of Devils Peak, a stretched row of three storied flats, painted beige, accompanying their rise along the steepening road; they could both see Table Bay beyond from their elevated positions.

"You see there," Thembisa's guide waved his hand towards the view, unsteadied by the falter of the bus. "That's District Six. Sies. Or it was! Those fancy flats, they're just a front, a Potemkin village! Bah!" he got up and pointed through the pulled down window, "you see that barren section?"

"Yebo," Thembisa had also risen to see better.

"The Nats bulldozed down everything in the sixties. Sixty thousand people had to move, my family included," he took off his cap and fanned himself and sat down in a slump.

Thembisa followed suit and craned her neck, again sneaking a look at her fellow traveller who was struggling to light his next cigarette. Striking match after Lion match, breaking each one as it caught fire.

"May I help you, Sir?"

He passed her the matchbox, upon which Thembisa deftly extracted a match, struck it once against the box's side and satisfied them both with its sulphur smelling flame. The wiry man took a deep toke, and, drawing strength, continued.

"This is Devil's Peak, and over there, on my side, you can just see that red roof, on that white building, and that water tower. That's Groote Schuur Hospital, and here's Hospital Bend. You see those little crosses on the grass verge. Many, many accidents."

The bus gathered pace as the road curved down on to Settler's Way, leaving the Table Mountain range behind and descending on to the Cape Flats over the Liesbeeck River and beyond to the Athlone power station. Its two enormous toilet-roll-shaped cooling towers creating steam that imprinted passing shadows on Langa below, unfortunately, affording its residents only passing relief from the searing African sun.

"And why are you here?" the wiry man had dropped his burning cigarette butt and was grinding it beneath his worn veldschoen. "We're here. This is Bhunga Avenue," he turned to the schoolgirl.

"My parents want me to go to school here. I must live with my uncle, Mr Dlamini. Do you know him?"

"There are many Dlamini's. But... so... you must be black. Anyway, look around at your new home."

The scenery had certainly changed. They had driven through a steel entrance gate. A six foot tall fence stretched each side into the sandy distance, its wire netting had prevented windblown detritus from entering; the enclosure was plastered with newsprint and brown paper. And although the main road was covered in tar, Thembisa could see many side roads were unpaved, filled with garbage, and lined by dilapidated houses fronted by the occasional motorcar in various stages of repair. She saw the same mangy dogs roaming the side streets and decided that it was just like being back in Soweto, except for the remarkable view as they turned up into Washington Street, "Devil's Peak, Table Mountain, Lion's Head and Signal Hill," Thembisa clapped her hand to her mouth, collected her belongings after receiving directions, and made her way to her new home.

†

(August 1983)

"Thembisa, enough lying around, come and help me outside," Goodwill Dlamini was peering through the burglar-barred window into the bedroom she shared with her older cousin, Priscilla. The post matriculant was listening to a Rolling Stones record.

"Aikona, I can't hear you."

"Turn it down then," the huge man had tipped his head back to let his straw hat slip to hang by its leash around his neck glistening with sweat, like fine polished ebony, atop his flashy shirt. Uncle Dlamini had been wondering how to approach the next step with his charge. He had an idea but wanted Thembisa to be its author.

"Why haven't you found a job? Come and help me paint this banner," Dlamini was bent over a twice folded, none too clean bedsheet that he had put on a stretch of sooty concrete that led from the kitchen on to the rummage of his back plot.

"I haven't found anything meaningful to do."

"Meaningful? What do you mean?" Dlamini's plump lips pouted, his golden family ring flashed in the wintry sunshine, a passing biplane had left a trail of vapor fading against the untroubled sky.

"There's so many problems. The tsotsis roam free and I have heard of rapes. Just the other day... "

"Okay, okay, Thembisa," Dlamini held up the paint brush dripping with bright orange paint, "you got an A for English, what do I write?"

"Where are you going?" Thembisa flexed over, shook out her mane of tawny hair, whipped up straight again, and stroked it down to cover her shoulders and the apricot coloured straps of the smock that barely reached her midriff; her almond belly button was set off by tight jeans, her toenails competed with the bright colour of Dlamini's paint but were covered in garden dust.

"You'll find out."

"Aikona."

"You want meaning and purpose? We're going to a meeting in Mitchel's Plain. The United Democratic Front is being launched."

"But *I'm* not going?"

"Oh yes you are. That's an order. We must make a plan for you. Meaning and purpose, my foot," Dlamini swayed his head like a buffalo.

"Alright. Write: FREEDOM. No let me do it. Your hands are shaky; you'll mess it up."

†

The Rockland's Community Hall was filled to the rafters; there was insufficient standing space surrounding the raised speakers' platform, so some of the jubilant crowd had climbed on to the U-shaped parapet underneath its corrugated iron roof and dangled their legs over its ledges while others braced their backs against its supporting beams. Dlamini and Thembisa had taken position in a back corner spanning the painted banner between them, V-ed on two sticks.

The place felt hot with excitement, but Thembisa found the series of speakers boring, so she drifted, recalling the conversation they had had on their way in Dlamini's ramshackle car.

"Thembisa from now on, please call me Goodwill."

"Uncle?"

"No, I am old enough to be your grandfather, so just Goodwill will do. You are not like my daughter, Priscilla, she is wasting her life with frivolous things getting big and fat. I think you can do better. But it is dangerous opposing the state. So I am telling you this in the car, where no-one can overhear us; there are informers everywhere."

"Is that why you have a pistol in the cubby hole? And lock away cash in that safe of yours underneath the bed. Where did you get that from?"

"Oh, no... no..., that is not a question a niece asks. Aikona. You are getting too big for your boots. We have to do these things to make ends meet. To help you and Priscilla and others... And we must prepare against the white man.

"You forget, what happened to my sister in Soweto. I know about the white man."

"No I haven't forgotten about your sister. Oh no... I worked for the ANC, before it was banned, just like your mother."

"My mother in Soweto?"

"No, I mean... I mean, I shouldn't have said that. We must not name others. That slipped out. Please forget it," Goodwill changed gears with a crunch and peered through the grubby windshield. Drops of sweat suddenly appeared at the margins of his greying, peppercorn hair.

"I want to explain what you are about to see."

"I read the papers Uncle... I mean Goodwill," Thembisa dried her palms, rubbing her jeans.

"Do you know what the Tricameral Parliament that sits for the first time today means?"

"White, Coloured and Indian Representation."

"Yes, but Piet Wapen wants to shut us out completely. There is to be no Black representation. We must vote in the Homelands," Goodwill rolled down the side-window further and spat on to the passing pavement.

"No hope for the future. No justice. That's why I have joined the UDF. We must fight for the vote," Dlamini raised his fist through the car window and shouted "one man, one vote..."

Thembisa felt an elbow prod her ribcage, snapping her out of her reverie — she looked up and saw a caffeine coloured man with a helmet of tightly

211

coiled hair from which golden spectacles protruded, approach the microphoned podium, pat down his pale suit and straighten his black tie, and then pause to hold on to both sides of the lectern and clear his throat, waiting for the audience to subside.

"That's Reverend Alan Boesak. Watch him. He's going to lead the UDF, just you wait and see," Dlamini had cupped his hand to Thembisa's ear.

When the clapping had diminished, Thembisa caught only some of what the reverend was saying because Doctor Boesak had a high voice and a saliva filled way of speaking; his snappy words seemed to bubble rather than flow.

"We must create a united front of churches, civic associations, trade unions, student organizations, and sports bodies," Boesak stopped, looked around him, his extravagant brown eyes aflicker.

"Thembisa, I want you to join a civic organization. Grassroots, they have a newspaper, I'm on the board," Dlamini had cupped both hands to her ear having relinquished the banner to others earlier in the proceedings, "just say yes."

"Shh," Thembisa wriggled free, and put her index finger up against her lips, her crooked pinkie curling into her palm, "let me listen!"

"Three little words," Boesak's shrill voice was amplified by the microphones, "words that express so eloquently our seriousness in this struggle: *all, here,* and *now.* We want *all* our rights; we want them *here* and we want them *now.*"

The crowd echoed back the refrain; ALL, HERE,

NOW, stamping or clapping the time until Boesak raised his hand; his outstretched palm tripling as the sign of benediction, a call to arms, and a quest for quiet, after which he said:

"The time has come for the white people in this country to realise that their destiny is inextricably bound with our destiny, and that they shall never be free until we are free."

†

(October 1985)

Thembisa was tidying her secretarial desk at the Grassroots office in central Cape Town just after lunch when one of the freelance photographers, Stefan de Ruyter, stopped by. Dressed in a plaid shirt, regulation khaki bush jacket, and cargo pants tucked into rubber-tire-soled boots, he sported a bandolier of camera equipment strung around his chicken neck, a blond ponytail complimenting his swash-buckling image which was unfortunately ruined by a squeaky voice and eyes that could not fixate on any given point properly.

"Howzit. Sawubona, kunjani? Where's Jan?"

"You mean Jansen?"

"Ja, nee the reporter. There's going to be trouble in Athlone, I've got a tip off."

"He's not in today," Thembisa got out the contract files she was meant to complete and put her head down to work, her hair contained in a scarlet *doek* so that it didn't interfere with her typing.

"Well, I need a reporter," Stefan leant across Thembisa's broad desk, one of the cameras swinging free almost hitting her in the face but for her quick movement backwards.

"Aikona, you're in my space. It's not my problem!" Thembisa pushed back her chair and rose behind the desk, making sure that her black mini dress did not ride too high.

"Sorry, how else am I going to tell my story. Just photos are not good enough," Stefan tugged repetitively at his ponytail, fiddling with the rubber band that retained it while looking down at Thembisa until it snapped. "Agh, shit. Scheisse, can you help?"

"I've got a rubber band but I am *not* a reporter."

"But you type, write, do reports?" the photographer was adjusting his hairdo with the blue rubber band.

"Then you can be a reporter. Let me ask your boss. This could be a big story. Do you want to sit in this office and push paper around all day or do something meaningful. Make a difference?"

"My boss is out!"

"Well, make a decision. Do you have other shoes? You can't go in those pumps," Stefan had turned and was moving towards the door.

"Yes tackies. I'll bring my diary to write in."

†

Stefan, with Thembisa sitting next to him, had made their way to Athlone in the photographer's beat-up

Beetle and parked on Thornton Road. They scoped out the scene through the windshield before proceeding, alarmed by a pack of school children amassed at a nearby corner throwing stones at passing cars. They could see worried women taking down washing to avoid the smoke billowing from blazing debris fires that dotted the street. Opposite, and across the way, but at some distance from the stone throwers, a yellow police van, its windows protected by wire netting, had been parked with its blue light flashing; a blue clothed police officer was standing in the protective angle of its open door speaking into a microphone, its coiled tethering cable stretched to the limit. Homeowners were watching proceedings from their stoeps, or hurriedly making their way along the pavements that lined both sides of the busy street trying to avoid the broken glass, rocks and rubbish that littered the thoroughfare — the whole menacing scene was backdropped by the looming presence of one of the massive cooling towers puffing steam over the Athlone power station; the sun a burning ember in the soot filled sky.

"Thembisa, do you see that television crew? They're from CBS, take notes and follow me."

As they exited the Volkswagen, a muddy, orange-coloured government truck, it's open bed packed heavy with black crates and brown cardboard boxes trundled past spewing diesel fumes. The duo followed in its shelter, taking cover behind a garden wall as the service vehicle traversed past the pack of children protesting at the corner and continued on its way. They could hear the youths yelling abuse from their hidden position, so when the shouting lulled somewhat, Stefan stood up hesitantly, took a few close-ups of the rioters directly across from their position and noticed that, further down, the orange truck had made a U-turn and was making its way back up Thornton Road, just as slowly as before, but this time on the side where the motley crowd was hurling abuse.

Stefan ducked down behind the brick wall again, his ears sharp for the distinctive rumble the government service vehicle had made — only rising when the grind of its gear change signalled that it was drawing level. He was just in time to photograph a fusillade of stones cracking the oncoming truck's windshield, splintering off pieces of glass, one of which embedded in Stefan's forehead, another his unshielded eye.

"Thembisa, get down, get down," Stefan had abandoned his camera to swing around his neck, put one hand over his injured face and with the other pressed on Thembisa's shoulder forcing her to crouch behind the protective brick work, interrupting her concerted scribbling. They both sat back against the garden's retaining wall to take stock of the situation.

"Stefan, here, take this Kleenex for your eye, look," Thembisa was pointing at the house's front windows which reflected a view of the top of the orange truck: ten hidden policeman in khaki and blue uniforms had emerged out of the boxes and crates and were firing shot guns wildly in every direction. They could smell the cordite, hear the rapid reports of the weapons ranging overhead, as well as the anguished wailing of the injured, and could picture the surge of the protestors.

"Shit... shit... shit, those pigs," Thembisa sagged back against the warm bricks and continued writing.

"Thembisa, I've got to get a shot. The truck is like a Trojan horse. We've got to expose this. Let's go through this house's back garden, cut across to the street beyond, and see if we can head off the truck near where my car is. Too dangerous here. Keep your head down," Stefan met Thembisa's eyes, for once held fast, despite the bloody gash at one eyelid, and then gripped her sweaty hand, receiving a squeeze of acknowledgement for the plan.

Thembisa and Stefan crouched behind the Beetle, its cowling still warm and smelling of oil. Thembisa could see the approaching truck telescoped through the Volkswagen's front and back windows, its orange colour faded by enveloping dirt. The scene was one of bedlam; a one sided war against the people. She saw two school children lying motionless; one boy, one girl, on each side of the pavement. Many others were running, or cowering. One boy sat frozen on his bicycle in front of the truck which had stopped. The volleys of police shots were relentless. Too much to count or comprehend. Blood soaked clothes and spilled in the dust of the streets as people fled, while the fires in the gutters kept burning.

As the truck drew level with their car, Thembisa stood up trembling, holding her diary in one hand,

"You, you and you," she pointed to three white officers in turn "you bloody cowards."

One made to raise his gun, another restrained him shouting, "No she's press, we'll get the cops to sort her out," and turning to look at Thembisa, "Voertzek jy, bugger off, go back to your bloody homeland, we don't need your sort in the Cape."

Meanwhile, having documented the terrible scene to his satisfaction from his position next to Thembisa, Stefan was making conciliatory gestures at the policemen hovering above them and turned to usher Thembisa away hissing in her ear, "calm down, calm down we've got to get the hell out of here, with my camera intact. Get into the car, now!" And not a moment too soon, because as they were driving away from the crime scene, they could see a baton wielding policemen chasing the three man CBS television crew.

"They're going to take their video tape and then they'll having nothing to report, and we'll have the scoop," Stefan pressed his foot hard on the accelerator causing the engine to misfire provoking a jerk and reached out to Thembisa to stop her buckling forward, inadvertently clutching her breast.

"Hau, is that all you care about?

"No, that was a mistake."

"I don't mean *that*. Don't you care about the people that just got killed?"

"Of course I do. That's the whole point about reporting. To tell the truth. The truths that the government wants to hide. *That* deadly decoy truck wasn't meant to be seen by the press."

"I'm the press?" Thembisa undid her red doek and glanced at Stefan's grim mouth.

"If you finish the article to accompany my photographs you will be. I'll help you edit. But first, I must get this film roll developed to see what we've got."

"Is that why you're driving so fast? Thembisa reached over and rested her open hand on Stefan's thigh, pressing softly.

"No, I'm scared that the police will stop us."

"Well, slow down then," she pressed a little harder, and left her hand in place as they moderated their speed, "The race is not to the swift, but to the slow and steady."

Stefan relinquished his hold on the gear knob and placed his hand over hers.

†

It was only five years later that Thembisa and Stefan's paths crossed again; much had changed in between — Thembisa had learnt never to trust a white man, an aphorism that would prove to be fatally true.

It was not that their photo-report hadn't met with immediate success; the exposé was published in the Grassroots Community Newspaper, but the piece was eclipsed by the CBS camera footage which was circulated around the world with dire consequences for South Africa's reporters in their search for the truth. A state of emergency was again declared by President P.W.

Botha, all journalists and television crews were banned from townships across the country, and the offices of Grassroots were burnt to the ground; many of their members banned or taken into custody by the security police.

Thembisa, however, soldiered on spending more time as a community organizer than writing articles, having won respect for her bravery at a time when rioting in South Africa was as ordinary as sitting for a haircut, or taking the children to school. If one took a hike up Signal Hill, or Table Mountain, one could see the plumes of smoke marking the daily disturbances ignited across the Cape Flats. Sometimes the cause of the fires was the wanton destruction of property. At other times, a petrol-doused car tyre had been set alight around an informer's neck, condemning the victim to a horrible death called necklacing.

Community resistance had built to a fever pitch by 1989 through organizations such as the Mass Democratic Movement, Grassroots, the United Democratic Front and many others, but needed a coordinated focus point to create the change that the country so desperately needed. To that effect a national Defiance Campaign was launched to protest against the second election for the Tricameral Parliament, where, yet again, the black man could not vote — requiring locally organized co-ordination.

†

"We must *unban* the UDF and take the power. Without power there will *be* no justice," Goodwill Dlamini had needed his knobkierie to hoist himself up on to the podium in Langa township's hall and, now winded by the fervour in his voice, stood at an angle, one hand stented on the stick, the other resting on his pregnant sized paunch, "on this fifth anniversary of the UDF's genesis," he stretched out his arms to the rows of seated people — one ended in a balled fist from which the knobkierie suspended, the other an open palm, "We must gather at Saint George's Cathedral. Bishop Desmond Tutu has invited us to march." Dlamini swatted his brow with the hanky he had pulled up from the pocket of his navy blue, double breasted jacket, and continued, "the UDF is tired. Tired of Tricameral. Tired of still having separate beaches. Tired of still having separate hospitals. *Apartheid* makes me sick."

"It makes us all sick," a man dressed in a dark overcoat stood up, "we must march. We must march for justice. For power."

A few in the crowd ululated, while other's clapped to echo this sentiment.

Thembisa sat back in her wooden folding chair. She had taken a seat in the rear so that she could gauge the communities' response to her uncle's speechifying when something familiar caught her eye. A plaid shirt and a bush jacket. Although instead of a ponytail, Stefan now had a short back and sides covered by a rolled wool cap, the leash of a camera strap pulled taught across the scruff of his neck, as he adjusted an impressive looking lens and a flash erupted that blanched Dlamini's face, interrupting his train of thought for just a moment.

"The Arch helped release the protesters caught in Greenmarket Square. The pigs had water-cannoned them with purple dye. Now we must show solidarity with the Bishop, and Boesak, and march with them on September 13th. Will you join with me to end apartheid? Will you march to end injustice? Will you march for power? Power to our people. Amandla!"

"NGWETHU" the crowd responded, some rising to their feet and raising fists as Dlamini performed a slow, halted jig at the podium shouting "shoo, shoo, shoo," in time to pumping his knobkierie aloft.

Thembisa had stood up to get a better look at Stefan; he had been long in her thoughts, but short on presence since Grassroots had moved to Greenmarket Square following the torching of their previous office. Thembisa had lost track of him except for the occasional published photo-essay she had saved in her scrap book, each time reliving the excitement of the hunt for the truth, five years ago. Her heart beat at the shallow of her throat as she craned to see him, and then raced faster when she caught up with Stefan outside of the hall where he had escaped through an emergency exit and was reloading his camera underneath a sun battered awning. He had unrolled the black wool cap into a balaclava over his head, leaving only his slate eyes and pink mouth visible.

"Hau, why are you in disguise?" Thembisa had come to rest leaning her shoulder against the hall's red-brick wall, her black miniskirt a little longer than the last time they had met.

"And what are you doing here?" Stefan was looking down to wind his camera reel to the correct setting.

"I live here. With my uncle, you just took a photograph of."

"Who, Dlamini? Where?"

"Harlem Street. Why?"

"Oh... no matter, just curious."

Thembisa watched Stefan's eye's start their shifting and his lips purse through the balaclava's holes, *like the inverse of a skull*, Thembisa thought with a shudder and said, "curiosity killed the cat."

"But satisfaction brought it back. Thembisa, I must go, see you soon."

And with that, Stefan turned on his heel and hurried towards his Beetle which started after a second misfire and skidded out of the parking spot.

And three mornings later, at 4:30 a.m., Thembisa was awakened by a hammering that ricocheted around the Harlem Street house and threatened to take their steel front door off its hinges. She saw the intermittent flash of a revolving blue light cast through her open window. The smell of exhaust smoke and whispered voices mingled with the deep barks of a police Alsatian.

"Dlamini must be here, Stefan said so, try again."

The crashing on the door resumed. Followed by a shout in Afrikaans, "Open up or we'll break the door down. Open up."

"Stop, stop, stop," Thembisa heard Goodwill say from behind the closed door of her bedroom (her cousin, Priscilla, had long ago relinquished their shared room for a grander place). "I'll open up. I'll open up. These keys give no end of trouble," and hissed in the direction of Thembisa's room under cover of a great rattling of the bunch of steel "tidy bed... hide in cupboard... lock from inside... look after yourself."

"Come on old man. We haven't got all day what's the problem?"

"The key is the problem, and I'm not opening till you put that dog back into the van. I get an *asthma bors* from dogs."

"What's that? An asthma attack from police dogs? Never heard of it. Gerrit, put the dog in the front, you'll ride with the prisoner in the back."

An officer must have burst into the house because the next thing Thembisa heard from within the closed cupboard reeking of camphor balls was a loud slap, "Jou k....r, you give us shit. Get your passbook. Get your jacket and a toothbrush. You're going away for a long time. Where is that daughter of yours?"

"She's not here. Staying with friends, you know how it is, they grow up."

"Ja, ja. Gerrit, check the place out. I'll put Mr Dlamini in the van."

Thembisa, dressed in a turquoise nightie, was drenched in sweat in the dark. She sat on her bottom with arms around her legs folded into the foetal position and held her breath when she heard the crank of her bedroom's door handle. It needed oil. She heard the squeak of a rubbery footfall, the creak of a spring coil depressed on her bed, and a tug at the cupboard's door handle and could smell cigarette smoke. Thembisa didn't move, not even to exhale, she had a sense of suffocation, her diaphragm started to spasm, she felt lightheaded and feared blacking out, and was about to give up when relief came again in Afrikaans.

"All good, no one here. Let's get out of here. These shitholes give me the creeps."

And despite Goodwill Dlamini's disappearance, the protest march took place as planned. Starting at St Georges Cathedral, and led by Bishop Desmond Tutu, Doctor Alan Boesak and others, the thirty thousand strong crowd made its way peacefully down Adderley Street, and on to the Grand Parade; the police had been ordered to stand down, a new State President, F.W. de Klerk was in place.

Meanwhile, Thembisa had become frantic, frustrated by attempts to find out where Goodwill had been taken, and concerned about her uncle's already failing health, she had visited the Langa police station and been turned away; they knew nothing of the matter. She scoured the newspapers, asked around at Grassroots, and managed to secure Stefan's telephone number, leaving multiple unanswered messages on his answering machine. And, once, when he did pick up the telephone and must have recognized her voice, he did not respond in kind. Instead she heard a click, but nothing else. Repeat calls meeting only with a busy signal.

Thembisa started noticing disturbing reports concerning black prisoners in the newspapers. Up to now, such reports had not been the focus of her attention (although she was vaguely aware that similar bulletins had been there for years). She was far more interested in political developments. But now such news, always tucked into a small box in the lower corner of a middle page, captured her attention.

> Detention without trial:
> Prisoner tries to escape by
> jumping from John Vorster
> Square Police Station.

> Prisoner slips on soap in the
> shower and dies of head injury.

Thank goodness that this occurred further north in the country and not in Cape Town. Thembisa remembered again how Steve Biko had come to grief in 1977, in Port Elizabeth. *This must not happen to my uncle. After all he must be small fry. Or was he? Is he?* Thembisa corrected herself.

Thembisa had visited multiple police stations: Bonteheuwel, Athlone, Pinelands, Maitland, and Salt River often getting a similar response, varying only in the sympathy with which it was rendered, depending on the colour of the desk officer's skin.

"Sister, what can I do for you?" the black police officer had lifted his cap to swipe the perspiration of his forehead with the flat of his hand.

"Officer, I am desperate. My uncle has disappeared. I have a photo. Here."

"When?"

"Eight weeks ago."

"How?"

"I don't know, I came back to our house in Harlem Street and he was gone."

"Is that the truth sister?" The officer put his cap back and straightened it, first aligning his sight with its rim and then pierced Thembisa's eyes.

"Aikona, can I trust you? Yes...? He was taken away by the police. Our place was raided."

The officer looked left and then right and beckoned by flexing four fingers of his drying hand for Thembisa to lean over the counter so they could not be overheard.

"That's the Security Branch. You must go to Caledon Square in Cape Town for that. Go and ask there. They will stone-wall you though," the officer muttered, "you will not get the truth if he is there."

"I feel so powerless," Thembisa said, "I have written articles. I have done community work. I have joined the UDF, but nobody listens and I can't get a simple answer. Where is my uncle and what has become of him?"

"The only way," the officer leaned in further, "you know they are going to release Mandela. And we will get a new South Africa?"

"Yebo, I hope so, but will it be too late for my uncle?"

"I don't know but watch my lips. As I said, the only way to power for the likes of us, is to join the police force."

"The S.A.P.? You must be joking?"

"Oh no. Politicians come and go, but the police force stays. And if you become a detective, you can investigate the crimes. There is a police college in Bishop Lavis."

"Hau."

"Yes, but go to Caledon Square, behind the Grand Parade. You know where it is?

"Yebo."

"Well, go today. As soon as possible, it is good if they know someone is asking questions."

THE CAPE TIMES HERALD
January 22, 1990

Caledon Square Police Station: Prisoner falls down flight of stairs and dies of head injury.

---

†

11

Muizenberg, 1996

Quite out of the blue — Suzanne popped her page-boyed head into Doctor Pieter Marais' office — and he was back into the black, "I have Detective Dlamini on the phone. She says it is urgent. Can I put her through to yours?"

"Yes, but let me tidy my desk first, give me one minute."

"Doctor Marais?"

"Thembisa!"

"No, *Detective Dlamini*. This is an official call and so might be recorded."

"We must meet... ah to discuss developments. I am no longer the lead detective on the case."

"My calendar is full this week. Chock full," Pieter said, pressing the telephone handle close to his ear, "perhaps the week after?"

"The case will be brought to the Cape Town Magistrate's Court Monday September 30th."

"I will let Suzanne know. Is your weekend free?"

"Sunday, I will have to swim off all this stress."

"I *sea*."

"You will... Doctor Marais. Thank you."

†

So it looks like we're back in the game, Pieter thought, as he squinted through his windshield and parked next to a fire-red scooter at Muizenberg beach. He could see an expanse of yellow-grey sand stretching into the Indian ocean, and beyond that the Hottentot Holland's Mountain range just visible across False bay. The sun was at eleven o'clock in a fine, clear sky.

Getting out his shoulder bag filled with his beach gear, Pieter peered across at the freshly painted blue, green, red, and yellow bathing houses that fronted the seashore. He was just in time to see Thembisa's familiar face emerge from a curling wave, her shoulders propelled out of the foam, her dangling arms beneath her serving as a personal flotation device. She smiled when he walked up to meet her at the edge of the water, happy as a seal.

"Kunjani, kunjani," she waved, her other hand pushing down on the sea-bottom so she could leverage up and stagger out of the surf, her tangled hair slicked back in a tawny tumble and her vermilion bikini glistening in the sunlight.

Pieter had taken off his clogs, added them to a pile of clothes and a picnic basket piled on the sand that he assumed to be Thembisa's, and waded into the sea to meet her. He wondered whether he should stick out his hand and was pleasantly surprised when Thembisa did so first and pressed his palm and fingers through the motions of the African handshake: a three point movement that included the forming of fists in a black power salute.

"You've decided to trust me?"

"Maybe. I've learnt to never trust a white man, but we've established before at Blouberg, that you're putty coloured, off-white."

"I'm swarthy," Pieter smoothed his white shorts over his tanned thighs which were wet with salt spray; the smell of the sea they were still standing in, cleansing.

"So you say, but I need your help... in a big way."

"And you'll help me with my problem?"

"Which one is that?" Thembisa's hazel-flecked eyes met Pieter's brown ones, both flaring at the question.

"Whether to seek amnesty at the TRC."

An unexpectedly large wave crashed into their calves, unsettling them both. Regaining their balance, Thembisa continued, "For what?"

"I cannot tell you, until I know that I can trust you with my secret."

"And why me. I know I am pretty but... "

"Because you're *black*, Thembisa, and I must ask forgiveness from a *black* family. The black family that I harmed. That is the way the Truth Commission works. I need your assessment of whether..." Pieter steadied himself; aware of an oncoming wavelet, "... of whether I will be forgiven, to help decide what I should do. You're the only black person I know to ask."

"You know me? Please."

"I want to."

"Aikona, 'the lonely one offers his hand too quickly to whomever he encounters.' How can I know to trust you?"

"You can, I'm a doctor... with your life."

"Alright... but... if I'm going to, I go first. I'll listen to your troubles later. Let's get out of the water before we get plastered again and head up the beach, for some privacy."

†

It was quite a trek across long stretches of hot sand crunching underfoot to find their different notions of privacy; Thembisa was happy to sit in a gully of dunes, their tops tufted by spats of wild grass, frayed yellow-brown by the elements; while Pieter preferred a shaded site that he knew of, where Zeekoevlei passed brackish water via an outflow to the sea. But, because that was further along the bay, they decided to decamp at Thembisa's spot first so she could tell her story.

"Your father, the colonel, has decided to take me off the case," Thembisa was settling herself on a grey blanket she had unrolled from her picnic basket, "It's too big for me, I can't be trusted..."

"You can't be trusted? Why?" Pieter was crouching in his clogs, balancing his folded arms between his knees like a praying mantis.

"Did I tell you about the piece of garden hose, the second search team found? The search team that was sent when your father was unhappy with my report at the police meeting, that day you crashed into me. Like father, like son I say, bloody difficult," Thembisa shook her head free of remaining sea; droplets flew in every direction.

"Thembisa, that got me in the eye," Pieter rubbed it to clear the stinging, "what of it?"

"Forensics found my fingerprints on the hose; the colonel doesn't believe my story, that I am innocent — 'Why did I hide the hose away?' I think they want me off the case. Warrant Officer Jan du Plessis, who was already at the site when I arrived on my scooter, has been charged with the killing. I think, and so does my friend, Constable Thandi Matloapane, who was at the crime scene with us, that the police want to cover this up. An extrajudicial killing like in the old days; the new South African Police Service is no different from the old S.A.P., many of the same bad actors are still on the force, using the torture technics they learnt under *apartheid*. Only the governments have changed, but the techniques remain the same."

Pieter rose from his position quickly, disappeared around a dune, and Thembisa could hear retching, and not too soon afterwards smelt vomit so called out, "Pieter what's wrong, can I help?"

"I'll be okay. Food poisoning, I think. Came on suddenly," Pieter reappeared, patting a handkerchief to his mouth, his tangerine shirt wide open, a sparkle of sweat on his sparsely haired chest.

Pieter resumed his squatting position; his mother Marja always sat that way rolling one of her wrists, whenever she was in distress. She had told him that was the way Indonesian's sat; on their haunches, balancing their bodies on the balls of their feet. "Go on," Pieter took a quick glance at Thembisa.

"Aikona, you are not well."

"What evidence do they have against Du Plessis?"

"Well, apparently, his official police shift only started at midnight, but the previous evening someone remembers that Du Plessis *borrowed* a police car, and it's this van's backdoor canvas that was found sticking to a tree at the murder site."

"On Signal Hill?"

"Moreover, a few drops of blood found in the van matched the dead man."

"So, he must have known all along that the murder weapon was under the rock, you had them lift. What of the accomplices that you talked about that were needed to lift the rock?"

"Perhaps there were none, or only one; they may have rolled the rock on to the knife instead of lifting it."

"That's sharp, but where's *motive* detective?"

"I don't know. Rival gangs are in cahoots with the police. They want information from a perp. So they use police torture techniques that leave little or no trace. A wet bag over the face; slight marks at the crux of elbows and knees with the helicopter technique that only an expert like you can find. They don't leave burn marks from electricity to the testicles. Too easy to detect. After all, it will be your exacting report that will provide that information, doctor.

"Yes, that is why we are meticulous. But this team did leave burn marks though. But, no matter, where does that leave you and why are you still consulting me?"

"You offered your help. I'm in need of it. I must still give evidence of my findings from that morning's investigation. And here's the question I have for you. Do I admit into evidence that I saw Du Plessis flicking a burning cigarette butt, in the direction of the corpse, contaminating the scene? Remember three butts were found near the corpse, and DNA analysis linked them to Du Plessis. Or do I omit that evidence. I have done so before when your father asked whether I was witness to any contamination of the crime scene and I denied the fact at the police parade in front of everyone.

"So you have lied about it already."

"Yebo."

"Thinking back... if you could do it over. What would you have done?" Pieter asked.

"Knowing what I know now makes it different. Then I lied to protect a fellow officer from your father's wrath. Now that he's a suspect I would be withholding evidence, but the information could turn the case either way: it might provide evidence that Du Plessis was the perpetrator placing him at the scene of the crime from the two other butts, *or*, all three *stompies* could be explained away as contaminants, flicked there from the car park, when Du Plessis was waiting for me to arrive on my scooter."

"The other police officers that were there might refute or confirm that fact, but how would you feel after your day in court, if you didn't tell the truth? Remember you're under oath and a detective in the police force, with a reputation to make."

Thembisa looked away, between the slopes of two dunes. She drank in the sea view, the crash of the breakers seeming louder and the smell stronger when you emptied your thoughts letting them in. She got up off the blanket and walked, then jogged, speeding to a sprint before diving headlong into an oncoming wave; all that was left behind for Pieter was her musky smell and an invitation to join her.

†

"You never answered my question about telling the truth," Pieter repeated.

Thembisa had returned dripping wet from her swim, arranged her possessions into her wicker picnic basket, hooked it over her shoulder and having shaken her hair free of water, jogged down the beach in the direction of Zeekoevlei, stamping her feet into the sand and waggling her arms to be shot of the feeling of salt on her skin. Pieter had followed soon after and had caught up from behind her, catching her hand in his as he tugged her to a stop. He pulled her gently in to him, feeling her hot body, warmer than the sun. They were both panting and smiling; perfect white teeth from the brown side and horsey alabaster ones from the other.

"Not so fast. I'm not so fast," Thembisa said.

Nonetheless, Pieter planted a kiss, Thembisa's mouth barely open to receive it, she flattened her hands against his sweating chest and lightly lengthened her arms and said, "I'm not sure what I'll do."

"Tell the truth, it will set you free. That's from the Bible by the way."

"Not from Nietzsche? I was reading up on him."

"So I noticed. No, Saint John 8:32. Tutu likes to quote it: "And ye shall know the truth and the truth shall make you free."

"I thought you didn't believe in God?"

"I don't. But you should still tell the truth; it provides credibility."

After walking a while, sufficiently close for companionship, yet insufficient for a relationship, they had rested under a Port Jackson willow grove just up from Zeekoevlei's outlet into the sea — its coppery water had carved away bevelled layers of sand and become lost in the vastness of the foamy ocean.

"Pieter, look over there," Thembisa pointed her nose in the direction of the confluence where a handsome couple were casting what looked like white roses, from their distant view, into the water. Both African, the woman wore a lavender gown that trailed in the wet sand, had on a bifold headdress shaped in two varicoloured half cones, and had slung a similarly coloured shawl around her neck, while the man had on a white cassock from which a clerical collar protruded. He clutched a black book under his armpit and was peeling flowers from a bunch, alternating between handing one to the woman, with pitching the next into the back and forth of the outgoing tide.

She was singing — Thembisa and Pieter could

hear snatches of a hymn — and proceeded to twirl her shawl, lassoing it above her head before releasing it into the surf amongst the outflowing flowers which, unbunched, were being consumed like ashes thrown to the waves. The flower casting complete, the couple stood together, while the cleric read from the black book.

Thembisa let out a soft cry, she was sitting hunched over, still in her bikini, with her forehead resting on her crossed arms like a slender table across her knees.

Pieter was overwhelmed with emotion; Thembisa was so beautiful, and so sad, he wanted to care for her like a patient, but more than that, his heart flowed out to hers, so he placed his hand to rest tentatively at the tip of her neck.

"What is it Thembisa? What is it...?

"You know why they're doing that?" Thembisa sobbed, raising her head to turn a swollen face in Pieter's direction, sitting next to her in the mantis position. "They don't have a body to bury or incinerate. No ashes to cast, so they use flowers instead."

Pieter stroked Thembisa's nape and whispered "Tidak apa apa. Tidak apa apa."

"What does that mean? Tidak apa apa."

"Oh, it's Indonesian, my mother says it all the time when I'm upset. It means do not worry so, things will be alright. Tidak apa apa."

They could smell the peppery sage of the surrounding fynbos and hear the breakers on the beach accompanied by the cicada's hesitant screeching, winding up in the heat.

"That's what I should have done for my uncle, the one who died in Caledon Square; they wouldn't give me the body," Thembisa used her index fingers to wipe each side of her face, blew her nose into Pieter's hanky and resumed her head down position.

The silence lengthened between them; the sounds of nature reclaiming the space, until Pieter couldn't contain himself, "Thembisa, when did this happen? How did he die? Do you have the same name, Dlamini..."

Thembisa sat up again and brought the past back to life.

"It was my uncle... and mentor and father, Goodwill Dlamini. He looked after me growing up in Langa... better than his own daughter," Thembisa turned her head away from Pieter and spoke to the sea so he could only just hear her: "He was high up in the UDF. We were organizing for the big march in Cape Town, during all the riots."

"There have always been riots, when was this? I cannot hear you when you talk to the waves... Thembisa."

She turned back to face him, the sadness in her eyes defeating him.

Thembisa was startled in turn by Pieter's evident anguish — his features were drawn, his lips thin and his snaggle teeth prominent.

"I'd say end 1989, there was a raid at our house in Langa. Uncle Dlamini told me to hide in the cupboard, so they didn't find me."

"Who?"

"The Special Branch, I think. That's what a Police Officer told me when I went searching for my uncle at Salt River Police Station. He told me to go to Caledon Square, but they knew nothing..."

"Agh... agh... Thembisa," Pieter's lips were bloodless, his face waxen.

"And then I found a report in the *Cape Times Herald*. My uncle had died in prison. He had fallen down the stairs trying to escape. Head injuries... that's why I have become a detective: to solve crimes."

This time Pieter looked away and up into a Port Jackson willow above them wrestling with the *berg* wind which was blowing out to sea. He inhaled deeply, summoning the past, "was there anything distinctive about your uncle? Something people recognized him by."

"Yes. The top half of his left ear was lopped off in a fight, many years before, you couldn't miss it, but he did. He said he could only half hear on that side... he made jokes like that all the time. Shoo, shoo... I miss him," Thembisa used her two index fingers like a windscreen wiper to clear her eyes again.

And the nightmare scene — that Pieter so wanted to forget — flooded back into sharper focus, *the upside down torture victim's half ear was not an acute injury but a* chronic *one; there had been a stream of blood there, but this must have come from the gash in the man's jaw and, because his head was shaved, was clearly visible.* Pieter looked away from Thembisa, over his left arm, his hands still pressed together in the form of prayer. His chest heaved involuntarily. He rose and retched into a fynbos plant beside him. The cicadas went silent. Thembisa arose too and pressed her spread out fingers around Pieter's rib cage from the back hoping to still its violent movements as, bent over from the hip, Pieter vomited again and again. Thembisa's hands were stretched to the limit to offer consolation.

"Shoo, shoo...shoo... this is too much," but she thought, *there is something going on here, I can smell it. And that's not a pun. Is it from when Pieter was on the border? He told me that he had gone* bossies *after his friend got killed in Angola; or is it this business with the TRC?*

"I'll be oorait... oorait, just excuse me for a minute. Can you pour us some coffee from my thermos, in the bag. I'll be back."

The cicadas had resumed their chirping whine and Pieter and Thembisa were sitting cross legged, across from each other, regrouped on the grey blanket. Dark coffee steamed in the plastic thermos flask cups that they had both taken sips from. Thembisa offered Pieter the roll of Marie biscuits.

"The trick is black coffee, it helps with food poisoning, settles the stomach."

"Is that a medical truth, or something you dreamed up?" Thembisa asked.

"A bit of both. Caffeine does increase stomach motility, in the correct direction i.e. downwards not upwards. Why do you think we have coffee after a big meal, it's just that."

"And cigarettes and ice cream do the same thing too, don't they doctor?"

"Yis, ja. These emotional things wear me out."

"But now to your troubles with the TRC," Thembisa put a hand on Pieter's thigh, feeling his muscles toughen.

"Thembisa, you said something just now that made me wonder. Why did you become a police detective?"

"To solve crimes, what else? You think I'm not going to be any good, because your father took me off the case? I'll show them."

"I don't doubt it, but, and may I be perfectly honest?"

"Yebo."

"Things do seem to go wrong around you. But was there a specific crime you wanted to solve?"

"Yes... yes," Thembisa at first leaned back, thinking, and then bent forward and put both hands on Pieter's kneecap, noting as she did so that his eyes glanced down to take in the deep curve of her breasts.

She tightened her hold to regain his full attention.

"Yes, I've not told anybody this before, but I am willing to trust you. I wanted to become a detective to solve my uncle's crime. I am convinced he was killed at Caledon Square. That is why I sought to be posted here."

"To do what?" Pieter asked, although he thought he already knew the answer.

"To find the Police Occurrence Book for January 1990, the month my uncle died, and then to find his

242

case files, if they still exist."

"Isn't that illegal?"

"But so was his killing, if that was what really happened — I must know the truth."

†

12

Thembisa Dlamini, 1996

"Thandi, will you help me?" Thembisa looked at Constable Matloapane, the well-built Zulu policewoman who had been the business end of lifting the stone off the murder weapon on Signal Hill that frost-bitten, moonlit night. They were sitting across from each other, sipping rooibos tea, over a scratched plastic table which just fitted in a hole in the wall space adjacent to the police cafeteria's tuck shop. It had become a favourite meeting place where the two rookies had fast become friends, ever since Thandi had loaned Thembisa her hat, and stood up for her during Colonel Marais's dressing down. The nook allowed private conversation, masked by the clatter of kitchen utensils and African loud, bantering.

"Help you with what? Is it important?"

"It is... very important."

"Well tell me then," Thandi said.

"I'm not hundred percent sure what I am looking for," Thembisa set aside her teacup and bent in nearer to Thandi, who these days sported a close-coiled Afro, broadened by her wide open face, which seemed permanently pressed into a beaming smile. "Can I trust you?"

"Depends on what with."

"Finding the truth."

"What truth? There are so many sides of the truth, so many perspectives..."

"The truth about my uncle. About what happened to my uncle. That's the one truth that I have come to Caledon Square to find. A record, that must be filed somewhere in this building, that documents his death. The newspapers said that he fell down the stairs trying to escape."

"Your uncle was imprisoned here? Here at Caledon Square," Thandi pressed two stubby fingers on the scuffed table's surface.

"Or up there," Thembisa tilted her head upwards, "I don't believe it: I believe he was tortured and killed here. And I want to get hold of the file and find out who did it."

"Whoa... whoa, slow down, you' re going too, too fast for me. What happened? Start at the beginning," Thandi, raised her palms to face Thembisa; the universal stop sign.

"Well, I lived with my uncle Goodwill Dlamini. I moved to Langa after the Soweto riots. I went to high school here and later worked for Grassroots in Cape Town. My uncle joined the UDF and was helping organize a protest march for Bishop Desmond Tutu, when, late one night, we were raided by the Special Branch."

"When was that?"

"Oh, end 1989, just before Mandela was freed."

"So what happened?" Thandi had placed both

hands flat on the table and was leaning closer to Thembisa, almost whispering.

"My uncle told me to hide, so they never found me, but the Special Branch took him away and I never saw him again. All I could find out about him was written in a newspaper article which related that my uncle had died from injuries sustained by falling down the stairs here at Caledon Square. I don't believe it. I believe he was killed here. I want to find my uncle's file to determine the truth. Will you help me Thandi?"

"But that's illegal. You can't just access police files without cause, even if you can find them," Thandi hissed.

"To solve a crime? Isn't that why we became policewoman, to solve crimes. Well, isn't it?"

"I suppose... but if we get caught, we'll be dismissed. All that hard work out the door. And even if you find the truth, you cannot use it, because it will expose us. Have you thought of that?"

"No, but maybe there is a way... just knowing the truth, if we find it, and... tell someone about it. Maybe that will work. The Truth Commission or someone close to it might wish to know. Anyway, I know it's a risk, but I must find out."

"The police occurrence records are your first best bet; they must be kept for at least ten years. You said 1989?" Thandi asked.

"Yes, that was the police raid, but my uncle died in 1990: January 22, 1990, to be exact according to the newspaper report."

"That's good, I mean that's bad... you know what I mean. If we can find the date your uncle was imprisoned here, and find the record, we'll get the case number and go from there.

"September 7th, 1989, that was the night the Special Branch raided our house in Langa."

"Well, that is a good start. The TRC sits again in the Cape in two months' time. Let me do some investigations. We'll need a set of keys, and I think I know just how to get imprints. I know who the man in charge is of the Record Room... just give me a little time. But we should probably do this at night, to let the truth see the light of day. Hau. Now I've got to go," and after engulfing Thembisa's shoulders within two hefty hands, Thandi did.

†

Pieter was intensely troubled by what he had learnt. Whenever his anguish deepened, he sought relief from the sea through windsurfing. As long as the wind was strong enough, Pieter headed through the crashing breakers and far out into Table Bay, becoming just a colourful speck amongst the foamy whitecaps whipped up by the Cape Doctor. The gale force south-easter that spun a covering of mist over Table Mountain like a cotton mill.

Pieter thought of windsurfing as a test of his strength, determination and skill. After negotiating through the giant waves that pounded the beach in a storm, he had learnt to navigate the enormous cold swells that coursed like watery hills across the ocean. Pieter used one to springboard his return journey, gathering speed down into its gully (where there was a fall-off in wind) to pivot the sail round for the trip back to the beach at Table View. He could see his block of flats in the distance; another larger one to its right, Witsand, served as a beacon.

Pieter knew full well that this water sport was dangerous; there had been recent reports of windsurfers lost at sea, only their broken equipment found at a far off beach. It was easy to drown in a gale if you lost your strength battling to get back on to the board in a futile water start, or if your equipment broke. But for that eventuality Pieter carried a flare in the back pocket of the harness snugged tight around his midriff. If for whatever reason he couldn't manage any further, he would shoot up the magnesium flare, hoping to summon the orange and white painted *John Rolf* helicopter that patrolled the seaside, or the NSRI Coast Guard vessel based in Cape Town's harbour.

As a consequence, whenever Pieter had completed the turn back and had set course for the beach, he felt a sense of relief from the danger; the pressure to concentrate and sail precisely at bay — that's when he could think things through. He was on automatic pilot.

It must have been Goodwill Dlamini that my father kicked in the face at Caledon Square that day, hanging vertically in the helicopter position. I never read the name on the death certificate he forced me to sign; all I wanted was to get out, to get out. Pieter tightened his grip on the boom, a gust of wind spraying salt water on his face and neck above his wetsuit. He licked the salt from his lips. *If Thembisa finds the certificate, that's it. I have no choice.* He smirked at the irony of the situation; his cheeks blowing out in the wind. *I certainly picked the right person to consult on whether I should apply for amnesty and get forgiveness at the TRC. Or the wrong one!* Pieter adjusted the sail's pitch to correct his course. *She'll never forgive me. Never. And... and I really like her; my insides are all churned up whenever I'm with her. I don't know what it is. I've not felt like this for a long time... I shouldn't have tried to kiss her though. I couldn't help myself.*

Pieter was gaining on the first set of waves rolling towards Blouberg Beach, catching up to them from behind, as they built to massive peaks which could no longer hold. *But Thembisa probably won't be able to find the police records. Many were destroyed with the change of government, so maybe there is a way forward... But no! If I ask for amnesty, I will have to confront the affected family: hers — there is no way out, even if she doesn't find the case files. I know the truth. My father killed Dlamini and I abetted the crime. There is no way of getting away from that.* Pieter rode up the back of a wave just as its tip curled over to break, and surfed down its face, speeding ahead of the churning foam, to muster enough speed from the thrust of the wave-propelled wind to turn and head out again, back for more punishment from the threatening storm.

†

"We must hurry," Thandi, dressed in full uniform like Thembisa, whispered "this could take us all night or longer." They were creeping down the darkened corridor that led to the Record Room on one of the upper floors of the Caledon Square Police Station. Not wanting to arouse suspicion by entering the building after hours and leaving a record of their entry in the occurrence file, they had bivouacked in different enclosed toilets at the end of the official working day and agreed to meet in the stairwell that ran up to the secure section of the building leading to the Record Room. Serendipitously, the regular night patrolman for the section of the building had called off sick — they had heard a request for a volunteer over the intercom earlier that day — and so with any luck, nobody was willing to pitch in and their work would be that much easier.

The police women used just their police torches for lighting; the set of keys had been unearthed through Thandi's undeniable charm. Her paramour had extended the tryst to provide the necessary pointers for their search. A how to, for finding a case record. The policeman had not bothered to ask after the purpose, so that he could plead plausible deniability. Thembisa and Thandi had rehearsed the process. First the occurrence books, by date. Then get the case number, and so try to find Goodwill Dlamini's file, and for good measure, photocopy whatever they could on the Xerox machine stationed in the room. Thandi had replacement paper in the police bag dangling from her shoulder, and Thembisa had brought her Polaroid.

"Shush," Thandi put her index finger to her lips, as Thembisa's rubber soles squeaked on the linoleum floor, propelled to catch up and kneel alongside her, they had both adopted a hand and knee position like sniffer dogs seeking their prey, "You pong of piss, what's up with you?"

"The toilet stall I sat in wouldn't flush, and I dropped something in the bowl so had to fish it out."

"What? The Record Room key?"

Thembisa looked away so that Thandi couldn't see her hangdog features.

"Well, the smell clings to you like that doctor."

Less contrite now, Thembisa swung back to look at Thandi, their eyes inches apart, "Hau, hau what do you mean?"

"You don't think it's obvious for all to see that you like him. I saw you with him at Le Café the other day, your eyes glued to his. And he's a white boy."

"Hau, aikona, so what, apartheid is over, the Immorality Act is long gone. We've got a job to do here, lets act like professionals."

"I know, I know... I'm just ragging you, letting off steam. You go first on all fours; you've got the key... I'll light your way, when I see you go in the door, I will follow," Thandi clamped Thembisa's shoulder in her familiar vice grip and then let her go. They were both sweating profusely, despite the cool weather.

Having gained entry to the room and relocked the door (nightwatchmen always check to see that rooms *remain* locked), their real work started, made even more difficult by the poor lighting in the large

251

room. Although one wall had innumerable windows and they could see the silhouette of Table Mountain backlit by a weak moon, there were thick steel grates covering them, obstructing the natural light, and, for obvious reasons, they couldn't switch on the overhead neon lights fitted for the exacting work of filing police records.

Thandi and Thembisa reconnoitred the rows and rows and rows of black and grey filing cabinets. Their torches played off sections that held: Police Administrative Files, Police Personnel Files, Police Investigation Dockets, Police Inquest Dockets, Police Case Files.... all with dates going back ten years, "the rest are kept in Pretoria," Thandi whispered, as they came upon the Occurrence Files section about halfway the length of the room, tucked away in a recess, that had not been visible when they panned their flashlights upon entry into the room.

Not a moment too soon for all of a sudden, they heard a key turn at the entrance door and shrunk back into the space. They were only just in time to hide themselves, nonetheless, allowing Thembisa to peek out undetected to deliver a whispered commentary.

"Fuck, it looks like Du Plessis. What is he up to?"

"Our colleague, the one charged with the killing?"

"Yebo, he must have got bail — on administrative leave."

Du Plessis was also in uniform, but this visit looked unofficial in nature. After quickly shining his torch around the room, he moved behind one of the filing cabinets and all Thembisa and Thandi could see was the occasional flash of light against the ceiling or glancing off the window. Thembisa peered out from the recess, carefully, in an attempt to observe what he was doing. Du Plessis seemed to be fiddling behind a cabinet. Thembisa could see his silhouette reflected back from the window which served as a shadowy mirror — she just caught sight of Du Plessis removing something from a file and closing and relocking its cabinet, after which, he shone his torch around, narrowly missing her, turned on his heel, walked out the door, and relocked it again.

Thembisa and Thandi both stood up from their crouched positions and embraced each other in relief.

"Shit that was a close call. Aren't you supposed to report on his case? Let's go and see if we can find out what he took," Thandi said.

"Aikona, he's guilty as hell, but that's not my business now... we must stay focused on the job: Occurrence Reports of Sept 7th, 1989," Thembisa unlocked the year's file (there was a key hanging on the wall adjacent to the row of cabinets) and found the day's file without too much difficulty, *the police clerks were more efficient than the present lot, it seems.*

Thembisa paged through the file with trembling fingers, Thandi lighting the way with a beam that was shaking too.

"Mr Goodwill Dlamini, born 1913," Thembisa read, "I didn't realize he was *that* old."

"Shush."

"Charge," Thembisa read the scrawled words

"Suppression of Communism Act" Case number 935200. Next of Kin: Faith Dlamini, Eugenia Dlamini, Priscilla Dlamini, Thembisa Dlamini, ..."

"That's all we need, take a Polaroid and lets go find his case file."

.....

"Come on, come on, Thembisa, take the photograph, we must hurry."

And, after many painstaking, sweat filled hours working through the files in tandem, Thembisa eventually found it; the hanging file was not in its proper place, but stood out because it was not as dusty as the rest. She took out the complete hanging file — leaving a paper marker to be able to refile it again — to better examine it on a table close to the Xerox machine and started to pull out each manila folder in turn. The first one entitled *Photographs*. There it was, a photo of her uncle standing on a podium, with a knobkierie. *That must have been Stefan's at Langa Town Hall. I knew he was up to no good.* The next was entitled simply *Interviews*, there was nothing in it. The next, *Personal Details*, had three sheets of information, which Thembisa promptly photocopied. The third copy became stuck in the belly of the Xerox machine and had to be laboriously removed after which the photocopier declared it was out of ink.

Fuck, Thembisa became ever more frantic; she couldn't find the death certificate folder. Had it been removed? The certificates were usually provided in triplicate: white – yellow – pink, coloured paper.

It was not there. Thembisa went through all the manila folders again, lifting each out of the hanging file in turn to no avail. *I've got to know how he died, someone must have removed the evidence, think... focus.* Thembisa wandered back to the original filing cabinet and shone her torch down into the space where she had left the re-file marker, on to a piece of crumpled pink paper. She lifted it out and flattened its creases and shone her torch. And what she read there turned her stomach, just as it had Pieter's, at Muizenberg, a few days ago.

†

The *Jan Hermanus du Plessis* trial conducted at the Cape High Court had been in session for quite some time when Doctor Pieter Marais was requested to summarize the autopsy findings by the judge who sat bewigged and berobed upon the high bench overseeing the proceedings playing out in front of him.

Pieter had dressed as he usually did for such occasions in his University of Stellenbosch blazer, matching maroon tie, white shirt, and grey flannels, feeling that it gave him the necessary authority to present the postmortem findings that could incriminate and imprison a man. He was standing in the elevated witness box, opposite to, and adjacent from a second section of seats that ran along both mahogany clad side walls — reserved for the press and police contingents — and so was positioned asymmetrically, allowing him to address both the judge and the central section of the court room.

Here two stenographers took turns clocking every word for the record, and two long tables were attended by the State Prosecutor and his entourage to the right, while the barrister for the defence sat on the left with Warrant Officer du Plessis who had been stripped of his uniform and wore an ill-fitting grey suit, a poor match for his Brillcreamed black hair and insufficient moustache.

Pieter was aware of the scatter of spectators. Some sat in the mahogany benches behind the two witness boxes (which were separated by stairs that led to the holding cells below the court room), others were sitting on seats that had been placed for the purpose on the balcony. A few wore sunglasses to dull the glare of sunlight that moved with the passage of time via the multiple skylights fashioned into the stucco plastered dome of the venerable building.

During his presentation, Pieter had tried to engage Thembisa, sitting across from him with the police contingent, her uniform freshly pressed, her tawny, braided ringlets pulled back into a tight ponytail, stretching back her caramel skin, softening the memory of her swollen face at Muizenberg. But not entirely. *Had she found the record? Did she know?* Thembisa would not enjoin his glances; her hazel-flecked eyes darted away from his advance, failing to be drawn, even when he came to the final words of his summation,

"My Lord, although there was clearly evidence of torture; the cause of death was a stabbed heart."

"Very well, you may step down, and now we call on Detective Thembisa Dlamini to bear witness to her investigation of the crime scene on," the judge looked down, "the sixth of August this year."

Thembisa and Pieter crossed paths as they exchanged positions in the witness box, but although Pieter offered a cracked smile in greeting as they passed each other, a dispassionate observer of the exchange could only have concluded that he had been rebuffed.

After Detective Dlamini had been sworn in with a hand on the Bible and had given her uninterrupted summation, including the important fact that Warrant Officer du Plessis had been the senior investigating officer already present at Signal Hill when she arrived a little late on her scooter, it was time for cross examination by the defending barrister.

An overwhelmingly obese man, belligerent and dressed in a billowing black robe, the defence burrowed for the truth like a badger.

"Submitted into evidence by the prosecution is the fact that there were three," he held up the requisite number of big fingers, "three stompies... three Lucky Strike cigarette butts, that on DNA testing matched the saliva of Warrant Officer du Plessis. Did you, or did you not see the Warrant Officer contaminate the site of the crime by flicking his stompie there, from the parking space on Signal Hill?"

Thembisa didn't respond immediately. She first looked at Du Plessis, who returned her gaze defiantly. Then at the barrister who was wiping his suffused face with a handkerchief, and then, finally, at Pieter, where she let her look stay, narrowing her eyes to dashes as she spoke, "I did *not* see Warrant Officer du Plessis contaminate the crime scene."

"Are you sure?"

"I am."

"Then... no further questions, My Lord." The judge banged his gavel on the resonant mahogany of the desk in front of him and announced, "We will recess; court adjourned till two p.m. Enjoy lunch and come back refreshed for more."

Pieter never left off looking at Thembisa, wanting her to come over to him. He watched as she gathered her notes from the witness box in one arm, pulled at her ponytail, and then took the three steps down to the courtroom floor, never looking up again, her eyes downcast on the burgundy polished floor, aiming for the door to the corridor outside just past the police section where Pieter had taken her vacated seat.

"Thembisa, we *must* talk," Pieter said as she tried to walk right past him and he restrained her by commandeering her arm.

"Not here!" Thembisa had stopped, but her head was still down.

"In Le Café for a samosa lunch? In fifteen minutes. I'll get us a seat?"

"Is your watch working again?" And with that she pulled from his catch and hastened out of the double swing doors that closed off the court room from the rest of the world.

†

Pieter was waiting in the corner seat, its angled mirrors bearing witness that he had combed back his hair, pulled loose his tie and released his jacket button. *This is where it all started,* he thought, *will this be where it all ends?*

He had two cappuccinos and a plate of minced-meat samosas waiting when Thembisa arrived, removed her police hat and sat down opposite him. She had applied new lipstick and eyeliner and loosened her hair. To Pieter she was beautiful, but he was upset and guilt struck so went over to the attack.

"Why Thembisa, why did you not tell the truth when you had the chance?" he leant back both arms resting on the top of the vinyl covered corner seats, like Jesus at the crucifixion.

"THE TRUTH? Why didn't you tell *me* the truth. YOU lied to me," all the beauty disappeared from her face, replaced by wrath. "You spoke to me under false pretences. You wanted to seek the advice of a *black* family member. That was the pretence. It was *my* family that you harmed by your false attestation on the death certificate," Thembisa glared and rooted in her handbag pulling out a piece of pink paper which she smoothed on the table in front of Pieter so he could read it, "here is the proof."

"Where did you get this?"

"Where do you think, and lower your voice please," Thembisa looked around warily, conscious that she may have spoken to loudly, "and read it under the table, I must recompose myself. I'll be back."

Pieter bent forward to read the crumpled paper lying across his knees, confirming what he had always suspected, that his forced signature had falsely attested that the torture victim killed by his father had instead died of head injuries sustained from falling down a stairwell; a futile attempt to escape from his captors. Pieter looked up from his reading as Thembisa retook her seat.

"I didn't know it was *your* family that was involved, how could I?" Pieter ran five fingers through his hair combing it back to a point in his neck and tucked his face into his curled up elbow. "This is the first time I have read this document. I was new... I had just started as a District Surgeon. My father called my office, told my secretary I must come in and sign a form. The regular DS was not available. I was late, as usual," Pieter stroked back his hair again, but this time, put down his elbow on the table and met and held Thembisa's eyes. She drew the back of her hand along one side of her face, leaving a streak of mascara in its wake.

"Go on," Thembisa said.

"I thought, I could make up time by running up the fire escape instead of using the lift to my father's office as I was told to. As I reached the final stairwell, I heard a slapping sound and then a mewling sound like a baby crying. I crept to the light that fell into the darkened corridor. I barged into the room. And there was a black man hanging upside down folded around a broom stick suspended between two tables. My father had kicked him in the face and he was bleeding."

Thembisa clapped her hands to her face, "Pieter, I can't take anymore, shoo, shoo, shoo give me peace," and started wiping her eyes with her index fingers, the tip of her bent pinkie at an angle.

"I tried to stop him... I tried to stop him," Pieter whispered, "but my father kicked once more... and your uncle was dead."

"Ayee...ah... Pieter... Pieter," a dreadful expression played across Thembisa's tortured face as she rose, took the pink sheet of paper, folded it carefully and then pointed it at Pieter. "You wanted to know whether to apply for amnesty to the Truth Commission to seek forgiveness from our family. Well here is your answer," Thembisa waved the pink sheet like a flag, "if you don't apply to the TRC, my family will prosecute yours in civil court. I know the law."

"Agh, Thembisa," Pieter, an expression of pain curling back his lips, made to get up from the seat.

"No don't rise, there will be plenty of opportunity for that. I will see you at the Truth Commission next month."

†

13

Pieter Marais, 1996

The blanket of cloud hurtling over Table Mountain cast a dark shadow over the city below; its inexhaustible mist fast evaporating in the gale force wind that had strengthened across Table Bay, churning the aquamarine ocean to grey. Huge swells accumulated mass. Squalls coursed furrows across the mounting sea releasing swathes of sea spray and propelling massive breakers to spend futilely on Blouberg's shore where the wind whipped the beach into runnels of low flying sand that beat at Pieter's unshod feet.

After Thembisa's dramatic exit, Pieter had called Suzanne to cancel the afternoon's appointments and driven home at speed, glad of all the signs of a strong south-easter blowing as he drove through Goodwood and then Milnerton — flags stretched out slapping at their poles, bits of newspapers and other rubbish blew freely along the road, and most importantly, *white caps.* Pieter kept his eyes tuned to the ocean for the trace of their foamy crests scudding across the bay, an indication that the wind was north of twenty-five knots.

But, judging from what he saw now, and sensed of the intermittent blasts of wind swaying his body and sand-blistering his feet where he stood poised to launch his buffeting windsurfer, it was close to forty. Maybe even fifty. A perilous situation. *Like my current state* he thought wryly. *Madness. A death wish? It's madness to go in now — Thembisa looked so disappointed in me.* And then Pieter thought of a Nietzsche quote *"there is always some madness in love,"* ... *but am I in love?*

A buffet of wind and an ice cold sea wavelet sunk his feet further in the silted sand forcing an adjustment of stance.

Maybe... but... if not yet... I certainly... care for her. How was I to know it was her uncle? But now the truth was out. My father killed Dlamini. I have no choice. I must ask for amnesty and so must he. But... he won't... too proud — "the ends justified the means"" He'll say. He was doing his job. The total onslaught. The communists were taking over the country... the only good k....r is a dead k....r.

Pieter stood swaying in the deepening tide embedding his feet further in the sand as the water rose up his calves. He was sweating hotly in his wetsuit, his body aching for the cold comfort of the sea water when he plunged in. *But I will have to tell him of my plan. That's only right. I can't face him. He'll blow up — throw back at me that he was doing his job for the country. And what did I do?*

Fuck it. I died for the country. Inside. On the border. Pieter was already addressing his father. *You forced me. I never wanted to go, but you forced me. I went to the border and killed someone. And then you killed Dlamini right in front of me.* And then Pieter yelled into the howling wind, "Stop... stop...stop. *Those were the last words I said... six years ago... I can't face him. I can't face him.*

Pieter adjusted the angle of his board and sail, as a furious gust ripped past.

And the shame of it all. At the TRC I will have to admit what I did in front of the T.V. cameras... in front of the family... Thembisa's family... in front of colleagues... in front of Bishop Tutu... its unbearable.

Pieter launched into the raging sea. He coursed out-out-out, way beyond the vast breakers to the depths of Table Bay. The snarling storm enveloping him in a grey cold mist that had spread in patches across the ocean. He continued on and on. He didn't want to turn back. He feared falling in the bumpy turn. In the gully of a ten meter swell — the lull of the wind in its lee insufficient for the water start that was the only way out if he crashed and fell off the 'sinker' board that he so loved.

I could just keep going straight past Robben Island, Pieter mused as he ripped along, *lost at sea! No-one except Thembisa the wiser. No further shame. No confrontation with my father or the Truth Commission. Who would really miss me? Marja no doubt; not my father... Suzanne... and maybe Thembisa.*

Pieter coursed on, the wind buffeting the sail, his body juddering on the boat, Table Mountain packed over with grey-black clouds, threatening, dark and distant becoming ever closer, until...

.....

Pieter thought better of it and started to risk a turn,

264

bouncing down a gigantic cross swell to gain enough speed to pivot his sail and set it for the return journey in the relative calm of its gully. But, misjudged. The boards prow ploughed and submerged, hurling him into the seething sea beyond his windsurfer.

The only way up and out now, was to float up to the apex of an enormous roller buoyed by the board beneath him, and at just the right moment lift sufficient sail out of the water to catch a slip of the gale to propel himself back on to the windsurfer, hold tight in the foot straps, and manoeuvre his midriff harness' hook into the leash that hung from the boom, balancing his body backwards on the board to avoid being catapulted forward into the sea on top of the sail which had ballooned out of control from too much wind — having to start the exhausting process all over again.

Shit, Pieter breaststroked back to his board, bobbing at a distance, but took a gulp of water when he tried to manipulate the sail — which had started to sink — back into position so that he could attempt a water start, bringing on a spell of coughing. He thought of Thembisa telling him that seawater was good for you as he let himself float up to the apex of a wave, gaining his rasping breath — a rush of wind strengthening as he rose in the sea — he readied the sail at an angle for a water start and, at just the right moment, lifted the mast so that the sail caught just enough wind to lift him out of the water. He could hitch his harness hook in place, but he stubbed his toe on one foot hold, destabilizing his footing and was catapulted headlong back again into the sea, becoming ever more exhausted each time he unsuccessfully attempted another water start — he lay winded on the board, now becoming colder despite his heavy duty wetsuit.

Pieter was frightened now; for his life. He reached back to his harness for the flare that he carried there, adjusted its complicated mechanism while bobbing on the board in the relentless surge and shot it off into the grey sky above. It arched up in a blaze of orange-yellow phosphorous, a futile gesture in the squall that just then burst above him; the sweet rain mixing with the salt water on his face. He licked his lips for some relief, and a sudden wave separated him from his boat, plunging him beneath the sea and tumbling him down-down-down so he became disorientated. Luckily, he had taken a large breath of air before he became submerged, and the overhead squall had allowed in a shaft of sunlight. Pieter had been plummeted deep down into the ocean, but because of the sun's rays could see where he had to go. Where up was. He was running short of oxygen. Very short. His chest was starting to heave, his body felt tingly all over. *This is what torture by asphyxiation must be like* he thought in a flash, *what a waterbag clapped around a victim's mouth feels like. The screaming terror of death.* He struck for the haze above but couldn't seem to get there. He thrashed harder. He felt more tingly, his heartbeat pulsing in his ribcage. He started gagging.

He had stopped believing in God. *This must be*

hell; knowing where to go, but not being able to get there. Striving but never arriving. The readings of Nietzsche had convinced him. God was dead. Pieter would become the *Uber mensch. But Nietzsche was wrong! Pieter was not super human. He didn't want to die. Like Corli. Like Cherise. Like Dlamini. What a waste!* He said a silent prayer. *God if you help me — I will bear witness to the truth...I will bear witness...* and blacked out.

.....

Pieter's curved body, flooded with adrenaline, ascended slowly and broke to the surface like an octopus — his arms and legs trailing — to lie bobbing... When... all of a sudden, an enormous wave dumped Pieter back, face down in his grey wetsuit, on to the yellow board. The force of the impact expelling some of the sea from his waterlogged lungs, starting a convulsion of coughing that gradually brought him back to life. Pieter regained consciousness, his upper body askew on the boat; a counterpoint to the rigging — the mast and sail floating off to the other side, like a Christian suffering on a cross. He hoisted himself fully on the boat and lay the length of it to rest, floating there for an hour or more as the sun started to clear the storm clouds and the wind and waves subsided to a more manageable level.

"I survived", he thought. *I promised God and I must do it... face my father ... tell the truth. I will go to the Truth Commission... redeem myself with Thembisa?... maybe not... I must try.* Pieter regained his breath, lying panting. *I must get out of here... without me, the*

truth is dead. My father will deny it... the copy of the death certificate that Thembisa has found does not tell the truth. It is a lie. A lie that I certified to be true.

†

Pieter slammed the car door on his way out of Zeezicht's driveway, leaving his safety belt, unfastened, dangling outside. He was in a rush to get the confrontation over and sped down Blaauwberg Road, between the lovely rows of willow trees that lined each side, helped on his way by the fact that he was driving against the rush hour traffic; the other side of the road was clogged by those returning from work. Pieter had wound down the car window, *to get extra oxygen*, but had to reverse that plan to stem the inevitable petrol fumes when he turned left at the refinery onto Plattekloof Road; the acrid stench added to the sense of nausea he had had after making up his mind as to his course of action. From there it was but a fifteen minute drive to Parow to his parents' house. Pieter maintained a good relationship with Marja, despite his estrangement from his father, sustaining that with occasional phone calls, walks in the Durbanville hills, and visits to nearby coffee shops, but had not visited their home, ever again, since the breakup with his father. Hence it was with some surprise that Marja opened the front door to Pieter's agitated knocking.

"Coming, coming, coming... oh it's you! I thought it was your father. Locked out. Come in, come in,

Pieter. You look terrible, like something washed up."
Marja was barefoot, wore a long yellow frock that
stroked the floor, her jet-black hair coiled up high,
escaped wisps floated about as she moved her head.
"Here let me give you a hug." Marja stood on tiptoe,
reached under Pieter's arms and pressed his shoulder
blades crimpling his light blue shirt, pulling a section
loose from his denim jeans in the embrace. "Come,
come sit down, I'll make a pot of tea. What brings
you here? Your father will be home soon."

"Yes, mom, I have something to tell you both."

"It must be serious?"

"Ja, it is." Pieter kicked off his blue clogs and
sagged down into a tan leather lounge chair across
from the centred table which had been covered by
a batik imprinted with brown and black wayang
patterns, upon which lay an open photo album.
Walms of musty incense smoke wafted from an array
of sticks stuck in a clay pot alongside. He stretched
out his feet feeling the variegate cowhide which
served as a rug, put his hands behind his head, and
extended his arms back to try and relax himself. He
could hear Marja busy in the adjacent kitchen and
looked around at the familiar surroundings: episodes
of his youth displayed in photographs on the mantel
piece above the fireplace; a water colour painting
of the mustard veld surrounding a farmhouse at
Caledon; a black and white self-sketch by Gregoire
Boonzaier which had been the inspiration for
his own drawing; and at the mountain sketch by
Pierneef of 1942. He looked over at the dining room

table, the scene of many altercations with his father. He thought of Cherise and the Sunday lunch when they were medical students and his father's diatribe against the blacks. Pieter put his hands over his ears, screwed his lips tight over his uneven teeth and bent forward; he moved his hands over his beard into the prayerful position and narrowed his view to take in the pictures stuck in the photo album in front of him. He swivelled the album around on the table to better see and zeroed on to one, marked 1960.

A tall man, Pieter judged him to be in his thirties and a doctor given his stethoscope and white safari suit, was flanked by Marja in a yellow sarong on one side, and a black woman in a black dress with a mane of tawny hair on the other. The doctor had cupped his hands over both woman's shoulders like pale epaulets. Both women smiled broadly, while just a hint still showed on the man's face baring his horsey teeth.

"What are you looking at?" Marja was carrying a teapot on a tray. Putting it down hastily next to the album, a spout of tea spilled on to the photograph in question. "Aitsa, look what you've made me do Will... Pieter, I mean that is Willem."

"Who? asked Pieter.

"Let me wipe it clean first, with this tea cloth, that's my most precious photograph."

"Why?"

"That is... eh... Will...eh... the doctor, Willem Jansen, who saved my life," Marja dabbed away the tea with the cloth, having knelt beside the coffee table "and that is the nurse who helped him."

"You never told me the whole story. Why you needed cardiac surgery; how you came to marry dad," Pieter put his arm over Marja's shoulder and studied the photograph, the spill had not enough time to leave a permanent mark, it just raised the surface of the photograph like a scar.

"I promised not to."

"Who?"

"Your father, Pieter."

"Well, you know what I think of him. He's a terrible man."

"Agh, we all have our faults, Tidak apa apa, tidak apa apa," Marja started salaaming back and forth, her frock softly crinkling while the motion propelled the incense smoke this way and that.

"I thought I did the right thing. I did it for you." Marja started picking at her right wrist with her fingers as if unravelling a knot, having disposed of the cloth on the table.

"Did the right thing? How?"

"By marrying him, Pieter, so you could be a white son. Look at the year Pieter. 1960," Marja continued, worrying her wrist.

"Sharpeville?"

"Ja. Nee, but there were also riots at Langa."

"But that's a Coloured township, you wouldn't have been in a Coloured township?"

"I was. You know where I come from, from Indonesia."

"Duh... of course, I've suffered from incense

sticks ever since," Pieter waved away a wisp of the offending fumes.

"But I didn't tell you that my father was a Dutch captain and my mother Indonesian. I was born an Indo, and settled in Cape Town after the war, in District Six. I married another man before your father. He was killed at the Langa riots and I was stabbed in the heart."

Pieter sat back, tugging his brown beard to a point with his right hand, a perplexed expression on his face.

"So that's why I'm... I'm not completely white. Swarthy. Do I have dark blood in me, a touch of the tarbrush?"

"Ja, nee."

"No, mom, it's ja or nee, yes or no, not both," Pieter, had bowed forward again and was kneading Marja's shoulder.

She turned up to look at him from her kneeling position, engaging his eyes, "I promised your father not to tell," but nodded affirmation and then turned to look at the photograph again, the constant pinching of her flesh had raised a brown welt on the back of her wrist.

"Stop that mom, you'll hurt yourself with all that fidgeting," Pieter stroked Marja's shoulder with one hand and bent forward again to arrest the nervy hand activity with the other, taking a closer look at the photograph as he tried to soothe her.

"The black woman is pretty, as were you mom. What's her name?"

"Agh... Pieter... her name is Promise Madiba..." Marja bowed her head, and shoulder's narrowed, let out a snuffle.

"What's the matter mom?"

"Marja looked up, tears brimming, "Promise was imprisoned by the apartheid government when they bulldozed down the house we are standing in front of, there. It was in District Six, high on a hill, with a beautiful view of the harbour below. I've never seen her again. I think she left the country." Marja grabbed the tea cloth again, dabbed at the corners of her eyes, leaving a trail of black marks sullying its soft surface.

"But I've heard that name, recently... where?... ja... ja... at the Truth Commission."

"Promise Madiba? Really?... Promise? Are you sure? Marja's features were transformed, "then... then... if she's alive there's hope."

"Yes, she was giving evidence, and... that's what I've come to speak to you and dad about... The Truth Commission. I must ask for amnesty. But let's wait till he's here, I'm not looking forward to the agro. But tell me first what happened to Doctor Willem Jansen. Don't you think he looks a bit like me? I know he hasn't got a beard but, big teeth, thin and tall and good looking?"

"He was blonde Pieter."

"Was?"

"Agh, het is te verschrikkelijk, he died. Climbing Devil's Peak, the day before being acquitted. He had been prosecuted under the Immorality Act."

"That's terrible. Terrible," Pieter raised his head and looked over at Boonzaier's self-portrait hanging on the wall, and then down at the photograph in front of them, "I bet I can guess who he was prosecuted with; he's standing awfully close to Promise on this photo. I must say she is really lovely; looks a little like someone I've recently met, but darker," Pieter picked up the album to have a closer look.

"So... I have the doctor to thank for my life," Pieter said.

"What do you mean?" Marja started tweaking her wrist once more, salaaming furiously.

"Well if he hadn't saved yours, I wouldn't have been here."

Just then, there was a frantic rattle of keys, the front door was flung open, and Pieter senior stepped into the varnished slasto foyer that led directly into the lounge. Dressed in full police uniform, he launched his cap on to the deep-green couch set across from the coffee table at which Pieter and Marja huddled together, both making to rise from their positions, till they were cut short.

"Marja, you promised," Pieter senior smoothed his displaced bush of hair back with one hand while pointing with the other at the photograph, "that was our arrangement."

"Not to tell the truth?" Pieter had got up from his seat equalling his namesake in height and anger. "I suggest that you sit down on the couch and listen to what I have to say."

"What? You talk to your father like that. After all

274

I have done for you."

"I'm sick to death of hearing what you've done for me. You've made me lie to save your skin, that's what you've done for me," Pieter said.

"What does this mean, what does this mean?" Marja looked up at her husband, "PLEASE sit down. I'll pour you a cup of tea, here, it's still warm."

Having both accepted the refreshment and drunk from their cups, the two Pieters squared off again across the table having calmed down just a little in the process. Marja adopting the mantis position, sat on her haunches like a referee between the two sides. She asked the question again, "what does this mean?" her eyes flicking from one to the other till Pieter responded.

"Mom, I don't think you know the half of it. What a monster you have for a husband, and I for a father," Pieter looked first at Marja and then turned and fixed his unblinking glare on Pieter senior. "He tortured and killed a black man in front of me in 1989 and then forced me to certify the death certificate. I suspect there were many others."

"Is this true Pieter?" Marja turned to her husband, shrinking smaller as she asked the question.

"No, I didn't force Pieter, he signed of his own free will."

"The rest is true?" Marja again.

Pieter senior pressed back embedding deeper in the dark-green felt, withdrew his glasses and polished them with his handkerchief.

"Well," Pieter, exposed his teeth, "I am going

to apply to the Truth Commission for amnesty, for false testimony. I want to come clean. Nietzsche said 'Silence is the worst of all. Truths that are kept silent become poisonous.' Dad, you poisoned me."

"I had a job to do, and I did it."

"Was the job to torture and kill?"

"We had to extract information. The person in question was an organizer for the UDF and a crook besides. You know they found hidden pistols and bags of cash when he was arrested. And he wouldn't provide answers. So we had too... had too... He wouldn't provide."

"You kicked him in the face, hanging upside down. You killed him!"

The two Pieters continued glowering at each other, like opponents in a judo joust. Marja looked at the one, then the other, and then back again — all the time salaaming slowly, the incense sticks continued to burn, now releasing a sour odour; two had burnt down to their wooden stalks.

"I have to confess... I can't live with the guilt any longer," Pieter said, his eyes starting their nystagmus movements. He was feeling nauseous again.

"Confess, confess, confess, that's all I hear about at the Truth Commission. Pieter senior pulled out two cigarettes, put both between his index and middle fingers, lit them and took a double draw. "The bloody politicians are leaving the police out to hang and dry. I saw the former foreign minister, Pik Botha, give evidence the other day on T.V. Bah! He knew nothing. It was us he said. The guys in the trenches that did the dirty work. That made the death decisions. The politicians didn't order it. They just commanded that the person in question needed to be 'eliminated'. If that didn't mean killing them. What else did it mean? The top brass are leaving us out in the cold. To fend for ourselves. I'm not going to confess. To belittle myself. The blacks got what was coming to them. We had to stop them." Pieter senior leaned forward on the couch, took a last draw of his double cigarette, blew out the smoke through his nose and past his teeth, and stubbed both out together in the saucer of his teacup.

"Well for me it is not just a matter of guilt, but of honour," Pieter had crouched low in his seat. "I heard on the radio that there are a group of academic doctors that are calling for a separate Truth Commission to bring to account all physicians that aided and abetted the S.A.P. — that provided false testimony like Doctor Ivor Lang and Benjamin Tucker did with Steve Biko's murder. I did that for you with Mr Dlamini. It's against the Hippocratic Oath; I must do my duty."

"How did you find that name? The records were destroyed." Pieter senior blinked, the movement exaggerated by his thick lenses.

"Verschrikkelijk, verschrikkelijk, too terrible," Marja said, "Pieter," she stopped ringing her hand and placed it over his where it indented the soft leather of his chair, "I will support you. You must do this. How can I help?"

Pieter sandwiched his second hand over Marja's,

curled his upper lip to push his snaggled teeth beyond the ring of his brown beard and replied, "I must put in an application for amnesty. It is lengthy... and send it to the Truth Commission offices in Cape Town. If it is accepted. I will have to appear at the Truth Commission with an attorney to put my case. Haven't you followed the proceedings on T.V.?"

"Nee, nee Pieter, I watched part of one once and it is too verschrikkelijk, too terrible. All those families gathered on the podium, trying to find out what happened to their loved ones. The crying and the horrible stories of torture and killings. I can't bear it."

"Mom, that's what I have to do, ask for forgiveness from the Dlamini family for my role in Goodwill's killing."

"Goodwill?" Marja extracted her hand from Willem's clasp and moved it to pinch her throat instead, "Goodwill Dlamini?"

"Ja. That was the name on the..."

"On the what?" Pieter senior snarled.

"Dad, you should apply for amnesty, otherwise you will be prosecuted in civil court" Pieter gesticulated at his father.

"No, never. Haven't I made my self clear enough," Pieter senior lit yet another cigarette. Only one this time, keeping it burning between his fingers in front of his mouth as he spoke, "I will not ask for anything from the Truth Commission. It is a political sham. To shame us Afrikaner's who were doing our job. The communists were trying to take over the country. We had to stop them. The ANC was just as bad. Do you know what they did to their own people; the torture and the killings? You know that don't you Pieter? Don't you?" Pieter senior had risen from the couch, the tenor of his voice pitching ever higher. "You just keep my name out of it. OUT OF IT, you'll never see me there. Over my dead body. Marja show Pieter out, I need to find my other pack of Winston's. This one is finished. He threw the scrunched up red and white packet on the floor.

†

14

Promise Madiba, 1996

Thembisa rushed out of Le Café in a quandary after she had given Pieter her ultimatum. She looked up at Table Mountain as she crossed Buitenkant Street over to the police station. A wash of dark cloud was spilling over the mountain's plateau covering all but the cableway station at its tip. Although the wind had not yet picked up strength in the city bowl, if the south-easter became worse — and it showed every sign of doing so — no-one could remain unaffected.

Having made her way to her office, taken off her cap and put it on her desk, Thembisa sat down to think, critically aware of the stolen document hidden in her satchel; she had the habit of hording some of her most valued possessions — the sketch that Pieter had finally surrendered, prized photos, birthday cards — rather than have to remember where she had filed them later (when the bag became overfull, she would eventually purge it, and file the contents: Bag no 1. Bag no 2. etc. at home.)

Now I've got to find the rest of the Dlamini family, so that they can come to the Truth Commission with me. Thembisa pulled the satchel on to her lap and rummaged through her set of Polaroids stopping for a minute to look at the one of Pieter taken at Blouberg

Beach. *Was that just six weeks ago? It seems much longer.* Thembisa put it down on her desk to have a better look. *There's a glimmer of a smile; he's trying to cover his crooked teeth. He's good looking... no matter what he did.* Thembisa put the photograph away and continued searching through the stack, freed from the green and red elastic bands that held them together, eventually finding what she was looking for: the photo that she had taken of Goodwill Dlamini's case file, the one with the detail of the next of kin. She took it out and turned it upside down on her desk. Thembisa packed everything else away, inhaled a deep breath, let it out slowly through her nose, and then looked around to see if any of the other police officers were taking notice of her frantic activity.

Only Constable Thandi Matloapane caught her eye, got up from her seat, and ambled over to lean above the desk. She put her chubby arm around Thembisa's shoulders and whispered in her ear.

"You're being very secretive, what's up?"

"I am trying to find the Dlamini family, or what's left of it. Here look," Thembisa turned the Polaroid photo over and they both silently read each name, Thembisa pointing to each in turn, announcing who each were in sequence: Faith Dlamini, "Outa, my father in Soweto," Eugenia Dlamini, "Mamie," Priscilla Dlamini, "Goodwill's daughter, my elder cousin. She left the house in Langa when I grew up there with him. After Goodwill's death, I felt it only right to go and live somewhere else." Thembisa Dlamini, "me of course." Umfisi Dlamini, "I have no idea", Zondi Dlamini, " I can't even guess."

"Perhaps Priscilla has moved back," Thandi hovered over the desk, let's look in the phone book, do you know the address?"

"Yebo, 17 Harlem Street, Langa. I lived there for years."

"No," Thandi had opened the yellow telephone book and was tracing down the length of Dlaminis with her finger, running through two pages before she got to the P's, "I see no Priscilla, did she get married?"

"And divorced; apparently there was some problem, she couldn't have children."

"I can't find anything under the U's and Z's; a small family then," Thandi stroked the back of Thembisa's hand, the one with the bent little finger.

"Yebo. I haven't had contact with my parents in Soweto for many years, they don't have a telephone, and I'm not sure if letters are delivered."

"Send them a telegram, that *has* to be delivered, and, you know what I would do?"

"What?"

"I would go out to your uncle's place and find out what happened to Priscilla. If she's not there the neighbours will know something."

"What now?"

"No time like the present. I will cover for you here. After all, you're out doing detective work, aren't you?"

†

Despite the increasingly inclement weather — Table Mountain's cloud cover was becoming denser and darker, an ominous sign — Thembisa rode her bright scooter along Settler's Way and turned past the mist covered Athlone Power Station into Langa, and then rode on to Washington Street and parked outside the house on Harlem street where she had lived with Goodwill.

Although six years had passed, since that time, the house was still in good repair: the wire netting fence, centred by a lopsided gate, had been freshly painted with aluminium spray, and the sparse block of grass that it protected, had been mowed recently. Thembisa appreciated the tangy smell. The gate had squeaked on its hinges as she made her way over the familiar brick path to the front door. The two square barred windows separated by the dull-red front door, topped by the cranberry coloured roof always put Thembisa in mind of a dwarf's squat face; the scrape of bushes each side of the walking path serving as a giant beard.

Thembisa was nervous. She hung her satchel leash over her left shoulder, the bag bumping at her right hip, took an elastic band from her wrist, took off her helmet, pinning it under her armpit and tied back the frizz of hair that had been rendered shapeless by her head protection. She fretted whether she should have brought some flowers. *For what... it's not a celebration. Anyway, I wonder what Priscilla looks like now; she was taller... yes! And had a buxom bottom... oooh yes.* Thembisa knocked twice with her index knuckle and stood back. She looked up at the sky and strained to listen for signs from the house's interior. Rain was imminent, and the wind had freshened. Thembisa could see rubbish starting to pick up speed as it blew along the streets.

She knocked again, this time louder and thrice.

"Aikona, aikona, I'm coming; the lock is a bit rusty." After which the steel door was opened with the tear of oil-free hinges.

Thembisa took a step back on the foot path, almost tripping, her police boot had caught on an irregular stone. She recovered just in time for the next surprise: an elegant Xhosa woman, around Thembisa's height, with a mass of braided hair turning grey running to her shoulders, stood in the doorway. She had a fawn shaped face, offset by hazel-flecked eyes that were angled like a doe's and wore a long grey scarf to her knees, part covering a slim black dress, but was barefoot.

She looks familiar, Thembisa thought, *and it looks like she recognizes me.* "Good morning, I am Thembisa Dlamini. I used to live here with Goodwill Dlamini, and I want to speak to Priscilla."

"She is out working. But can I perhaps help you? You look so familiar; are we perhaps acquainted? My name is Promise Madiba."

"Hau, I heard you present at the Truth Commission, I was part of the police detail seconded there. I have just become a detective."

"Please come in," Promise raised her left hand closed in a fist in the direction of the dull sky, "it

284

will rain soon. Can I make you a cup of tea and then we can talk? Please sit there," Promise pointed to a green/aluminium chair pulled from under a shiny Formica table of a similar construction and then absorbed herself with water, kettle, and stove — all the while studying Thembisa carefully in the wall mirror.

Thembisa, at first, focused on the opposing wall on a painting of an African woman sitting patiently outside her house, and then looked out the kitchen window where the impending storm was in evidence from the erratic movement of the overhead electric cables, the flexing of a threadbare tree in the back garden, and the hue of the sky which had deepened.

Thembisa is a mirror image of myself when I was young, Promise thought as she poured the tea into earthenware mugs, *when I visited this house with Willem at the invitation of Goodwill, so... so... so... long ago,* but asked, "Thembisa, why are you here looking for Priscilla?"

"It is in connection with a family matter, but may I ask why *you* are here; I heard from your testimony that you are living in London."

"To testify at the Truth Commission."

"Yes... yes... but why are you staying in *this* house, Goodwill Dlamini's house."

"Goodwill was my benefactor. I stayed with him in District Six, when I came to Cape Town to become a nurse.

"Hau, he was my benefactor too, or at least my uncle." Thembisa's eyes flickered up to meet

285

Promise's — equivalent in colour — both dilating upon recognizing the fact.

.....

Promise broke the trance.

"Why did you come here, if Goodwill was your uncle?"

"Oh, I lived with my parents, Faith and Eugenia Dlamini in Soweto first, till after the riots when I moved over here."

On hearing this, Promise got up from the table, turned away from Thembisa and folded her hands across to each shoulder clasping her chest. She looked out the window at the building storm. And then looked back at Thembisa in a strange way, eyebrows knitted, she put a fisted hand to her face.

Thembisa hesitated where she sat; *what have I said?* She took a sip of tepid tea from her mug but found it hard to swallow. Returning the mug back on the table Thembisa continued.

"But I hope that you don't mind me asking about your testimony before the Truth Commission, you must have suffered so. Shoo... shoo... solitary confinement... and you had to give up your baby."

"Hau, hau, I can never forget that day," Promise rotated her head in a circling movement, her mouth opened to a wide O. She pushed her fist into her lips, and then on retracting her hand, slightly, continued. "It was very hard. We both cried. My baby must have known what was happening. I'm sure of it. They wouldn't let me keep her in prison; the pigs said they put my daughter with family. What family?"

Promise's eyebrows lifted. "At the time my father and mother were both long dead in Pondoland where I come from. I couldn't even start to look for my little one because I escaped to Zambia, to work for the ANC in exile, and when that became unsafe, I moved to exile in London where I have made a new life. I have tried to forget the past. Forget South Africa. Forget... but I can never forget my children." Promise placed her hand over her nose; her rapid breathing audible as a soft whistle between her fingers. "Forget those that I loved here. And... abandoned... I could do nothing other but try and forget the past." She dropped her hand from her face to rest at her side. "But then I heard about the Truth Commission. I would have to face my past, to tell my story, so that the truth of what happened can come out. The hearings have brought me back home. South Africa is my true home... perhaps I will also find my way back to the others; the one's I love that I left behind. Then... then... maybe... I can move back, permanently." Promise regained her seat, putting her left hand underneath the table and the right, palm upwards, on its battered surface. She turned to look again into Thembisa's eyes. Holding her gentle look, Thembisa placed her hand over Promise's — Thembisa's crippled pinkie looked like a question mark cupped in Promise's hand lying open beneath it.

A deluge of rain, clattering on the corrugated roof, made speech quite impossible, so they just sat for a while in each other's comforting warmth, and when it stilled, Promise asked another question, agitation raising the register of her voice. "When were you born Thembisa?"

"July 31st, 1967."

At this response, Promise lifted her arm from underneath the table and placed her hand carefully over Thembisa's, their two bent little fingers matching each other perfectly, but for the lighter tone of Thembisa's skin.

Promise angled her head up where she sat, looking at the overhead light bulb, attempting to restrain the emotion spilling down her cheeks. She sniffed in a long breath, and moaned on its release, "my child, my child, Thembisa, my child."

Thembisa sat stunned, the fingers overlapped exactly, a living replica.

"Aikona, aikona," Thembisa shook her head, her ragged ponytail swivelling above her uniform's collar, it took all her power to keep her hand where it lay under Promise's. "How can you know? How can you be sure? This is too, too much. Too fast."

"I suspected it when you first came into the house. And then when I looked down at your hand, I saw that your pinkie was bent like mine. Thembisa, your pinkie was crooked from birth. It runs in families." Promise pulled Thembisa up by the hand to stand in front of the decorated mirror that was a large fixture on the side wall.

"There Thembisa, now we can compare notes. There's the truth that you are my daughter. I had given up all hope of ever finding you."

And there was no question that there were many similarities. The evidence was there for Thembisa and Promise to behold. The thick hair. The highish forehead and slanting eyebrows covering hazel-flecked eyes that glowed with excitement. The doe-ish face and slightly pointed nose covering full mouths. Thembisa started crying. "But we need to be sure. "I... I... always wondered whether Outa and Mamie were my true parents. I even asked them."

"Why?"

"I didn't look like them. They were much darker like my sister Lindiwe."

"You have a sister Thembisa?"

"No...no... she was shot in the Soweto riots." Thembisa drew a handkerchief from her pocket, dabbing her face.

"Aikona... aikona, so you have suffered too," Promise waggled her head, they continued regarding each other in the mirror, while holding hands — Thembisa's left deformed one crumpled in Promise's good right one; they shared that too.

"Shot by a white man following orders?"

"I had given Lindiwe a red scarf for her birthday. She had put it around her head like a turban, I still feel guilty..."

"You must not!" Promise tightened her hold on Thembisa's hand, "we are not to blame. That's why this Commission is so important."

"Yes, yes, but I need more proof. I want to know the truth, I'm a detective. I must know if you really are my mother."

"You don't believe what you see?" Promise guided Thembisa to sit back down at the kitchen table. Thembisa bowed her head as they settled.

"No, it's not that. It's just too much to take in. Shoo... shoo, I have often wondered... whether... Eugenia was my real mother. What... what you would look like if she wasn't. I searched for faces like mine in crowds... never knowing whether you were out there for me to find. Now I need proof." Thembisa leaned closer to Promise and wiped the back of her hand softly down the side of Promise's face, attempting to dry away the tears that were now in free flow, to no avail. Promise leaned over the table corner and embraced Thembisa, where she sat, having to rise slightly to do so, their foreheads touching at their hairlines, cushioned by their abundance of hair, they sat in a huddle, and listened to the rain abating above them.

"I know what," Thembisa said, shifting back in her seat.

"What?"

"How we can know the truth."

"How?"

"We can do a DNA test. We use them in the police lab. All we need is to sample our saliva with a cotton wool stick and then we can confirm the truth."

"You don't trust me, Thembisa?"

"I... I... do, but we've only just met."

"No we haven't. I gave birth to you. I loved you the first time I saw you, especially with that crooked little finger, that marked you as mine. They took you away from me... and I had to leave the country. I never thought I would find you again. Now, I am sure. Just look at us; we are so alike.

"Yes, but..." Thembisa looked away and out of the window: *are the clouds clearing? Can this really be my mother? Is it true?* Thembisa turned back to look at Promise, there was a softness in their tortured eyes, "let's do the test... just to be sure... that I can call you Mom... just to be sure of the truth."

"Won't there be a problem, with the lab, to get this test?" Promise held Thembisa's scrutiny with an enquiring look.

"Maybe, but I have a colleague, Constable Matloapane. She can figure out anything. She sent me here in the first place to look for Priscilla, she'll know what to do when I tell her about this."

A larger question still loomed that required reconciliation. A question as to who the father was. A question too delicate to ask by a daughter, who had newly found her mother, but not for a police detective who was investigating a case. Thembisa continued her forensic role and raised her hands in Pieter's prayerful position, placing her elbows splayed like a bipod on the table, and contracted her eyes in concentration.

Promise had anticipated the question from the build-up, "Thembisa," she said, "I was raped in prison by a white man. I never saw his face, they blindfolded me first, but he felt and smelt like one. I have knowledge of such matters; I had a Dutch doctor as a lover once, and he fathered a boy, coloured light like you, but never lived to see him... Doctor Willem

291

never lived to see him..." Promise stooped forwards and intertwined her fingers as a covering over her fore-head. She sat and stared at the Formica table, the incandescent bulb above reflecting a green patch at its scratched centre. Thembisa got up to provide emotional rescue, enfolding Promise from behind; she knotted her hands together gathering in her mother's bosom and hugged, swaying slightly where she stood and whispered "Tidak apa, apa. Tidak apa, apa," in Promise's ear.

"What? What did you say?"

"Tidak apa, apa, its Indonesian for do not worry so."

"Yes, yes I know that expression, but where did you learn it?"

"From a doctor, I am working with on a case... well more than that, it has to do with why I am here looking for Priscilla."

Promise had started back in her seat, forcing Thembisa to relinquish her hug and reposition herself in her former chair. "What's his name?"

Thembisa was rummaging in her satchel. She had ripped the rubber bands off the Polaroids in her haste, "Doctor Pieter Marais, here's a photograph that I took at Blouberg Beach where he lives."

Promise took the picture, held it up between index and thumb at two corners, and studied it in silence, her face slack and without expression, she let the image wash over her, absorbing each detail, *but for the brown hair and beard he looks just like Doctor Willem; same nose, horse teeth, ugly, but striking.*

Promise pressed her eyelids closed, opened them again, a distorting film was marring her sight. She opened and closed her eyes until it disappeared, her nose felt full, her breath came quickly.

Thembisa was getting worried, "Promise, I mean Mom... can I call you that? What's wrong?"

"Nothing."

"Nothing doesn't look like that. Doesn't make you cry. Does it?"

"What did you say his name is?"

"Pieter... Pieter Marais."

"And you say you like him?" Promise's mind was racing as she figured out the truth; she knew that name from the past with Marja back in District Six.

"No I didn't say that, but I kind of... kind of... do."

"Why?"

"He's handsome."

Promise allowed that with a nod but continued to study the photograph intensely.

"The problem is we are on opposing sides."

"You sound like a real policewoman. What does that mean? Opposing sides?"

And then as the sun started to gain the ascendancy over the Cape storm, both in Langa Township and out over Table Bay where Pieter Marais was recovering on his windsurfer, Thembisa told Promise the story that had brought them all together. The torture, death and false certification that had been visited on Goodwill Dlamini at the hands of the Marais family.

Thembisa ended with the fact that Doctor Pieter Marais was applying to the Amnesty Committee to ask forgiveness from Goodwill's family. The reason she had come searching for Priscilla, to make sure that her cousin would attend the Truth and Reconciliation hearing slated for late November.

And so, at the end, with the truth laid bare on the table, Promise looked at her daughter, some of her long lost fire rekindling.

"Thembisa, you know now that I am part of this family. Your test will make that incontrovertible. I must attend the hearings. In fact nothing will stop me." Promise pushed back her seat and rose, "Nothing ever has. We must find reconciliation or lose everything the ANC fought for. We must atone and move on. We must recognize the past to go into the future. Amandla," Promise raised her left hand in a fist, tightening away the little finger that tied them together.

†

15

Truth and Reconciliation
Commission
Athlone
Cape Town, November 1996

The Truth and Reconciliation Commission Special Amnesty hearing of Monday 25th November was held at a different venue from that of the Human Rights Violations hearings that Pieter and Thembisa had attended in Bellville at the far larger University of Western Cape Great Hall three months earlier.

A far more intimate venue thought Doctor Pieter Marais, as he was being patted down at the staff entrance, by a black policewoman with a handheld metal detector. He looked into the sun shriven space; a bank of windows had been opened at its far wall allowing in a fresh morning smell and the churn of Athlone traffic outside. The venue put him more in mind of a comfortable auditorium rather than the tribunal the country had pinned its hope on to foster reconciliation. He was standing alongside a series of five transparent telephone-box-styled translation cubicles, arranged along a side wall, already busy with interpreters, and could see that the room's low ceiling was supported by two sets of three parallel posts either side of a central parquet pathway that led from the podium at the front and sloped up to the public entranceway at the back. He judged the distance to be about one and a half cricket pitches in length, either side of which a century of ruby velvet chairs where already being filled. A police Alsatian was irritating him by trying to lick his hand and sniffing at his shoulder bag.

Having rearranged his clothing after the frisk — the policewoman and her dog passing on to the next entrant behind him — Pieter stood to one side to survey the scene better. *Camouflage* he thought. Potted trees, bushy plants and ferns abounded the perimeter of the room's walls. The greenery had been placed higgeledly piggeledly between the innumerable T.V. cameras, trestled speaker boxes, and multiple photographic lighting stands, while posters had been plastered on white-washed walls declaring, TRUTH THE ROAD TO RECONCILIATION, and, REVEALING is HEALING, and, MURDER, ABDUCTION - TORTURE & SILENCE, sharpening Pieter's sense of guilt. He tried to mentally prepare for the ambush which was in store for him.

Although Pieter was wearing his freshly dry-cleaned navy blazer, he had cinched his maroon tie uncomfortably tight and so was anything but calmed by the horticultural display around him. He scuffed one brogue after the other along the back of his grey flannels to provide his black shoes a less than confident shine and was directed to be seated behind an oblong table, beside his lawyer, Jannie van der Merwe, who was already busily spreading out their papers on the green felt that had been fastened tightly over the table top to provide a smooth surface for the inquisition at hand. Pieter smelt a cloying whiff of floor polish as he pulled out his chair from under the table, mingled with the reek of yet another Alsatian. *Bomb sniffers,* he thought, the animal's stench reminded him of the border patrols where such dogs were used for the same purpose.

"So how you feeling?" Jannie asked, speaking past a paperclip held between flat lips. He had a buttoned down face, hollow cheeks, eyes set far too deeply, a snub of nose, and a blond crew cut leaving almost no hair to set off his pug-like look.

"Kak," Pieter sat down gingerly, wriggling his shoulders, "like I am on the border again, all hyped up. I feel like shit. I didn't mean to kill that terrorist. You know that don't you?"

"Ja, ja, of course not. I know that" Jannie placed a pale hand on his friend's shoulder, and then put his long beige-suited arm around Pieter to give a quick clench before turning back to his paper sorting, "and you didn't kill Dlamini either. Far from it. You tried to save him from your father. You are innocent. You suffer from PTSD and were coerced into false testimony by your father."

Pieter pointed to the black microphones, that had been placed in front of them, next to a glass of water each. "Are they off?"

"Ja, only when the red light is on are they active."

Putting his hand over the mike nevertheless, Pieter continued, "I cannot rat on my father. Jannie we cannot give up his name, no matter what."

"I know, I know, I don't think it will come to that. Is he coming?"

"Nooit," Pieter swivelled back to look at the auditorium filling up behind them, "too proud. He won't ask for amnesty; he believes he was doing his duty by the country. We have not been on speaking terms for years."

"Your mother?"

"No, no, if anything she will watch it all on T.V. She goes where he goes."

"Okay, although we have rehearsed this..."

"A thousand times."

"I want to point out what's going to happen."

"Those white draped tables on the platform," Jannie turned his face away from Pieter and raised his pug nose, "well the judge will sit at the head of the V, and the five commissioners, one of whom will lead the proceedings, on that side, on the right, where that camera crew is setting up the television apparatus."

"Judge?"

"Ja, you can see their names on the white paper cello taped to the tablecloth in front of their seats."

"I didn't know about a judge."

"Yes, the commission runs procedurally like a court. All of the commissioners have legal training too, so that's why the family members, who will sit over there on the left, will have representation as well. When it comes to that point in the proceedings, all of them may wish to cross examine you. At the cross, you are not allowed to communicate with me, i.e. seek legal counsel, unless you request it through the judge. But don't worry, we'll figure it out. Now I must concentrate. Twenty-five minutes to go. Just calm yourself."

Pieter got up quickly, turned from behind the table with his head hunched down, and walked back the ten feet to the first row of chairs, avoiding eye contact as he made his way via the parquet pathway to the back of the auditorium in search of the lavatory. He hurriedly passed rows of people settling in their seats, and when he had found a stall in the *Men's*, pulled open its door, closed it hastily, spun round and then retched into the toilet bowl — the smell of the vomit clinging to him, despite the water he had gulped down afterwards and splashed on his face. He looked into the mirror above the basin, combed his hair back over his ears and ran its teeth through his beard. *Like death warmed up,* he thought and then leaned in closer, his fast coming breath steaming up his reflected face, hiding it from view, before he turned round and retraced his steps to regain his place beside Barrister van der Merwe.

†

Thembisa Dlamini had also come in through the staff entrance of the building and together with Priscilla

Dlamini and Promise Madiba — the sum total of the Dlamini family she could muster for the Amnesty hearing — had been ushered to sit at the left side table of the V shaped configuration on the platform. Similar to the right side which had been reserved for the five commissioners, the white clothed table was festooned with the requisite four microphones, three white paper triangles embossed with VICTIM, as well as four sturdy glasses, an accompanying water jug and a newly opened box of Kleenex tissues. Both tables had been positioned so that they were within spitting distance across from the amnesty applicant's rectangular table where Thembisa could see a pug-faced man in a beige suit busying himself with paper work. Next to him was an empty seat in front of which hung a white piece of paper cello taped to the dark green cloth covering the table claiming APPLICANT as to the vacant seat's occupant. *Where is Pieter?* She thought.

The Dlamini family had joined their barrister, Lamprecht Labuschagne, who had represented the family in the past and had been volunteered by Promise when Thembisa had consulted her and been able to deliver the glad news that, yes, Promise was indeed her mother — the genetic test had proved it beyond all reasonable doubt.

Mother and daughter had consequently taken their places together, joining their barrister who sat closest to the judge's seat, while Priscilla had taken the fourth seat, on the outside. The three women had dressed in predominantly black. A casual observer in the audience would not be hard pressed to sense that Promise and Thembisa were relatives, separated by age; their shoulder length ringlets of hair, greying, and tawny brown respectively, had been pushed back from fawn shaped faces by black head bands, while their doe-like eyes flashed hazel in the bright T.V. lights that had been trained on them when they took their seats. They were almost mirror images, but for the effects of time; Promise had a darker more weathered complexion than her daughter and Thembisa was altogether of more sunny and lighter disposition. While, in stark contrast, Priscilla was created in the Dlamini mould, having been fathered by Goodwill, a man of buffalo proportions in his youth, which was retained in his daughter's features and substantial habitus.

"Welcome, Promise, Thembisa, Priscilla," Barrister Labuschagne had risen heavily from where he sat shuffling files, and nodded to each in turn, "please make yourselves comfortable." He was dressed in his characteristic, straw-coloured, bulging, linen suit, pink shirt and floral tie and had taken out a tartan handkerchief to dab his forehead, careful not to dislodge his ginger coloured toupee, a far too obvious subterfuge from his advanced age, which was not however reflected in the strength of his Afrikaans accented speech.

"Are you settled? Let me run again through the procedural issues..."

Thembisa had stopped listening. She was watching Pieter walking down the aisle. She grabbed Promise's leg underneath the table and said,

"There he is," softly.

Promise had turned away from Labuschagne, looked up to see Pieter advancing along the walkway lining the rows of chairs and then covered her mouth and nose with her hand, her bent little finger curling under her chin, her face pinched by emotion.

"What's the matter mom?"

"That's Pieter? He doesn't look well."

Pieter had regained his seat. He was saying something into his barrister's ear, holding his hand over the mike, less than fifteen meters away from them, and then reached down into his bag, pulled out a red canister, up ended a sprinkle of contents and daubed his neck to pat the scent into place. His head down, he looked at the table in front of him while completing the toilet seemingly oblivious to the fact that the Dlamini family had taken its place across from him.

"Old Spice, I can smell it. Pieter uses it to feel better about himself," Thembisa sniffed, and then asked again, "what's the matter mom?"

"I recognize the perfume; Doctor Willem used it."

Thembisa could see the swelling in her mother's eyes, the beads that welled at their corner angles. *Doctor Willem? The doctor Promise fell in love with?* she thought but was interrupted by the start of the proceedings. The spectators had risen in front of her on seeing the judge and commissioners filing from an entrance way off to one side; they took their respective seats, placing their multicoloured file-folders in front of them behind their angled microphones and adjacent to the glasses of water, that had already been filled in anticipation of events.

Thembisa thought that the five commissioners, all finely dressed, reflected the new rainbow nation rather well. There were three women, two men and Coloured, Black and White were suitably represented, with the Chief Commissioner, an Indian women, Doctor Fatima Cherian, dressed in a long multi-hued sari of elegant design, a bundle of exquisitely coiffed silken hair topping off her delicate, pointed features; all set off by gold ear, nose and neck jewellery, that sparkled in the glare of the camera lights, to a most beautiful sheen.

Doctor Cherian launched the Special Amnesty Hearing by first introducing the judge, Advocate Robert Balfour, a stick like presence with bulging eyes, and absent hair that put one in mind of a grasshopper preying at the apex of the two V aligned tables, and so positioned next to Barrister Labuschagne, who Thembisa could see had just got up a little to shake the judge's hand as the introductions were being made. Thembisa turned away to look at Pieter catching his eye for a second before he looked away.

†

Pieter felt a little better. The tang of Old Spice had supplanted the stink of vomit from his nose

303

and beard, allowing him to inhale more freely. He had been studying the opposition during Doctor Cherian's introductions. He read off the placard in front of the flamboyantly dressed man: Barrister Lamprecht Labuschagne was representing the family. Thembisa looked lovely in her black dress. And then Pieter cast his eye on the person sitting next to her. *She looks like Thembisa but older, same shape face, darker colour though... I've seen her before... where? And the other one, the big one doesn't look like them at all.* Pieter caught Thembisa looking at him so he looked away and focused on Doctor Cherian.

Doctor Cherian had risen from her seat to better introduce the special proceedings that had been arranged for today. She held up a microphone, which was unnecessary as her voice carried clearly throughout the room, setting off a skreich of electronic feedback. She replaced the offending device back on the table and turned to the translation cubicles across from her.

"Good morning and welcome. Translators can you hear me if I stand like this. Or should I lift up the microphone?" Receiving five thumbs up visible through the cubicle glass that enclosed their boxes, and various nods from the participants in the audience who had donned headphones, Doctor Cherian only slightly heightened the pitch of her voice.

"Very well. As a medical doctor, I am honoured, but also distressed at being tasked by Bishop Desmond Tutu to chair this Special Session. Honoured, because the practice of medicine is a high calling, but distressed that the state of medical practice in South Africa has deteriorated to this point. The point where doctors have trespassed the Hippocratic Oath and are not holding their patients safe from harm. Some in the medical profession have broken the people's trust in them, by aiding and abetting crimes against humanity by the police.

There was much nodding and shifting of chairs as well as a few muffled 'ewe's', 'yes's', and 'ja's' from the almost completely filled chamber.

"Many doctors have either not called out such instances of torture, rape or murder, or have provided false testimony, or certificates to hide the fact from public scrutiny, discovery and appropriate prosecution. At the instigation of Doctor Wendy Orr, a fellow commissioner, who has also served as a District Surgeon like our applicant today, Doctor Pieter Marais," Doctor Cherian stopped speaking and nodded in Pieter's direction seeming to lose her train of thought when she saw him avert his eyes and seek consolation in the papers arrayed in front of him, before, she swallowed, and continued in a louder voice.

"As I was saying... yes... Doctor Orr served in Port Elizabeth in the past, but through a much more recent investigation has managed to help uncover the malfeasance of two District Surgeons, Doctor Tucker and Doctor Lang in relation to Steve Biko's murder back in 1977. Doctor Orr has worked in concert with the Medical Association of South Africa to request that medical doctors who have erred in their duties to their patients during the apartheid era come forward by December 14th, this year, to apply for amnesty. This fact has been well advertised by the SABC through television and radio broadcasts, as well as widely called for in newspaper bulletins.

"Because Doctor Pieter Marais's application for amnesty was one of the first, we have received, the Truth Commission has accelerated the process to encourage others to come forward and so added a Special Amnesty Session today. This brings us to the present. We will dispense therefore with the usual practice of a prayer and singing...."

†

Thembisa had been listening attentively, her left hand still cradled in Promise's palms underneath the table. But then became distracted by a slight commotion about halfway into the auditorium: Colonel Pieter Marais in full dress uniform and a woman in a bright yellow sarong, her jet black hair stretching to her shoulders, were making their way to two open seats at the edge of a row, well in range of the bright glare that fell from the fancy lamp fixtures that had been attached to each of the six posts that punctuated the low hung ceiling. Thembisa noticed that upon the couple taking their seats, two African women, sitting next to them, collected their clothing and possessions in a huff, stood up, and moved out of the row in the opposite direction, making their excuses as each audience member had to stand up from their chair, to allow them to pass noisily. The two ladies' departure effectively isolated Thembisa's nemesis and the woman beside him clearly in the bright over-hanging light. Thembisa could see the flash of scarlet lipstick and matching nails as the lovely lady settled down next to the Colonel, and so clasped Promises' palm, and turned to whisper in her ear.

"That's Pieter's father, I told you about," Thembisa jutted her nose in the direction of the couple and was surprised by the intensity of her mother's palm clasp. "And... and... that must be his mother Marja. I've never met her. Hau, she's pretty." Thembisa turned her face to look at Promise. Her mother's features had starkened; her eyes drooped, her cheeks hollowed, and her mouth had fallen open. *A yearning look,* Thembisa thought, but just then the judge called the proceedings to order. Sitting just along from the family at the head of the V positioned tables, his reedy voice was again in no need of the microphone to carry.

"I'm calling this hearing to order," Judge Balfour remained in his seat and continued. "Doctor Pieter Marais, please stand, put your hand on the Bible we have provided and repeat after me. I swear to speak nothing but the truth, so help me God."

Pieter rose, his face an ashen mask above his beard, placed his trembling hand on the leather covered Bible and repeated the sacred words, after which he looked at each family member in turn in silence, pivoted to the judge and then focused on each of the five commissioners rotating his head slowly to do so. The auditorium was deathly quiet, except for the swish of revolving fans overhead, the creak of a few chairs, the whirr of the two television cameras that were trained from their tripod stands soaking up the proceedings, and the drone of passing traffic that could be heard through the opened side windows; it was summer and becoming hot in the room.

†

Doctor Cherian, as the Chief Commissioner, took over the proceedings. She looked across at Pieter and Jannie sitting behind their felt covered table, then ranged her view from left to right across the now completely packed auditorium behind them, and then turned her attention upon each family member in turn and then, to complete the exercise, addressed their lawyer.

"Barrister Labuschagne, would you please introduce the family of the deceased, Goodwill Dlamini, the victim of this application for amnesty."

"Yes, Commissioner, it will be my sad duty to do so," he mopped his brow with his tartan handkerchief, shifted his considerable bulk to sit more easily in the creaking chair and continued. "Next to me is Miss Promise Madiba. She was related to Mr Goodwill Dlamini, in so far that the deceased was a brother of Miss Dlamini's benefactor. She grew up with him while he was still resident in District Six before he was forced to move to Langa Township when his house was bulldozed down by the apartheid government of the time. In turn, Promise Madiba is no stranger to the Truth Commission as she presented at the Human Rights Violations hearings in Bellville just three months ago, occasioning her return to South Africa..."

"Keep it short please Barrister Labuschagne, we have till noon," Doctor Cherian interceded her will and jurisdiction.

Pieter had focused on Promise as Labuschagne spoke, recognition dawning. He looked at Thembisa, then again at Promise, marvelling at their likeness despite the obvious age difference and thought of the photo he had seen lying on his mother's coffee table. *Was this the nursing sister who had saved his mother's life with the Dutch surgeon? Was this the woman the surgeon, Willem Jansen, had been prosecuted with for the Immorality Act? The surgeon who had died. Pieter pictured the photograph again. The tall, stooped man, with teeth much like his own, at its centre between Marja and a younger version of this woman called Promise, who looked just like Thembisa now, then. Come to think of it, Promise Madiba, that's the name his mother had said, before his father had stormed into the house in a rage. Thank god he's not here to see this.*

"Next," Labuschagne had fully risen from his seat, making a quarter turn and pushing it back to create more room for the exercise, eliciting a stertorous sound from the slightly raised, wooden platform the tribunal were sitting on, "is Detective

Thembisa Dlamini. She was brought up by the deceased, Goodwill Dlamini, who was her uncle, after she moved from Soweto, after the riots there in 1976. And next to her," Labuschagne flourished a hand in the general direction, Priscilla Dlamini, Mr Dlamini's only daughter."

Upon the introduction, Priscilla bunched two fat fists on the table in front of her, leant forward, and peered at Pieter through horn rimmed spectacles from beneath a floridly coloured traditional head dress, ready to enter the fray.

"Very well, thank you Barrister Labuschagne," Doctor Cherian, now having taken her seat flanked by two commissioners on each side, turned to look at the rectangular table where the applicant and his lawyer sat, caught in a triangle, like a hyphen, beneath an upside down V that the table arrangement completed, "Barrister van der Merwe will you please lead your client through the testimony."

Pieter imagined himself sitting in the crosshairs of an ambush. The green-baize table behind which they sat, the centre of the attack. Ten sets of eyes and the two television cameras threatening him from the front, while a hundred pairs of eyeballs, bored into him from the back, and who knows how many were watching on T.V. He turned to look at Jannie, who was leaning forward on the table and had engaged the two microphones, their red lights shining, indicating that they were active and recording the proceedings. Pieter felt nauseous again. He laboured to still the motion of his eyes by concentrating. He took a deep breath for calm and placed his hands square on the soft felt in front of him.

"Commissioner, my client, Doctor Pieter Marais, will provide testimony of his own accord, but before he does so, I want to bring to the Commission's awareness that Doctor Marais suffers from Post-Traumatic Stress Disorder, PTSD, more commonly known as *Bossies* in Afrikaans, which he developed after his friend Cornelius van Wyk was shot dead through the head, next to him, in an ambush on the Angolan border in 1980 while he was serving in the South African Defence Force. As a result of this incident he suffers nightmares, depression, and is considered to be of a highly sensitive nature. And, as a consequence, has sudden panic attacks, sought the approval of an overbearing father, and cannot be regarded as having his full faculties in highly stressful situations like the one he is about to relate to you." Barrister van der Merwe paused, scanned the commissioner's and then the family's tables slowly, paused again, and then turned to look at Pieter. "Doctor Marais, will you please first tell us why... no start with your story first, we'll get to the why later. Go ahead," Van der Merwe, placed his hand over one of Pieter's and gave it an encouraging grasp.

Pieter swept his hand through his hair gathering it in the nape of his neck, looked up at the Dlamini family, focused on Thembisa, catching her shining eyes, diverted to look at Doctor Cherian, and then started.

"I wish to start with an apology to the family for their loss, and to the medical fraternity for my behaviour. I sought to apply for amnesty for my actions, not to avoid prosecution, but because I cannot bear to live without telling the truth any longer. I feel responsible for my actions notwithstanding what Barrister van der Merwe just said about my medical condition. I cannot live with this for the rest of my life." Pieter stopped, took a deep breath and exhaled in full, a sound audible to everyone that needed no translation.

"Go on. What happened on that day Doctor Marais?"

"I... I... had just started in my General Practice in Tamboerskloof. It was a very busy day. I also serve as a District Surgeon, chiefly, to perform autopsies at Salt River for the State as well as to look after prisoners at the Caledon Square Police Station. It helps to pay off some of my student loans. My secretary had received a call that I was wanted at the police station, to sign some papers. I should take the lift and go to the secretaries' office on the fourth floor." Another timorous breath was heard.

"I was late. I felt fortunate to get a parking place in the courtyard of the police station, so instead of taking the lift I ran up the fire-escape to the fourth floor. I came upon a dark corridor where a sliver of light shone out from a room, its steel door ajar, probably opened against the ferocious heat. I heard a mewling sound and shouting and decided to investigate. I looked into the room and saw a big naked black man, Mr Goodwill Dlamini, hanging in the helicopter position."

"Could you please explain what is meant by the helicopter position," Doctor Cherian had leaned closer to the microphone and stared at Pieter, her gold jewellery glittering.

"It's an awful torture. A broomstick had been thrust between the victim's elbow and knee joints and he was suspended between two tables. Mr Dlamini was hanging vertically with his shaved head down. He had been sjamboked, I saw the stripes on his back. He had been hit in the face. One eye was out of its socket. Like... like... Corli... ah... my friend on the border... there were weeping wounds from gashes on his forehead and there was blood and snot draining beneath him in a pool on the cement floor. I saw the white officer dump a bucket of water over the victim," Willem put his hands in the prayerful position, leaning his elbows on the table, his maroon tie swung against its green surface, his starched shirt sweat-stuck to his chest underneath his blazer.

"Go on, Doctor Marais, I know this is distressing," Doctor Cherian looked over at the family in front of her. Labuschagne was shifting papers head down. Promise had sucked in her cheeks, and with the back of one hand, alternated left and right strokes of her face to clear the wetness, while Thembisa looked fixedly at Pieter, watching his lips, and Priscilla sat back shaking her head, her looped earrings brassy in the glare of the T.V. lights.

"The white policeman had just kicked him, when I ran in, because Mr Dlamini was still swinging like a pendulum. A black officer in blood spattered

313

gumboots was mopping the floor. I could smell the carbolic soap and the blood. I know it well. It was overpowering. I yelled at the policeman to stop."

"What did you say exactly?" Barrister Jannie van der Merwe glanced sideways at Pieter.

"I told him to stop, or he would kill the patient... I mean Mr Dlamini."

"And did he? Stop." Van der Merwe again.

"No. He kicked him in the face again. The victim swung back from the force of it..."

A hullabaloo arose behind Pieter from the crowd seated in the auditorium: wailing, and cries of anguish and consternation interrupted his will to speak, but he pressed on when Van der Merwe carefully pushed Pieter's hands down from covering his mouth and patted them into place where they now lay crossed, sallow upon the green surface.

"And... and... stopped breathing. He didn't move again. He just hung there upside down. Dripping blood and snot and water on the floor." Pieter glanced across at Promise and then Thembisa, a hunted look in his eyes. He averted his gaze quickly from the hurt he sensed and returned to look at Doctor Cherian, the Chief Commissioner.

"Please lead your client, Barrister van der Merwe."

"Doctor Marais, what happened then?"

"I... I had a panic attack. I wanted to get out of there, away from the horror. But the white officer, who had left through a side door returned with a clip board and a pen. He told me to sign the Death Certificate. I couldn't read it; my eyes wouldn't focus. So I asked what was written there. The policeman told me that the document certified that the wounds that I had just seen were sustained by the prisoner falling down the stairs. I felt bilious. My jaw started shaking, like someone who has rigors. I said I couldn't. It was a lie, and against the Hippocratic Oath.

"Well then you will stay here until you sign," the white officer said. I hated him for that, but I was feeling like I had to vomit. I had to get away. I felt entrapped like in Angola. I had to get away. So I signed my name and left quickly. And I have lived with this... this awful death ever since," Pieter looked steadfastly at the middle distance in front of him, his face darkening.

Many in the audience behind Pieter were now standing up. Raising fists or waving handkerchiefs, or shedding words like "shame... it's a crying shame... Aikona... terrible, too terrible... there must be punishment."

Doctor Cherian rose from behind her table. "I must ask you all to settle down please. These are terrible events that Doctor Marais has disclosed. Terrible. Let us have a ten minute break and we will reconvene after that."

†

During Pieter's testimony, Thembisa had intermittently looked in Colonel Marais's direction, full-well knowing that Pieter's father was the white policeman that had forced him to sign the Death Certificate. She realized that Pieter did not know that his father was in the audience and Thembisa had been baffled at Promise's reaction to seeing Marja, Pieter's mother, after Thembisa had pointed the couple sitting in the auditorium out to her. Thembisa could only see Promise out of the corner of her eye, but could feel her body close to her and had held her mother's hand under the table throughout Pieter's testimony and so tried to make sense of Promise's reactions by the play of her enfolded hand grip as Promise's eyes focused away from Pieter's testimony and out across the audience in Marja's direction; her mother's clasp tightening and then releasing once Promise's eyes had settled on Marja. Thembisa used the break in the proceedings for a series of whispered questions.

"Mom, do you know that woman?" Thembisa had now turned, sitting slightly back in her seat, so she could fully see Promise's reaction. Her mother looked in a trance, far away. "Mom, do you know that woman?"

Promise's eyes refocused, her features reformed from a dream like state, she passed her tongue over her lips to rewet them, "Ewe," Promise nodded.

"Ewe, what mom?"

"A long, long time ago, before you two were born."

"Two?"

"*You*, before *you* were born."

"Were you close ?"

"Yes... yes... very, very close," Promise, wiped her

face clean of the tears that had returned with one hand, all the time tenderly stroking her daughter's hand underneath the table, when Judge Balfour called the Special Session back to order again.

"Before we get to the cross examination led by Barrister Labuschagne, I have asked Doctor Cherian to prepare us for this section of this Special Session."

Doctor Cherian rose again from her seat, elegantly rearranged her colourful sari, picked up the microphone, thought better of it, replaced it in front of her on the table, produced a black lip-sticked smile, coiffed her hair a bit and then started speaking slowly, going faster when she saw the audience warming to her message.

"When we hear such testimonies as Doctor Marais has just given, we feel loss in our hearts and anger in our arteries. But this Commission is not constituted to seek retribution... retributive justice... No! We seek another kind of justice... restorative justice that will induce healing... I would ask that the Dlamini family," Doctor Cherian turned her attention to the three members sitting in front of her, "consider being willing to forgive Doctor Marais. And... although this is not a precondition for amnesty to be granted, to know that no one... I repeat no one... goes off Scott free from such proceedings as we are together witnessing right here, now! Today. The applicants, like Doctor Marais, have to face this hearing and the full glare of the television," Doctor Cherian, waved her hand in the direction of the cameras focused on her, "and the palpable opprobrium present in this room at this time. I can feel it myself! Barrister Labuschagne please conduct the cross examination."

Labuschagne lumbered to the standing position. He had coached the family and they had rehearsed their questions.

"Doctor Marais, the family wish to personally question you, but before they do, I feel compelled to get to the heart of your case. The heart of the matter that brings you before us today. Could you tell us again why you applied for this amnesty?"

"Guilt, sir."

"Guilt? I thought it was the Hippocratic Oath. Could you speak up please."

"No, guilt. As a doctor, if you lose a patient or anyone, one can feel a great guilt," Pieter had unsteadily risen behind the desk, looking first at Thembisa, then Labuschagne, and then at the green baize in front of him — upstanding but bowed. I too have lost friends; my buddy on the border, my girlfriend Cherise to cancer. Was there something I could have done to save them? I don't know," Pieter looked up again, this time catching Promise's eye, with a beseeching look, uncertain why she held his gaze — a line of tears streaking her ebony skin. He continued speaking to the empathy he caught there; a distant memory triggered of a much younger, similar face in District Six, bending towards him as he ate his putu pap. "Could I have stopped the killing of Mr Dlamini? If I was more resolute, more forceful in my objections."

Thembisa watched Pieter's lips again, as he bared

his jagged teeth, she felt the guilt for her sister's death in Soweto. For stealing the red scarf that marked Zindiswe and attracted the rifleman's gun shot. She had buried that long ago, but now it re-emerged. She softened her face and leaned forward, focusing intently to try and attract Pieter's attention, to still the anguish that was contorting his features. Thembisa remembered one of Bishop Tutu's quotes she had heard on television: "It is as if suffering has ripped them open with empathy." Thembisa experienced that as she turned from Pieter to glance aside at Labuschagne who returned to the interrogation.

"Sister Promise Madiba, as the most senior member of the Dlamini family would you please start," he put his freckled hand on her grey shawled shoulder.

Promise seemed distraught. Her eyes had followed Pieter's like a sad hush puppy; she had sunken into herself, looking as if she had aged further during Pieter's testimony.

"No... I am afraid, I must decline."

"Do you mean you do not wish to cross examine despite our rehearsal?"

"Yes... ewe... yes, you must not have heard me. I do NOT want to proceed." Promise drew her shawl tighter across her shoulders, her face set with determined passion.

Labuschagne flinched back in response, knocking his microphone to the floor, and his chair back, causing a grating noise on the platform, amplified by the mike that had come to rest next to it — an escalating feedback loop of sound that became an excruciating clamour in the close auditorium until a technician could set things right and quell the disturbance.

Recovering both his microphone, composure, and standing position, Labuschagne turned to Thembisa, "And you, Detective Dlamini?"

"I decline too... like my... I...I... decline too," Thembisa spat out, looking across the auditorium, she singled out Colonel Marais, for a withering stare. A television camera encamped on the platform, focused first on Thembisa and then panned out over the auditorium to try and capture the object of her derision, coming to rest on Pieter's parents — the overhead lighting arrangements showing off the sweat that beaded the policeman's forehead beneath his mane of combed back hair, only a hint of a dent remaining from the colonel cap that now rested on his knees.

"Well, then it's up to me," Priscilla Dlamini had clicked on her microphone, and lunged forward in her seat to speak into it while fixating on Pieter, who had sat back in his chair, clearly disturbed by the turmoil that had been launched at him from the platform. She turned to her left, her colourful headdress fluttering, "Promise... and Thembisa... what has become of you? Our plans for the cross..." she turned again to look at her quarry.

"Doctor Marais, I understand that if amnesty is even to be considered," Priscilla raised a pink, tremulous, meaty palm, "then full disclosure is to be provided, WHO WAS THE WHITE POLICE OFFICER WHO KILLED MY FATHER? WHO?"

Pieter started feeling nauseous again, his nystagmus returning, "I cannot disclose that."

"You cannot, or you will not?" Judge Balfour stretched his insect neck beyond his black cloak. His nude head and bulging eyes captured ably by a T.V. cameraman.

Anticipating Pieter's response, Thembisa looked again out at the colonel and pressed her mother's hand still clinched underneath the table, to draw her attention to the couple bathed bright in the overhanging light. Marja appeared agitated and was whispering something into the colonel's ear.

"Both." Thembisa heard Pieter say as she continued to look at the two-some. Marja had raised her left arm to shoulder level and was furiously wringing it again and again, within the clinch of her right index finger and thumb, her features fraught, she kept on mouthing something into her husband's left ear.

"Well, the family demands justice," Priscilla spluttered, "an eye for an eye. We demand the truth. Isn't that what we are all here for? Truth and Reconciliation."

"The truth, the truth," a person in the back started up the refrain which was taken up by an increasing number of the audience members, "the truth, the truth, we want the truth. "The truth, the truth, we want the truth." Until the locust-like judge raised his hand for quiet and upon the auditorium returning to a low hum of dissatisfaction, he turned again to Barrister van der Merwe. "Jannie, may I suggest that you confer with your client."

"I will Your Honour."

Priscilla however could not contain herself any further, she seemed to become bigger with her brewing anger. "Your Honour, on behalf of the family and my murdered father. I must insist. Bishop Tutu has said that the truth will set us free. We must know the truth to set Doctor Marais free. I feel for him too. Just like my family," she turned left, where both Thembisa and then Promise nodded their agreement, and then again levelled at Pieter, who was bent over a paper bag, his mouth and beard ringed by its edges. His blazered back heaved, ribs showing through the tense navy cloth.

"Please," Van der Merwe said, "please let Doctor Marais compose himself. But I know his answer, he cannot... cannot disclose the police officer's name."

.....

"BUT I CAN," there was a disturbance from the back as the colonel had stood up, after putting on his cap. Marja rising next to him, her sarong a-sheen from the spotlight over their heads.

"I was that police officer. God help me and be my judge. Doctor Pieter is incapable of such... such... cruelty. I must set him free from his bondage to me. I did it. I tortured Mr Dlamini. I did it. Not because I am a bad person. But for the good of the country. I was following orders from the minister. We thought he was a communist, a terrorist. We needed information and Dlamini wouldn't give it. He was a very brave man."

At this, Promise stood up behind the table raised her hand and pointed a well-manicured finger at the colonel, her eyes flicking from his to Marja's and back again. "You want to set Doctor Marais free from his bondage to you? I know you. You arrested me when you bull dozed down Marja and my home in District Six. It was you that separated me from my son, Willem."

"You are right," the colonel bristled, "I admit it, but it was all for the good of the boy. If Marja married me, he could be classified white. That would be better for him and I loved you then," he looked down at Marja, standing next to him, "but now I no longer care." The colonel had squared his shoulders and looked back up at the five Commissioners "you can take your vengeance out on me. Forgive him. Set Willem free of the burden I put upon him." The colonel then looked down at Marja again, who seemed to have shrivelled in her sarong, "And you... you are free of me too... "

The film crews, photographers and the translators were having a field day as the spectacle unfolded in the sweltering room and Promise stepped carefully away from the table, loosened the grey shawl from around her neck a bit, and took the one step down from the platform and the three steps it took to stop and stand in front of Pieter who had stood up to meet her and had unbuttoned his blazer to give his quaking chest some room. The auditorium hushed at the drama. Promise and Pieter stood there looking at each other — sensing each other — over the intervening green-baize table, the red light on the microphone still burning between them. Pieter bowed his head. Then Promise held up her shawl in a U-shape and placed it gently over the nape of Pieter's neck as if in benediction and then bent her grey head towards Pieter's brown-bearded one, their foreheads coming to rest gradually against each other as Promise tightened the bond between them. They stood in this position for some time, the hubbub that had arisen in the surrounding space, seemed to ebb away from them as Pieter came to the certain knowledge that had been building throughout the day's proceedings.

.....

And although Promise spoke in a low whisper, her words were megaphoned throughout the room and beyond by the public address system:

"Willem... you are my long lost son. You are as strong and true as your real father, Doctor Willem Jansen, may he rest in peace. Of course... of course... of course... Thembisa... your sister... and I... forgive you. What else is there left for a mother to do."

†

16

Letter
Cape Town, 1996

November 26.

Dear Marja,

It was only when I saw you yesterday in the auditorium that I realized how much I have missed you.

You are just as lovely and beautiful as ever.

My abandonment of Willem to you was unforgivable, and I still feel guilty because of that.

But I thought it was the right thing at the time; to protest the destruction of our house: my role in the ANC's Struggle made that an imperative.

And of course it had consequences for both of us.

For me: I was imprisoned, raped by a white warder, and separated from Thembisa after three months. The Police took her away and unbeknownst to me settled Thembisa with Faith and Eugenia Dlamini in Soweto. She grew up believing they were her real parents and after her sister was shot in the Soweto Riots, Faith and Eugenia thought it better that Thembisa move down here to grow up with Goodwill Dlamini in Langa Township.

After several years of imprisonment, I was released and immediately banned, and so eventually escaped to Zambia and then to set up a new life of exile in London. I thought of you, and the two children often, but that slowly slipped away as I settled into a new relationship with a girlfriend. What had become of Willem and you I know now from yesterday. I did not know that you married Pieter Marais for Willem's sake.

What had become of Thembisa, I learnt only in the last few days.

Quite by chance? Or was it always meant to be? Willem and Thembisa had started meeting. Thembisa had become a police detective. Her motive pure: she wanted to find out the truth about Goodwill's death. She met Willem, while she was investigating her first case, because he had done the autopsy on the crime victim. Apparently, they were attracted to each other.

So why... I can hear you ask, why... did I come back to South Africa?

It was for the TRC.

I had made a new life in England. I had started nursing again at Great Ormond Street Hospital and had British citizenship, and a steady relationship. But that changed. My partner died of cancer last year and just after that, I read about the TRC. Bishop Tutu was inviting us back to give testimony.

So, I resigned my job and gave testimony in Bellville around 3 months ago. I was staying with Priscilla Dlamini in Langa in Goodwill's old house wondering whether I should stay permanently. It brought back such memories. Doctor Willem and I had celebrated one of Goodwill's birthday parties there back in 1960, the year before Willem's death. I remember our very first dance together as Miriam Makeba's click song (the one you liked so much) was bursting from the loudspeaker that had been hung from the ceiling.

Well, three weeks ago, who comes to the front door dressed as a policewoman?

"Thembisa" she said. I had called my baby that. Its Xhosa for Promise. But it couldn't be, or could it? She looked like me 30 years ago and, when I saw her bent little finger, the one you used to tease me about... shoo... shoo... I almost fainted. Lucky we were sitting at the kitchen table by then.

Well, she being a police detective and all, did a genetic test on our saliva and confirmed the truth; I was reconciled with my long lost daughter.

And then yesterday, I was reconciled with my son.

Marja, I am writing this letter, because I hope there is a future for me here back with my family. I would love to hear whether you think so too. Will you meet me at the Rhodes Memorial Tea Garden for lunch, Friday December 7?

I'll be there from midday, whether you decide to come or not.
I hope you do!

Love
Promise Madiba.

†

Acknowledgements

Prime acknowledgement goes to Ulane, my wife. Ulane has helped shape this story and has provided innumerable ideas for, and critiques of my writing.

Obviously, this historical novel required a great deal of reading (and video viewing) to situate Promise's, Marja's, Thembisa's and Pieter's fictional stories within the historical arc of the time, hence I have been most grateful for the many resources that I have tapped; only a few of which are listed below.

Firstly, I am indebted to Max du Preez's erudite reportage on the Truth Commission's Hearings presented on Sundays by the South African Broadcasting Corporation from 1996 - 1998. This work and the unspeakable atrocities there witnessed was harrowing in the extreme. The participants who gave testimony are to be honoured for their courage in bringing their stories to the world.

Gillian Slovo's *Red Dust*, Antjie Krog's, *Country of my Skull* and *A People on the Boil* by Harry Mashabela were all important books as was *A Human Being Died that Night* by Pumla Gobodo-Madikizela who served as a Truth Commissioner. *The South Africa Reader* by Clifton Crais and Thomas V McClendon as well as *Shoot to Kill: Police and Power in South Africa* helped to deepen my understanding of the country's history.

Truth & *Conciliation* was also greatly informed

by many a further visit to *Wikipedia*, *YouTube*, and the other wonderful resources that are available to a writer connected with a computer to the internet.

Special thanks go to Robert Welsh and Kim Nall for insightful comments as well as to Johan Coetzee and Karen Cronje from Naledi.

For all those who have not been acknowledged, and have wittingly or unwittingly helped inform this book, thank you.

Berend Mets. MB.ChB. PhD. MFA.

†

Author

Dr. Berend Mets was born in Indonesia of Dutch parents, has lived on four continents, and amongst other countries, grew up in South Africa under *apartheid,* where he became a doctor, anaesthetist, and scientist at the Universities of Stellenbosch and Cape Town. He is currently a Professor of Anesthesiology at the Pennsylvania State University. Berend came to writing fiction after a career of medical, historical and scientific writing having acquired a Master's in Fine Art degree from Carlow University in Pittsburgh. He has published two non-fiction books: *Waking Up Safer? An Anesthesiologist's Record.* And, *Leadership in Anaesthesia: Five Pioneers of the Deadly Quest for Surgical Insensibility.*

Truth & Conciliation is the sequel to *Immorality Act.*

Berend divides his time between America, the Dutch Caribbean and Cape Town, South Africa.

†

naledi

www.naledi.co.za

facebook.com/naledibooks

www.ingramcontent.com/pod-product-compliance
Lightning Source LLC
Chambersburg PA
CBHW071441260626
47170CB00008B/2791